Worlds of Power,
Lines of Light

To John Sabby,
one of the sweetest, kindest people
bravest + I, have known.
this world, + I,
You are a hero, John, + I warn you —
you're going to show up as such is
the next book.
love,
Devi

Other works by Devin Starlanyl

"Fibromyalgia and Chronic Myofascial Pain Syndrome: A Survival Manual" by Devin J. Starlanyl and Mary Ellen Copeland, ISBN 1-57224-046-6 New Harbinger Oakland CA.

"Chronic Myofascial Pain Syndrome: The Trigger Point Guide" 2 hour video ISBN 1-057224-076-8. New Harbinger Oakland CA.

"The Fibromyalgia Advocate: Getting the Support You Need to Cope with Fibromyalgia and Myofascial Pain Syndrome" ISBN 1-57224-121-7, New Harbinger Oakland CA.

Worlds of Power,
Lines of Light

Devin. J. Starlanyl

A Devstar° Book

Worlds of Power, Lines of Light. Copyright 1999 by Devin Starlanyl.

ISBN 0-9671157-0-1

Cover art by Linda S. Wingerter, www.sover.net/~wings

The text of this book was composed by Pagesetters Inc., Brattleboro, Vermont.
Printed in the United States of America by Quebecor Printing Vermont, Inc.
Amber silver Kellierin spiral designed by Robert Borter of Brattleboro.

°Devstar, Division of Central Agency for Transworld Sciences

99 00 01 02 03 °devstar° 10 9 8 7 6 5 4 3 2 1

Dedication

To the real Tav, and the Teek, and all who walk the Path of Light with me, I dedicate this book.

Thanks

I want to thank my partner Rick who has helped me through this effort, and all the many people (furred and unfurred) who have helped me in my research, especially the librarians at Brooks Memorial Library and the Army Corps of Engineers Cold Regions Research and Engineering Laboratory, for there is much in this book that is not fiction. Thanks to my illustrator, Linda S. Wingerter; the editor of my non-fiction books, Kayla Sussell, who gave me guidance; and Pagesetters, Inc. and Quebecor of Brattleboro for bringing this dream to reality. Great thanks also to my proofreaders and friends Susan, Linda and Betty, for I am spelling-impaired. Great thanks always to Drs. Simons and Travell, who taught me so much. Every person in this book is fictional, although art always imitates life to some degree.

Prologue

My name is Ari Seeg, and I have a story to tell. That's what I do, I tell stories, and folks back home say I'm pretty good at it. It's made me a living, anyways, and took me further than I ever dreamed. Yours is a new planet for me, but I heard a lot about you from the Tavs. Hang in and I'll fill you in with some background.

First off, back home folks would say "You call this place Earth". Here you say "This *is* Earth", paying no heed to what the rest of us call it. That sets up a road block to other ways of talking and thinking. You're not alone in the universe. There are other ways in the universe besides your own. Get used to it. You're entering a time of extreme change, and terms like "information superhighway" and "cybernet" are being bandied about. If you want to travel a cosmic superhighway someday, get rid of your self-imposed roadblocks.

Now imagine a world where information is currency, and curiosity is the driving force. So it was in the Golden Age of Metrowyl, before the Great War. Metrowyl was a magic planet then, part of a loosely bound trading group of solar systems, located fairly close together, as intra-galactic distances go. If you look at the night sky, in the direction of what you call the Great Nebula in Orion, that's where the trading group is. Of course, they'd be on the other side of the nebula, as you see it from Earth. We call that nebula the Freel-Omar.

Intelligent beings come in all colors and configurations, and most travel the star lanes with some degree of regularity. Whether tentacles, hands, cilia, paws, or other manipulatory appendages initiate the launch, it doesn't matter. Curiosity fuels more space exploration than any type of propellant. It has been said that the first word uttered by every child on Metrowyl is "Why". That truth has never been disputed.

Knowledge pumped the economy of Metrowyl, and knowledge fueled its exploration branch, the Survey Service. Scout ships scoured the galaxy finding new colony sites, but mostly looking for new materials and information to trade. Other races of the Seven Suns joined the quest: the mystic felinoid Tav, the mercantile Riunor, the secretive cloaked Cytherians, the flamboyant blue Orelians. Some ships eased slowly out near the boundaries of charted space, increasing their spheres of knowledge cautiously. Others ventured fearlessly, risking long hops through uncharted space. With the development of the Quantum/Time Matrix Drive, the range of these scouts expanded. For explorers daring and skilled enough to risk it, the Q/T matrix, fluxing through space/time, allowed them to cross vast reaches. Rules and regulations stretch thin in uncharted space, and all too often explorers came face to face with conditions not covered under "Survey Service Protocols and Standard Operating Procedures (SSP/SOP)".

All beginnings are difficult, and maturity comes not without price. For the youth of Metrowyl, the individual cost is the "Season of Change". During most of their physical growing, our young have none of the drives and challenges that disrupt the turbulent teenage years on Earth. Most of our physical and emotional development takes place during the span of a few months to a few years. It is often accompanied by severe pain, stress, and general confusion as the body and mind find their own information superhighway seriously disrupted. Evolution, or the Guardian of the Universe, often advances some part of a population ahead of the others, to prepare them for massive change to come. At the time of this story, the people of Metrowyl were at the brink of such a great change.

Several generations before the War, the first of the Empaths of Metrowyl began to emerge. Without the proper medical support and understanding, they went unrecognized, and serious mental and physical trauma, at times even death, resulted. Then the Tavs arrived, and taught us what was happening.

When the body talks to the mind, and the mind talks back, neurotransmitters are the language they use. Remember when you were small, and you lined up with friends and whispered a message down the line? That message became so garbled by the time it reached the end that it was funny. That's what happens during the Season of Change, only it isn't funny at all. The messages between the body and mind get garbled. Once you know what is happening, healers can help modulate differences . . . but that is beyond the scope of this story.

The Change can be buffered as maturity sets in, by forming a supportive "two", which is what we call a mated pair. A healthy sexual relationship helps balance the neurotransmitters. The twos may form for life, or as a "temp two" for the duration of the Change.

Our bodies are a lot like yours. Bundles of electromagnetic energy. The more electromagnetic sensitivity a person develops, the tougher the Season of Change for them, *but* the more likely he or she comes out of Change with psychic/empathic talents. Fortunately, neither political faction realized the potential use of these sensitives until it was too late to grab the hot talent, again, thanks to the Tavs.

You need to know something about Tavs, since they come into the story. They look sort of like big cats. They're good folks, mostly. You don't want to get on their hissy side, though, 'cause they make formidable foes. They travel the space lanes farther and faster than just about any other species I know, and they are more ecologically balanced than the other races I've met. It was humanoid students of theirs who started the Equalist movement, and changed the way the Survey looked at alien life. The Equalists also started the rift between the Survey and the Royalist faction, and an even bigger rift between the Riunor faction and everybody else. The Tav look upon the Riunor mercantile developers in the same way your own kitties view the stuff they cover in their litter boxes. I have never seen *any* Tav mention terms like "developer" or "advertising executive" without visibly expressing their claws. That gesture alone speaks volumes.

Tavs started funneling emerging raw empaths to places where neither the growing Royalist military complex nor the Riunor corporations could lay their grubby little mitts on them. That hiding place, for the most part, was the Survey Service, although some wound up here on your planet. But more about that later.

The initial recommendation on any survey, and thus the future of a surveyed planet, rests on the shoulders of the seven to nine beings who make up the Survey scout crew. The crew is led by one Chief Master, and consists of Academy graduates in various stages of some of the toughest and most interesting on-the-job training the galaxy has ever known. This is the story of one of these ships.

Worlds of Power,
Lines of Light

Chapter

1

This was shaping up to be the worst day in his life. Until today, that life had been well structured and financially secure. Then came the messenger, bearing dark news. Still half-asleep, he, Crensed Jorien, had been unceremoniously hustled into a darkened flitter. He was given a packed bag, a Survey Service uniform and manual, and specific orders to evacuate Metrowyl ASAP and keep his mouth shut. As heir to the Jorien empire, he was used to better. Now he was headed into deep space, and deep trouble.

The shock that grabbed his conscious mind refused to let go. He stared at the bulkheads for hours, his normally adaptable mind refusing to engage. When the comm blared, signaling to prepare for docking, he did so. A few shifts of position and a solid clunk told him docking had been achieved. He pressed the comm link. No answer. He unwebbed, and pressed the comm link again. Nothing. The compartment opened, but no one greeted him. Now what? He sighed, picked up the bag and manual, and entered the corridor. He tried the comm on the bulkhead.

"Ah, I'm sorry, um." he said tentatively. "I don't see anyone. Do I get off now?"

The bulkhead viewscreen cleared. The face that looked out at him was dark, triangular, and furred. Golden slit-pupil eyes regarded him gravely. Cren shut his eyes tightly and struggled to control his thoughts and feelings. Tavs! This long dark day suddenly showed every indication of becoming worse.

"I see no problem, Commander. We can hold them for a time. Their ship's a floating salvage yard. Accidents happen." Krel Dorvin, adjuvant commander of HomePort docking operations, dropped the compadd on the console and leaned back in his seat.

"That they do, Mr. Dorvin. That they do." The commander rubbed his balding forehead. "But with this bunch," he sighed, "they tend to happen to other people."

Dorvin's deep-set eyes narrowed. "What do you mean?"

"Read this, Mr. Dorvin." Commander Garefin picked up a silvered-grey hardcopy on his station, and tossed it over to Dorvin.

"What is it?" Dorvin asked, fingering it nervously.

"It's 'need to know', Dorvin. You need to know. Holding that ship is your responsibility."

Dorvin flipped it open. He whistled out a breath, and then looked behind him at the door. "Ho boy. I'm glad you're jamming the bugs." He read.

> *"Official Personnel Roster: Survey Service Scout Craft #192, Metrowyl Military Intelligence Eyes Only, Blackstar Clearance*
>
> *Chief Rial Jennery: 40 years Survey Service, Chief Master rating. Specialty: Multiple Science, Communications, Engineering. White Team Leader. Highly successful at training superior explorers. Innovative. Something of a legend. Unorthodox methodology. Allegiance suspect.*

"Suspect? Jennery? He's fringe, Commander, but they all are in Survey. That's why they're good at what they do. He's loyal to Metrowyl, in my opinion. And he's the best."

"I'm aware of his record, Mr. Dorvin. Read."

*Dalrion Darnel: 14 years Survey Service, Command rat-
ing. Specialty: Multiple Sciences, Xenobiology, First Contact Liaison. Blue Team Leader WARNING: Empath of
unknown ability: extremely high potential. Assume Tav
partisan. Possibly still undergoing Season of Change. DE-
TAIN IF POSSIBLE. ALL PRECAUTIONS.*

Dorvin's head cocked sideways. "Well, now." He chewed his lip.
"*That* empath. I've heard tales. If the stories have a grain of truth.
'Tav *Partisan*'? Last I heard, the furfolk were still teaching over at
the Academy."

"No more. They left during the unofficial military takeover."

Dorvin looked over his shoulder at the door. "How in the hell are
we supposed to detain an empath of that power?"

Commander Garefin sighed. "I commed them to that effect. It
does say 'if possible'. That may be an out. Intelligence is due here
before the ship docks. This scout ship is approaching as of now,
and they're short one crewman. We've removed their replacement."

"Removed"?

"That, you don't 'need to know'," he sighed. "Continue reading."

*Renzec Zimman: 11 years Service; 4 years Engineer HomePort,
remainder Survey. Senior rating. Specialty: Engineering,
Oceanography, Astrophysics. Red Team Leader. Temperamental and can be disciplinary problem. Possible use.*

"Rennie Zimman? I know him." The adjuvant frowned. "We've
been out drinking." He looked up in exasperation. "What is going
on here?"

"I'm going to miss this old tub," Renzec reached out, patting the
antiquated bulkhead with the flat of his agile hand as he grinned.

"Huuh, I never thought these ears would hear *you* say that!"

Chief Master Jennery laughed, his blue eyes squinting slightly as he eased the creaky ship into her final docking.

"Tis true, Chief." The engineer leaned his lanky tallness against the side of the view port, observing the activity outside. Most visible bays were filled. Support crews bustled about, mostly in military grey.

"I know, old son. I just never thought I'd hear you say it. " Jennery eased his hands off the controls, and the scout ship gave a final shudder and came to rest. He looked around wistfully. The compact Chief Master had run her for 30 years, and she had become part of him. "You've kept her going, Rennie. Patched her so much, you built me a new ship."

"New? Chief Rial! She's the old lady of the fleet, by far." Koren Greval shook her long auburn locks free of their space snood. "Perhaps they'll make a museum of her.

"Museum? There's too much life left in this old girl. She'd make a superb training vessel!" Jennery insisted. Then his normally cheerful countenance changed as he joined the others to assess the activity on the other side of the view port.

"Training for what, Chief?" Renzec grimaced and turned his back on the port. " She's obsolete from tip to stern. Maybe I can get a life now, instead of an endless repair gig."

Koren looked up at her teammate and smiled suggestively. "I can think of a thing or two for you to do with your time."

Renzec grinned and answered with a wink. The two had been an item, off and on. He opened his mouth to comment, when an incoming signal hooted at them. Koren leaned over gracefully and pressed the retrieval pad.

"HomePort Central greets you, Ship 192." The tightly clipped and regimented military monotone colored the standard welcome a dark gray.

Koren wrinkled her nose in distaste, and stuck out her tongue at the comm, but kept any trace of resentment from her voice. "Ship 192 acknowledges."

The comm crackled. "Stand by. U-messages". This brought raised eyebrows and immediate attention.

"Standing by". Rial leaned over abruptly and pressed the "Hold" command. Urgent messages, necessitating immediate verbal response. What now? "Don't let them get to you," Rial ordered softly.

"They already got to us, looks like, "Renzec muttered with an oath.

"I was speaking to myself, " Rial explained in a low tone.

Renzec grunted. "This place is an armed camp. The vibes must stink! Dal won't sleep 'til we clear HomePort."

"If I don't miss my guess, that will be the least of his problems. And ours." Rial hit the intership comm. "Dal?"

"Here, Chief." The empath answered evenly.

"We need full crew up here, son. U-messages."

"On the way." Within seconds, the hall to the aft cabin filled with crew. Leh Torvah, contact/xeno expert, came in first, her smooth dark skin contrasting pleasantly with her medium blue jumpsuit. In Survey, the darker the uniform, the more senior the rating. She had their apprentice crewmate in tow, Naui Dagoz. Naui's Orelian skin was a slightly lighter shade of blue than her pale suit, but not much. Following them, at a much slower pace, came Melion Haekay, geologist and physicist. Melion's bronze face was etched with lines of pain. Spacers undergoing the Season of Change had a tougher than usual time acclimating to full grav after weightlessness. In her arms she cradled Katayan, a genetically engineered Tavian catabit. The golden ball of fluff with distinctive brown markings was ship sentinel and mascot. His elongated ears flicked about as his esper senses flooded with tension overload, and his small nose twitched. Dalrion Darnel and Kimmer Sierk came in last. The handsome empath looked determined, and his eyes narrowed as he saw the port activity. Kimmer, the crew medic, botanist and xenoecologist, kept an anxious watch on Dal.

Rial briefly held the eyes of each member of his crew complement. "Is everything ok out there, Dal?" he asked.

"I think not. Let's find out for sure," Dal replied softly.

The Chief released the Hold, and the messages commenced.

"U-Message One: Replacement ship # 963 Model M-100 release will be delayed for approximately one week. Contact Military HQ for specifics."

Renzec grimaced and swore silently. Frowns deepened all around.

"U-Message Two: Molecular physics and electromagnetics expert Quer Dendries is no longer available. Contact Military adjunct for replacement."

Rial looked around at his crew sternly, silencing incipient complaints with a finger to his lips. "Why? Do you finally have a Tav for me?" he asked the comm.

"That request will remain unfilled. No felinoids HomePort or Metrowyl."

"Understood." Rial was grim.

"U-Message Three: First Officer/Empath Dalrion Darnel report to Mil/Psych ASAP."

Rial hit Hold again. "They mean business this time, Dal."

Dal reflected on his options. Then he sighed. "I do too, Chief". He said deliberately, "Tell them I am coming out of Change, and my reporting will be somewhat delayed."

Kimmer grabbed Dal's hand. "You can't mean to go to them!" she insisted.

"Calm your body, Kim, " Dal insisted firmly. "I can handle this."

Rial studied Dal's face. The empath's message was true, of course. Empath's didn't lie. He had no wish to lose Dal to that bunch. But he trusted his second in command. He replied as requested.

The answer was immediate. "Understood. Inform the First Officer/Empath to report within three days. End of U Messages. Prepare to receive recorded mail."

"Understood." As soon as he turned the comm to autoreceive, Rial blew air through his lips and shook his head. "Comments?"

"We need a crew replacement for Vors before we go spaceward." Leh sat at her console, absently petting Katayan. The catabit mewed. His ears and nose continued twitching with the mounting tension in the room.

"Agreed," Rial said.

" Dal can't go to them, " Kimmer insisted again. "Once they see the talents he's developing, we'll never get him back."

"Agreed."

"And this new ship? " Renzec blurted. "The one they say *isn't* ready yet? Like the specialist we picked *isn't* available? They knew we were coming, and when, and what we needed. They're stalling."

"Again, agreed." Rial looked around expectantly. Everyone looked totally bleak, except for one. And to that one the chief turned his attention. "What do you want to do, son?"

"We have time." Dal said cryptically. Katayan swivelled his head, and pointed dark ears at Dal. Dal laughed and reached out to scratch the semimane behind the catabit's head. Katayan closed his eyes in bliss and purred loudly, all tension momentarily forgotten.

Kimmer looked up at him anxiously. "You *told* them you'd report! Three days!"

"I did not, Kimmer," Dal said evenly. "I said I'd be *delayed* . It was *they* who specified the time, not me. I intend an *extended* delay. *Very* extended. There may yet be Tavs in-system. If so, we have hope. Chief, if we can get *secure* messages out, I have a plan."

"Ship 192 is gone," Commander Garefin said in a strained voice. "Without supplies, replacement or clearance. No approximate flight plan. No warning. Irregular, but not illegal. They can't get far."

Colonel Lar, Chief of Military Intelligence, steepled his long fingers. He glared at Garefin. He stood, and Garefin leaped to attention. There were only the two of them. Dorvin was . . . gone. "I will have them," Lar promised, clenching his long fingers into a tight fist. " And this time, I will tend to it myself."

"We're closing on Ku'Fenn. I don't understand why you had us overshoot the base. Dal, you think we'll get away with this?" Renzec glanced at the sensors. This satellite was not as obviously bristling with military as HomePort, but that was rapidly changing. "We've reached the coordinates, but there's nothing here. We need our replacement, and we need supplies."

Dal didn't look up from his screen. "Modulate your mood, Rennie. The military must be spread thin, monitoring people going *out* of the system, not *in*. The Chief arranged for our crew replacement."

"Whatever you say, Dal. Ok if I go aft?"

"Go back and get some sleep, Ren," Chief Rial called from the cabinway. He appeared rested, but tense. "Dal and I will be busy for a while."

"You figure they'll let us pick up what we need and take off?"

"We're not docking, Ren," Chief Rial explained. "We're for a rendezvous."

"Isn't that illegal?"

"Unconventional," Dal corrected.

"And then? This bucket can't go anywhere the military can't follow."

Dal's eyes glazed over. Then his focus returned. He grinned. "They're coming."

Renzec looked at the forward sensor array. Dal activated the screen to aft. Nothing. Then, in the upper right corner, a small ship with rounded lines materialized. Tav!

Renzec whistled. "I don't want to know." He speedily went aft.

Shortly, the commlink blinked. Without a word, Rial moved to Dal's station. Dal activated the link. In the commscreen, a dark grey feline face appeared, with a black Chief Master Survey stripe on a V-shaped throat collar. No words were exchanged, but the Tav yawned widely. Dal smiled in understanding. All was going according to plan. Dal raised a hand in greeting, and the Tav Chief responded with a raised paw and a nod. He expressed claws but with his toes very wide-spread. Then he withdrew the claws. Dal nodded and stretched his fingers as wide as they could go. The screen went blank. No verbal communication over the comm. The ships docked. Supplies were ferried to the ancient scout. The Tav Chief followed, to confer briefly with Rial and Dal.

"Sset up jumps as I dirrected, and no one will follow. Then the long hop. Be warry with this new one. Therre is darrk in him. He is not as he sseems." Dal nodded acceptance. Tavs often talked in riddles. He would ponder the words later, when he had more time. "I'll deal with it," he promised. The object of their discussion, novice Crensed Jorien, boarded shortly after the Tav left, and the docking coupling was disconnected. By this time, Dal and Melion had started calculations for the long series of hops. Within minutes, the Tav ship was gone. Ship 192, complete with supplies and full complement, followed shortly thereafter.

Chapter

2

Not bad. Sort of floaty. Cren Jorien allowed one of his tightly clamped eyelids to slowly release its hold on his eye. Death was a blurry thing. He opened the other eye and his sight cleared. He focused on the tag end of a strip of hyperilon tape patching a worn bulkhead. The tape had lost some of its hold with time. Long fingers of frayed insulate poked out behind it, giving it a grizzled look. Cren took in the dilapidated interior of the archaic scout ship. His teammates attended their consoles, monitoring screens and murmuring to themselves. Cren let out a long-held breath. So he was not dead. Yet.

He connected with the floating feeling. Labeled it. Null-grav. He looked at his aft viewscreen. The Freel-Omar Nebula hung suspended. It looked the same as it had from the other side. A ball of dirty fluff. The other screens were blank.

"I never thought this bucket would get us through," he sighed.

Chief Rial Jennery acknowledged the remark with a grunt and a shake of his head, but his eyes remained focused on his moody Matrix drive. "Don't sound so disappointed, lad. Adventure awaits. And don't use that negative tone of voice when you call this scout "old". She's vintage. Proven trustworthy. She'll need a little coddling, son, that's all. With luck, we'll find a suitable planet, and we'll be off this boat. Cut your teeth on a new world, and let go a little.

The Chief's fingers flew lightly over his sensor board. "Scan to your port side, Cren. See if you can sight our next heading. Now that we've 'survived' the hop through the Freel-Omar," he added dryly.

"Nothing on port scans, Chief."

"It's there, Cren," Rial Jennery said patiently.

"They're blank. I swear it, Chief!"

"You're squeaking lad. Like a baby yorbu. Scan the electromagnetics."

"I'm scanning, Chief. Honest. I'm not getting *anything*! What's a yorbu, anyway?"

"Complex beasts, they are. Complex," the Chief muttered as he keyed in changes to balance the overheated drive. "The port screen has an object clearly visible," he added.

"Not to me," Cren sighed.

Renzec Zimmen groaned as he unstrapped from his station. He kicked free of his console, and pushed over to troubleshoot Cren's scanners.

"No wonder the fardling port screen's blank! It's not activated, Cren! You were looking at an old pict! Get your station up!" He grimaced and his eyes rolled in exaggerated disbelief at Cren's blank look. "What do they teach at the Academy!" Renzec's long fingers moved expertly over the controls, pressing sensor pads. Three screens blossomed with rapidly changing data, and a brilliant light appeared on the visual scanner showing far to port. Next to it was the aft screen with the nebula. Cren glanced doubtfully at the sensors, and then back at the screens. Mollified, he looked up at the engineer.

"Thanks, Renzec. This, uh, set-up is older than anything I saw at the Academy. Even in the museum."

Renzec cawed at that.

"I guess that's our target right there." Cren squinted at the blob of light, checking scale. "Guardian, it's huge." A look at the incoming data told him nothing understandable. "We're going there? What is it?"

"Huge, Cren." Renzec's lopsided grin split his face wide. "And yes, it's probably our next destination. Can't tell much more for sure, from out here, but look at the EM!" Renzec eased his long body back into his station and resumed his job.

Cren wiped sweaty hands on his pale blue stretchsuit, studying the object far to port, carefully avoiding screens depicting only deep space. He had gazed too long into the emptiness once, when they first broke orbit for deep space, and he had nearly been lost to it. Dal had thrown him a mental tendril, and pulled his mind back inside his head. "Space Rapture", Kimmer had called it. Dal had been intrigued with this awareness of the depths of space in a non-empath. Cren could do without it.

The object to port did have a walloping electromagnetic signature. But it was bizarre EM, skewed, as if the sensors weren't calibrated for what they were receiving. Heavy grav pull, too, for it to register on this scale out here. Cren could make out vague colors as he searched inside the brilliance. He felt his stomach starting to roil with the perceived motion.

"Hey, my screen is frizzled," he complained. "This thing to port looks as if it's moving!"

"No frizzle, Cren," Renzec clarified. "I see it too. I think it's a star field. An extremely abnormal star field. I'm guessing that we could actually be seeing EM flux in motion. The books say we can't, not this far out, but . . ."

" '. . . the stars don't read the books' ", the rest of the team chimed. One of Chief Rial's innumerable axioms.

"Kind of a smoothling thing to watch, though," Renzec mused, "once you get accustomed to it. It looks as if there are living things crawling around in it, just slightly below perception level. I like it."

"That would figure," Cren groaned dismally as he tried to gain a measure of control over his growing nausea. He closed his eyes and reached hard for that place within. The safe place Dal had helped him build.

"Are you all right, Cren?" Kimmer asked. The diminutive medic appeared at his shoulder, medkit at the ready.

"Thanks for the thought, Kimmer, but I don't take meds," Cren insisted. "I'll work it out."

Kimmer looked dubious as she placed her hand firmly on Cren's arm. "I can't have you barfing in null-grav. It reflects poorly on my skill. Anti-nausea patches are standard for the first deep space voyage. I don't know why you're so stubborn."

Renzec muttered strong agreement. "You make a mess this time, you clean it yourself, kid."

"No meds," Cren insisted.

"Fine Cren," Kimmer said grimly. "No one will force you." She looked at the flickering, rapidly changing sensor displays. "But Rennie is right." She flipped her scanner over Cren's head and frowned. "Your neurotransmitters are all over the place. You barf, you clean. Here, let me restrict your screens to processed data." Her hands moved efficiently over Cren's console.

"That will simplify your input. Breathe deeply and slowly for a bit," she cautioned. "You're even paler than usual." She ran the sensor once more over her newest charge. "I guess you're ok, considering."

"Considering my growing desire to barf?" Cren smiled wanly.

"Considering you've refused the standard neurotransmitter balancing for novice crew members. I suppose you have your reasons, and I'll respect them, but they do have consequences."

"Wish we had that new ship, or at least a new analyzer," Renzec said wistfully as he scratched a rather large ear. "Cren's got a point. The readings I'm getting just don't mesh, Chief."

"I have faith in you, Rennie. You'll cope."

Renzec groaned. "Blind and hobbled", he muttered to himself.

"You doing better, Cren?" Koren Greval asked a little later. She paused from her tasks to turn and flash an encouraging smile.

Cren returned the smile, hoping for help and a little sympathy, but Koren had already returned to her board. She, along with Cren and Renzec, made up Red Team, a third of the scout complement and the only one technically on duty. Kimmer Sierk and Leh Torevoh were at stations only because they were awake, wanted to be useful, and there was no place in the universe they would rather be.

Cren tried again. "Actually, Koren, I can't make sense of this stuff. It's coming in way too fast. It's all new to me!"

The Chief intercepted the dialogue with a piercing whistle. "Cren, m'boy, of course it's all new. We specialize in "new". Downscale your sensors, lad. We'll go over the data when we're secured from Matrix transition."

"I *have* scaled them down, Chief. Honest. Twice already. I *know* electromagnetics." Cren twiddled some dials. "We could be missing important stuff, the way the graph markers are drifting. Look. There goes the marker, off the chart again!" Cren's movements became frantic as he tried to adjust. "There's too much data to manage."

"Two things you never have in Survey," Chief Rial intoned, "are . . ."

". . . too much data, or too much time to interpret it," the crew called out in unison. Cren had fallen into another axiom.

"Try to catch the highlights, if you'll excuse the pun," Rial added, his eyes twinkling. "You aren't supposed to 'manage' the data. It's all any of us can do right now to pick out bits of interest from the initial deluge. Except Dal, of course."

"What does Dal do?"

"He accepts it, Cren, as it comes in," Kimmer explained. "He allows his subconscious to fit the pieces together. He says most people try to group data too much, and miss important connections."

"But I don't *know* what could be important!"

"Cren, you're observing what your crew mates also receive. Make a note of your questions, and we'll discuss them later."

"Chief, why don't I wake Dal? He could help me *now*."

Rial just sighed.

"Give the guy a break, Cren," Kimmer warned. "Dal is exhausted after setting up the Matrix. He and Mel are going through Change, remember, and Change is extra hard on an empath. That's why I'm on Blue Team with Dal and Mel. Changers need medic support around the clock."

"Yeah, kid," Renzec agreed. "Dal has been awful patient with you. This stuff can wait."

Cren's lips quivered, while his eyes narrowed and his jaw set. "I only want to help."

Rial sighed again. "Calm it, Cren," he ordered. "A crewman in a
in a snit is only marginally better than one in a freak-out. You want
to contribute, I'll give that to you. You simply don't know how. You
never completed field training, did you, lad?"

Cren dropped his eyes at the Chief's accusation, but said nothing.

"As far as I know, it is still required at the Academy," Rial said
thoughtfully. "Even for those not assigned to Survey duty. Your father has a lot of pull. I was surprised to find a message from him
waiting for me at HomePort. Maybe the military didn't have anything to do with the fact that our chosen crewman decided on another posting."

Cren cringed mentally, but said nothing. He didn't know.

"It was a trade off for us, taking you on, Cren. I made a deal with
your father, because the military tried to lift my empath, and he had
a secure channel. I schooled Dal, much as I could, without their
help. It should be his right to decide where he goes and who he goes
with, and when. I'd do just about anything to protect that right. Including taking on a recruit who seems singularly unsuited for Survey work." The Chief's blue eyes lazered into Cren.

"I'm sorry for any trouble, Chief Jennery. But Dal's taught me a
lot. He always helps me right away." If Cren could have squirmed
in null-grav, he would have.

"You're too dependent on him, son. He's Blue Team Leader, and
second in command. He's a naturally compassionate young man, but
in all honesty, some of that help was self-defense. Guardian knows
I'm as close to empath-null as they get, but the negativity you broadcast affects even me. It has to be agony to a hypersensitive like Dal."

The Chief let his eyes mellow, and he smiled at Cren. "I don't
know your story, boy, but we can help you, if you let us. You could
repay Dal's help, if you'd let Kimmer moderate your fear and anxiety. You've been obstinate in refusing even the mildest calmative,
or anti-nausea meds. It might help if we understood why."

Cren said nothing, and hung his head. His jaw tightened even
more.

Dal's early assessment haunted the Chief. The boy's exception-

ally bright, he had reported. Gifted, in some areas. He means well.
Then he added the kicker. But he's hiding something, Chief. I can't
get down to it without destroying his trust. Let me wait for the right
time, for his sake.

Rial's silky white hair formed a halo in the null-grav, and his eyes
looked tired. He fingered the pause-lock on the Q/T Matrix, and began unstrapping. He moved with an easy familiarity, and his trim
body looked as if it had been made for his black Chief Master's uniform.

"I must be crazy, taking a kid who's spent his whole life in the underground warrens of Metrowyl, and carting him out to deep space.
Cren, there'll come a day when you realize you've shipped out with
a whole bunch of crazies. By then you'll fit right in. Don't know why
your dad picked us though." He gave Cren an encouraging smile.

"He heard something, ah, rather exotic about this ship."

Renzec hooted. "Exotic. That's a new one."

"Father said this ship is the safest in the fleet. People leave your
service *at their own discretion* in most cases, Chief. You know?"

"I know what you're trying to say, but you're expending a lot of
time and energy walking around it. People die in space, Cren," Rial
sighed as he caressed the old Matrix panel lovingly, and then
launched himself in a gentle glide across the cabin. "We just make
it our business not to join that group. We do that by teamwork, by
careful preparation and planning, and by respecting our teammates
and crewmates." He effortlessly hooked his leg around a support
and eased to a stop. "Now, let's take a look at what's tilting your
galaxy. Whatever it is, it's been there for millions of years. It'll be
content to wait a few hours longer, or however long it takes, before
it is understood by such as us."

He examined Cren's screens carefully, and then slipped some of
the hard copy out from under a clip.

"I made copies of those frames when something came up I
wanted to ask about," Cren explained tentatively.

"Ummn. Good for you, lad." He studied the copy silently for a
while. "I was hoping for a habitable planet for the Tagur colony, you
know. They've been heavy on my mind. This stuff, though, doesn't

look promising. See these hot points on the edge, Cren? They'll cool down into solar systems of their own, in eleventy-million years or so. The big blob in the center, that's so many proto stars so hot and so close that we can't distinguish them individually. The gravity, now. . . . I don't know about that. There's got to be something else we can't see."

He handed the hard copy to Cren. "Continue to follow the EM. Maybe you'll get that scientific paper you want. Your dad would be proud of that, right?"

Cren's eyes cleared and he nodded.

Rial sighed. "I've been training Survey crew for forty years. I've always thought it kept me young. Sometimes I'm not so sure. I've aged quite a bit these last few weeks."

Cren had the grace to blush.

"Think of a new site as a lazcut puzzle, lad. Pieces are coming in fast now, but not all of them, and not in order. Once we get close, we'll start organizing the borders of the puzzle. Before we leave, we'll have a fairly good picture for a SiTeam to follow. That's if we get a habitable planet or potential resource that calls for further investigation. I sincerely hope we do.

"What I can't figure is how the Academy let you graduate. Your records were sketchy. Due to circumstances, we couldn't call up what we wanted. They did indicate specialties of electromagnetics and molecular physics. Which, *just by chance*, was what we needed. Your dad was pushing hard to get you into deep space. *Very* deep space. Immediately. Is there something that Councilman Jorien knows that we don't? Something that we *should* know?"

"You must have heard talk," Cren said as he fine-tuned the electromagnetic sensors.

"Talk? There's always talk at HomePort. Sometimes I think that's what they built the satellite for." Rial hung over Cren's shoulder, thinking aloud.

"Seems like whenever the political factions get edgy, war rumors start. A city-world is real vulnerable to war, and to rumors, too." Renzec added.

"Maybe King Klev just wants to expand the military."

"Oh, he's doing that, Cren. I am not unaware of the changes on HomePort and Metrowyl. All the Tavs have gone."

"So who's training the empaths? And what did Dal say about the Tavs leaving?"

"There aren't any empaths left, Ren. Military's got 'em. Dal got vague and mystic on me, Ren, when I asked him about the Tavs leaving." Rial smiled sadly and ran his fingers through his hair-a futile gesture in null-grav. He took another glance at Cren's scanners and his eyes narrowed. "What do you see that has you in a tizzy now, lad?"

"You'll say it sounds silly."

The Chief skewed Cren with his blue-eyed stare. He waited, silence his best argument.

"See that irregularity on the hard copy? It's small. You can't even see it on the sensors anymore. It's blanked by EM. You know an overload can desensitize instruments after a while. Especially old ones like these."

"I'm conversant with their workings," Chief Rial said dryly. He had designed most of them before he took to Survey.

His satire was lost on Cren. "Well, this just doesn't fit in with the big picture. It's got to be an anomaly. It can't be natural, but its big."

Rial peered at the graph. The bushy eyebrows went up again as he studied it. "Yes, I do. Hmmn. Input 4928. Check it out, Rennie. Close to the edge. Relatively, of course. Everything is relative in space. Could be an artifact. Maybe a cloud, or some small, irregular nebulosity. It's cold, though. Comparatively, that is. Good catch, m'boy." Rial tapped Cren's shoulder gently,. and pushed over to his engineer's console.

"Really?" A slow, tentative smile fought its way across Cren's face.

"Ren, any theories on how such a thing could exist on the edge of a birthing field? The violence of star formation should preclude such a thing."

"Well, Chief, the thing is, it's at the edge of the field. Something is keeping the cold area separate." "My guess is, if this is real and not an artifact, there's *something* generating its own field. And it's a doozy of a field. Sensors indicate a cloud of some kind." He grinned his wide, lop-sided grin. "It begs to be investigated close-up." Then his face grew serious. "There may be a problem."

"And just what would that problem be?" Rial asked.

"There's a tremendous mass, way beyond what can reasonably be expected, in the same direction as the proto stars."

"Any radio waves out that way, Rennie?"

"Lots, Chief. We could have a Cosmic String, sitting on the other side of that field."

"That would fit," Chief Rial agreed. "The nebula we crossed could even be a part of the network. Dust. The gas. Hmmn." He looked up and his bright eyes twinkled. "We'll check that String idea as soon as we find out what's with this cloud. From a safe distance."

That brought smiles all around, except from Cren.

"I guess it doesn't matter what I feel," Cren said in a low tone.

"What makes you think it doesn't matter, Cren," Chief Rial asked.

"I'm new. And, I'll admit it, I'm scared. What if it's dangerous?"

"Look, Crensed, I haven't been Survey that long myself. You think I never get scared? I just don't spend my energy working myself into a panic. You can if yourself into a frenzy. The only way to find out is to check it out." Naui Dagoz sized Cren up, large turquoise eyes mirroring the frustration she felt about their newest crew member. Naui's features were decidedly Orelian. High cheekbones and delicate planes, born to space. She looked good in her new, darker outfit, and she wore it with a flare, no longer the new kid on the ship. "Why are you out here," she insisted bluntly, "if not to explore new things?"

"See," Crensed said pointedly, "you *don't* understand. It's raw out here. Hungry. I don't know how to express it."

" 'The infinite, haunting depths of space, where the touch of darkness seeps inside to quench the soul's true light' ", Kimmer quoted, and she smiled gently at the look in Cren's eyes as she spoke.

"Yes." Cren said with surprise, and his eyes widened. "That's it! Part of it, anyway. Where did that come from?"

"Dal wrote it. He wrote a whole book of poetry his first year out. Maybe he'd share it with you, if you're interested. We've all had feelings about the enormity of space. Honest, Cren." She gave a warning glance to Naui, who was about to object. "At least, those of us who spent our early lives on Metrowyl. But we chose Survey life." She smoothed down her jumpsuit unconsciously. "We're proud of what we do. Sure, we were spooked by the enormity of it all at first, but each of us had meds to help us adjust to deep space. The emptiness. We're forced to confront how insignificant we are in the scheme of things. Take it in a little bite at a time, Cren. You might try writing your own journal," she suggested. "It may help you with your feelings. If you have valid scientific reasons for us to avoid the anomalous area, let us know. We'll listen."

Cren thought for a moment, still unsure of himself. "I can't put my finger on it, but it scares me."

"Cren, we have to get closer to get any more data," Kimmer explained. "We need more data to arrive at any meaningful hypotheses. All else is abstract speculation. I want to go in."

"Me too," Rial responded. "Although I wouldn't want to disparage enlightened 'abstract speculation'. It has its place." He glanced at Crensed. Color was returning to his face. "Let's pull in closer. We'll wake the others when we've stabilized. Maybe Dal will be able to sense something when we're closer."

A mellow glow spread over Kimmer's face. Rial smiled inside. That relationship was deepening, as he'd hoped. Medics and empaths often made stable bonded twos.

"What do *you* think it is, Chief?" Koren wrinkled her nose and frowned. She was a slim, elegant young lady with golden skin and enticing green eyes. She had a kind of offhand sensuality about her that generated its own kind of magnetic field. Rial had thought for a while that Koren would two with Dal, but it hadn't worked. His emerging powers spooked her. But Koren never had a trace of fear when it came to space. She tended to take too many risks, in fact. But she had trouble making up her mind, and a tendency to depend too much on others. She had a good brain. Time she learned to trust it.

"Ah, Koren. I think it's something brand new," Rial said softly. "Something I've never seen before.

"Ok, Rennie," he ordered briskly, "set it up. We're going in."

Chapter

3

Alarms blared as the scout broke Q/T Hyperspace. Dal and Melion pulled themselves onto duty stations, with Katayan soaring swiftly behind. His "wings", lightly furred membranes stretching from the edge of his forelegs to the outside of his hind legs, were set taut to maximize glide. He started to furl them as he eyed his newly preferred landing spot. "*Riaowwww*", he howled.

Cren looked up and groaned. Dal glanced briefly at the tableau in formation, and spoke a brief command. Though no human could hear Dal over the wail of the alarm, the catabit abruptly changed angle of flight by snagging a protuberance briefly with an extended paw. With a frustrated cry and an observant eye Crenward, he engaged his claws to settle on the padding behind Dal's chair just as Dal finished checking radiation levels and aborted the alarm. The main screen was filled with a blazing gem of crackling energy, set in a backdrop of velvet darkness. White and Red Teams remained in the command cabin, absorbing data on which to fuel their dreams.

Naui was nearly on top of the screen, unable to contain her excitement. "Look at it! Look at it!" she kept yelling.

Katayan narrowed slanted eyes to a bare slit, and settled down, muscles twitching briefly from the positive emotional onslaught engendered by his crewmates.

Dal glanced at the sensors, gave a low whistle and laughed. "We just hit big time."

"The star field?"

"That too. I'm more interested in the anomaly, Chief. The solar system. It shouldn't be there. Could you see it before the hop?"

"Cren spotted it."

"Good man, Cren!"

Cren stared at the main screen as a red flush spread up his cheeks. Then he sighed deeply. Katayan fidgeted restlessly, widening his eyes at Cren. The little being bunched his legs, preparing to leap. Dal looked at the catabit meaningfully and thought some heavy thoughts, and the little creature closed his eyes again and settled down.

"First impressions, Dal?"

"Main Sequence, Chief! G2, no less. It can't be, but it is." Dal had unconsciously tensed his muscles in response to heightened adrenalin. Now he had to close his eyes a moment to get his neurotransmitters under control, breathing in careful, slow rhythm. Once he was in balance, he blinked once, and then smiled. "I bet we'll find this system has planetary bodies, as well."

"Why planets?" The Chief wasted no time getting over to Dal's station. He hung over Dal's shoulder, maintaining position with a light hand on the back of the chair. His left hand brushed Dal's shoulder and the empath registered his own remaining muscle tension, took another deep breath, and willed his muscles to relax. There was no reason to stress his body. Katayan rumbled a low purr, and opened slitted eyes.

"Just a hunch, Chief. Look at the precise border of the clear area. This is not cosmic business-as-usual. This star has a set of fields all its own. I never heard of an energy field in the shape of a spiral before. That field, plus the cloud, is putting a buffer on the proto stars. The raw power of the protostars is awesome, even out that far. Equally awesome, although not as spectacular, is the way the star is protected from it. The star is protected. Why *not* planets?. Finding out how and why this system exists should be our priority."

Cren smiled weakly. "Let me guess. You want to go closer."

Dal looked questioningly at the young spacer. "Stars don't birth gently, my friend. The star isn't *that* close to the field, Cren. It is actually much further away from the field than we were from it when we first stopped to check. It just looks close comparatively. Yes, there is radiation and toxic sulfur coming from the protostars. But we are here to increase knowledge. Our ship is well shielded. That inner cloud is nearly pure hydrogen peroxide. It keeps any toxic sulfur from the forming protostars off the system's perimeter, beyond the cometary belt. The boundary is clean, chemically reducing the hydrogen sulfide." Dal pulled back from his investigation of the sensors, and closed his eyes momentarily, correlating the data. Katayan closed his pale blue eyes as well, joining in the mental gymnastics. Then they both blinked and opened their eyes. "There's only water vapor left on the inner edge," Dal reported. "Totally safe. There was a theory on that, at the Academy."

"Oh yeah. I remember," Renzec agreed. His own eyes stayed glued to his screens. "It was supposed to revolutionize the production of hyperilon, if it could be applied. By Beierhof, I think."

"That's the one! Hydrogen peroxide will buffer sulfur given the correct astrochemical parameters. This is her proof, right here." Dal pressed a few sensor pads quickly. His whole face lit up. "Incredible! Look at that solar wind! Too intense for words."

"Reminds me of someone I know," Kimmer interjected dryly, but she was grinning too. She reached over to skritch Katayan's chin. She was rewarded with a brief purr and a twitch of the long, furry ears as the catabit leaned into the skritch, maximizing his enjoyment, and Kimmer's as well, as she basked in the glow of radiating catabit pleasure.

"We might be able to rig an energy tap, if we find a habitable planet," Dal said seriously, not to be distracted. "This is going to be interesting!"

"*Weehu!*" Chief Rial exclaimed as he eyeballed the monitors. "My Grandmother's cross-eyed yorbu, now *that* was interesting. *This* place requires additions to the vocabulary!" He rubbed his hands together in delight, and his eyes shone with a steady, hungry fire, equaled by all his crew-save one. Cren was staring at the floor, his face getting longer by the minute. "Any reason for extra precautions?" Chief Rial asked, more to give Dal a chance to soothe Cren's fears than for any concern of his own.

Dal took in Cren's apprehensive posture. His face became pensive, with that slightly out of focus look empaths have when their feelers are out. "It should be perfectly safe inside the protective envelope," he said carefully. "The area feels stable to me. Sensor readings lead me to believe these conditions have persisted for ages." Dal gave a slight tilt to his head and his deep golden eyes looked meaningfully at Rial. The Chief felt that all the indicators weren't in on that last statement, but that Dal couldn't verbalize without further disturbing Cren.

"Move us up then, Dal," Rial ordered, "to about one-half light year from the star."

"You're on," Dal agreed, keying in the drive sequence.

Hours later, Dal grimaced as he stretched slowly from his console chair, easing the cramping of his tight, spasming muscles. Muscles loosen in free fall. The myofascia, that sticky, flexible film that wraps around the muscle fibers, fiber bundles and the muscles themselves, releases much of its tension in null gravity. Even tendons and ligaments, themselves composed of myofascia, relax slightly. This helped those going through Change. During the Season of Change, myofascia was stressed, thickening and tightening protectively due to mixed messages sent by neurotransmitters. Myofascia lost elasticity, and formed painful lumps and ropy, constricting bands of trigger points (TrPs). TrPs caused pain of many types, plus bizarre symptoms, as various nerves, blood and lymph vessels and even glandular ducts were constricted. When Changers returned to full-grav after a period of free-fall, they were burdened with spasms, contractures, and a generalized worsening of symptoms.

Dal glanced at Melion, and caught her rubbing her small, russet wrists. He projected a blanket of soothing, comfortable warmth, and sent it and a smile her way. She looked up and managed a subdued, measured smile in return.

"Thanks, Dal. I'm one big ache. Time speeds up when you're absorbed," she sighed, pushing back heavy auburn hair, streaked with white and brown. "If I'd remember to move around more often, I wouldn't hurt so." She stretched cautiously and then groaned with the pain of returned movement. "Even my brain cells want to cramp."

"Me too," Dal agreed. "At least the cyclical nature of the Change gives us some relative relief in between flares. I wish we could program the Crises to come during boring periods of the mission. Maybe some day." He started working on the hardened nodules of TrPs in his upper arms that were hampering his ability to grasp. "If I drop one more thing, I'll have to take a break."

"Dal, you aren't heading for a Crisis too? That's usually a bad sign."

"No, Mel. I've just been overworking. I may have to sneak some of the magic C."

Melion laughed. "Choc! What would we do without it. But don't let Kimmer catch you. I love it too, but it's no good for us in the long run."

"Ah, but it tastes so good! And gives instant energy. You're right, though. I can't afford the brain fog and reflux it causes. The Change is a rough road, but the Guardian must have reasons. The more talents we develop, the later and more difficult the Change." He groaned. "I'm developing talented hands! Or maybe just developing patience and perseverance, of which I've had ample need lately."

"You have had more to deal with than most," Melion observed softly. "One could indeed wish for an easier time of it," she said pensively, and then stared off into space for a moment. Then she brightened. "The youth of the Kowla peoples must devour their teachers before they can fully mature, so I guess our rite of passage isn't so bad, comparatively, at least for the teachers."

"I heartily agree," Chief Rial said as he entered the command cabin, carrying Katayan on his shoulder. "Dal, make a note for me. Never ship with Kowlini. I don't fancy the thought of ending my days as main course at a pubescent brunch. Speaking of which, the rest of us have fed, rested and refreshed. What have you found while we did so?"

"Enough food for thought to make me hunger for answers, Chief. Will you call a briefing?"

"You're in charge this trip, Dal, for as much as you want to be. Grab some command experience while these old bones are still around to guide you. You never know when Melion could pick up ideas from the Kowlini."

"You have been putting on a little weight, Chief," Melion teased.

Rial patted his relatively flat belly. "Not enough to spare something for you to cook up, child," he warned. I've been lifting weights," he explained as he hoisted the gold and brown ball of fur off his shoulder and onto a more stationary perch. "Stay there, Katayan," he ordered, and the catabit humpfed, but he stayed where ordered, albeit with blazing eyes. "Dal has even less excess weight, so go easy on him, Melion. And Dal, don't let me catch you doing the same for the crew. Be strict. They need disciplining."

Dal smiled. "I'll be tough, Chief. Just like you." He had been expecting to take on this extra duty. He'd have his Master's rating soon, and his own ship, if he wanted it. "Melion, get the others in here, please. Got to whip everyone into shape."

Dal partitioned the screen while the others gathered around. He brought up a computer projection of the edge of the star-field. "This is how the target area would appear if we were approaching from above the plane, instead of from the side," he explained for Cren's benefit. The screen looked as though some monstrous galactic creature had taken a bite out of the edge of the a starfield. Only a dimly glowing crumb remained in the center of the space thus created. The star.

Chief Rial pursed his lips and sighed. Then he gestured at the screen. "People, that's tomorrow, and it's staring us in the face. What do we know, Dal?"

"It's a stable G2, with a larger than average ecosphere," Dal reported. "Koren, how close must we be for a comprehensive inspection?"

"Within one million miles to be absolutely certain of planetary habitability," Koren said, making a notation on her comppad.

Dal's eyebrow raised, and his eyes twinkled. "What do you mean, Koren, by 'absolutely certain'?" The darker the uniform, the more time spent teaching. Dal's uniform was deep indigo.

"Poor choice of words," Koren wrinkled her nose and shook her head slightly. "What I mean is, at one million miles out we can locate major planetary masses in the ecosphere. We'll be able to tell if they have the proper characteristics we seek; suitable gravity, reasonably circular orbit, and so forth, to allow for the possibility of carbon based life. We'll orbit each planet for a full surface scan before we know approximately what's waiting down below, before we consider landing."

"That's correct," the Chief nodded. "Melion, what's the scope on the EM?"

"There are several separate but interacting fields," Melion replied in clipped tones. "The stellar field is strong, but I can't get a solid reading from this side of the cloud. I don't know what to make of its spiral patterning. I've reviewed the Beierhof paper. I have not found any natural reason why such protection would exist in this context. I deduct that answer lies with the star, and not with the cloud or proto star field."

"Mel, do you think the inner field might block emanations coming from the proto stars?"

"That may well be, Dal." Melion drew a deep breath and smiled contentedly. Her love was geology. She could wait for the starfield.

Dal focused kind eyes on Cren. "You've done a lot of EM work. Do you have a comment?"

Cren shrugged. "I can't believe we won't be able to see anything that hot," he pointed to the radiating proto star area. "You really want my opinion?"

Dal's eyebrows went up again. "I asked."

"Ok then. We were talking big time for a while. The sulfur and radiation shielding, they could be heavy-duty money-makers. Think of the implications in hyperilon manufacture alone! It's the hazardous sulfurous by-products that limit our production of the most versatile building material known. *That* should be our number one priority. Now you say we might not even be able to study the cloud from within the G2 ecosphere. So why bother with the star? The Tagur settlers have been orbiting Metrowyl for over a year. They can wait a little longer. Let another ship find a home for the refugees. This G2 is just another star."

"But *what* a star, Cren," Dal said earnestly. "By its placement alone, it's worthy of study. And from what I hear, the Tagur refugees need a home *now*. Tagur was passed by both Survey and Science Divisions, but became the worst disaster in colonization history. Survey let them down. *We* let them down. It is our responsibility to make amends, in any way we can, as soon as we can. *That* has got to be our first priority. And," Dal continued, "we're here to gather information, not enhance our personal economic security, even though that may happen in the process. It's up to the bureaucrats on Metrowyl to turn our data into cash flow.

"Besides, I feel that Mel's impression is correct. That star holds the key to the sulfur displacement. For some reason, that star, and that star specifically, is being spared not only the sulfur cloud, but all the heavy ionization from the proto stars."

"The star is positioned way beyond the edge of the new-star field," Cren pointed out.

"Good point," Dal admitted. "But the displacement field still takes a decided bite from the cloud mass at the edge of the star field. No Main Sequence star could have evolved there."

"Did it *EVOLVE* there?" Renzec mused. "Or maybe there were other Main Sequence stars in the area, even a globular cluster. Say something initiated the birthing field, and somehow the cluster was devoured. The G2 happened to be left."

"That wouldn't explain the cloud," Leh said thoughtfully. "Only the position of the G2." She pursed her lips and rested her chin in her hands "What could cause the G2 to develop a hydrogen peroxide envelope?"

"No idea," Renzec stated flatly. "If we knew that, we'd be rich." He leaned over and tousled Cren's hair. "Wouldn't we kid?"

Cren batted at Renzec's hand, but kept quiet.

"I agree with Dal," Koren interjected. "We have to go in there to find the answers."

"I concur," Chief Rial nodded. "So we split back into three shifts. Standard approach routine. At least one shift *must* be resting at any given time, people!" The groans welled up around him. "Adrenalin can carry us for just so long. You need sleep."

"I don't think I can sleep, Chief Rial," Cren admitted with a sigh. He looked warily at the seething star field.

"Cren, just like we needed our Q/T Matrix to cross the nebula, we sometimes need medication as a tool. We've accommodated your wishes thus far, Cren, but now I must insist." Rial glanced at Dal, and the empath nodded reluctantly.

"Think what it is like for Dal when you generate negativity. And Leh is developing new empathic talents as well. Consider the poor catabit. Katayan spends far too much time in the aft compartment lately, unless you're there. He avoids you, except when you're out here with Dal. Then he tries to sit on your head when you're upset. Which is often."

"So I've noticed," Cren said glumly. The remembrance of Cren with the catabit's furry "flying skirt" draped over his head brought muffled giggles from the rest of the crew. "I don't get it. I mean, he isn't heavy, and he's careful. He keeps his claws in. But why does he *do* that?"

"Negativity hurts the little guy, Cren," Rial explained. "I'm sure it wouldn't be his first choice in seating arrangements. Dal tries to buffer your negativity, like the cloud is doing for the star, to keep it from being amplified and bounced around, but that's taken a lot of his energy. He has none to spare right now. Katayan is only trying to block your negativity from hitting Dal. Negativity is destructive, Cren. Ultimately, it hurts you most of all.

"Our empathic talents need to have their minds open right now, free to be seeking and sensitive for what might be out there. Your negativity threatens their ability to use their talents."

Cren hung his head for a minute and thought. "What about meditations. Why can't I use those, Chief Rial?"

"We've found meditations worthwhile, Cren, but learning the art is time-consuming. You don't take a meditation like a pill. They require dedication, patience and self-discipline. You, like some others," he added as he glanced meaningfully at Renzec, "need help in those areas."

Renzec mumbled something to himself.

"Cren, Kimmer will give you something to promote deep sleep, the same kind of med Dal uses when the pain and distractions of Change affect his ability to meditate. You need stage 4 sleep, Cren. You're moody and irritable and negative". He peered closely at the worried novice. "You couldn't be starting Change, Cren? If so, tell us *right now*."

"No, Chief. Definitely not," Cren said.

Rial looked at Dal and then at Kimmer, and received confirming nods. "It seemed early to me, as well. But we vary. From person to person, we vary. Trust your medic, Cren. We've managed to survive the meds she's whipped up thus far." Kimmer chuckled at this. "Besides of which, we have no more time nor energy for gratuitous suffering." Cren nodded in reluctant agreement, but looked apprehensively at the medic.

"Trust me," Dal reassured. "I've studied meditation with the best, the Tav mystics, and I needed sleep medication during the Change. Still do. Otherwise, I'd suffer from chronic sleep-deprivation and be no good to anyone. We're a team, remember?"

Cren nodded grudging assent. "All right. But make it mild."

The Chief looked satisfied. "Maybe your team should take the first sleep, Dal. I want you on-shift and sensing after the next hop. Have you caught anything? Anything at all?"

Dal's warm, golden-brown eyes assumed that dreamy, inwardly focused look as he reached far out for contact. The rest of the crew silenced, waiting. Katayan leaned toward Dal with his eyes closed, silent.

"What's going on?" Cren whispered to Leh.

" Shush! Dal is trying to make contact," Leh replied softly.

"Who with?"

Leh's face lit up with mirth. "*Shuush*, we'll explain later," she whispered. The others remained quiet, respectfully waiting.

After a few moments, Dal's features relaxed, and he shook his head. Nothing yet. Then he smiled and shrugged. "I'm no Tav. Couldn't feel a thing. We're too far out." Katayan opened his eyes and shook his head, and gave a plaintive sounding mew.

"That's ok, little guy," Dal said as he rubbed the velvety fur on the catabit's head. "We have to get closer. That's all."

"So what's the story?" Cren insisted. "Who were you trying to reach?"

"Not a who, my friend, " Dal explained. "I'm hoping for a planet out there. Once I reached a certain level in my Change, I noticed that each world has a certain specific vibration. A resonance. It's hard for me to explain. There is no term for it really, in our language. The sense of every world is different, and totally unique to that world. Even the lifeless worlds have this."

"Dal feels that if we could analyze the essence of each world, we wouldn't need to rely on sensors. It would tell us everything," Leh said wistfully. "Imagine, being able to listen to the story of a planet!"

"Can you do that, Leh?"

"Oh, Cren! I've never heard of anyone but Dal who has this ability Perhaps they just don't talk about it," she mused. "I'm just beginning in this journey of the mind. I think I can feel something, sometimes," Leh murmured. "On some worlds. Dal is trying to teach me more. It would make such a good story, if I could do it!"

"Renzec, do you feel comfortable taking us through the cloud? The drive's all set." Dal stood up and stretched carefully, and Katayan did likewise in like manner, a perfect mimic, and everyone laughed. Naui went over and picked up the catabit, cuddling him in her arms. Katayan stretched his head up and rubbed his gold and brown chin on her pale blue face. She cooed at him, and was rewarded with furry arms wrapped around her neck in a hug, and the long ears rolled up in a sign of bliss. One soft paw patted her cheek, and she giggled.

"No problem, Dal," Renzec said. He started to move his angular body over to the engineering console when Koren touched his arm.

"Can't go yet," she insisted. "We haven't named the star."

Cren turned with surprise. "Name, Koren? What's wrong with a number?" On Metrowyl, names were reserved for animate beings.

Naui looked at Cren strangely. "Where was your head in your senior year, Cren?" Her snub nose wrinkled in mirth. "We get to tack on all the names we want to out here. Seniors hold a contest every year to see who can come up with the most innovative names." She shrugged. "Of course, as soon as the SiTeam follows up, they pick more 'appropriate names'. Sometimes, though," she said smugly, "*our* names stick."

"Ha! I thought I heard name-babble being bandied about the cabin, Rial chuckled. "Some ideas certainly were original, although others would scandalize Academy scholars." He looked pointedly at Renzec, and the Red Leader had the grace to blush. "And *you*, Naui child! *Plan It* is not a proper name for a world. Although it does embody a sound principle."

"Actually," offered Kimmer, "We should honor our monarch."

Rial's face soured. "Klev has taken too many stars as it is," he objected. "Besides, I'm not enthused by his politics."

Cren looked startled, and his eyes quickly scanned the cabin.

"Smooth it, Cren," Dal advised gently. "We don't approve of spy devices. That's a perk of being on the other side of nowhere."

"Bugs on this craft would cramp our style, among other things," Renzec drawled. He clapped Cren on the shoulder. "It's my job to sweep the place after each stop at HomePort. Pest control. Besides, they make good raw materials for repair." He inspected his fingernails briefly, and then gazed about the cabin with a peaceful, smug expression on his craggy features. "Most ships do the same."

"How do you get away with it?" Cren asked suspiciously.

"Electromagnetic interference," Renzec grinned, and winked. "Funny what those pesky little Q/T Matrix fields can do. Especially the old ones."

Cren relaxed a little and sighed. "You and I should talk some time soon. I could use that expertise."

"Back to the name, folks," Kimmer reiterated. "I wasn't referring to Klev, the old lech. I mean Kellierin, our Queen. The 'Kellierin Anomaly' has a nice ring to it."

The Chief looked at Dal for his opinion. This would be a group decision, but Dal's input would weigh heavy. The empath thought for a moment before he spoke.

"Our young Queen is an unusual freethinker who speaks her mind. Rare in those circles. She's kept the special interests at a safe distance, like the G2 star and the proto stars. She's kept King Klev in line, as well as his poisonous court. I think it's apropos." Dal tilted his head slightly and smiled. "Of course, rumor has it the lady has a temper. We'll have to watch her namesake."

"She'd need one to match Klev's." Leh hooted.

"How disrespectful!" Rial chided sarcastically, wagging a finger at them. "Though true, I admit. Sounds good to me."

"Why don't you name the stars after yourselves?" Cren asked as the meeting broke up. "Why not a star named 'Jennery'?"

"Spare me, Cren," the Chief was quick to remark, and he held up his arms as if to shield himself. "I want no raw star system named for me!"

"Why?"

"We *never* name a new star or planet after ourselves, although it's been done by others." Renzec said patiently. "Would you want a world like Tagur four named for you?"

Cren winced, understanding. "Tagur looked like paradise. That's when it was named. Then, after three years, the colony got hit with that long wet spell." He shuddered.

"Exactly," Koren said somberly. "Windworms and whipsnakes." She shivered and hugged herself. "Ugh! I get chills thinking of it. By then the name 'Tagur' was written in hyperilon. I don't even know who 'Tagur' was."

"Probably some poor SiTeam guy in hiding now," Leh said sympathetically. "If he hasn't done himself in. Such a tragic story. Ironic, too. They're Unifieds."

"Yeah," Renzec affirmed. 'Oneness with nature'. All that kinda stuff. Started by human followers of your Tav mystics, I think." He looked at Dal, who nodded affirmation.

"They even had Tavs along to help them start the colony in the proper manner," Dal added. "Tavs are master gene modifiers. They designed plants and animals for the Tagur folk, gratis."

"I don't understand, Dal, why the Tavs didn't *know* that something was wrong with Tagur. They *are* mystics and empaths."

"Some of them," Dal explained. "Maybe not all. I don't know. We don't know all that much about the Tav, and their limits. Maybe they never made a "connection" with that world, like I've been doing. Maybe the connection harmony is a cyclical thing, like our Change Crises, on a planet that goes through weather and predator cycles like Tagur. Tavs wanted that colony to thrive. But they left after two years, when it seemed established. The Tav don't interact well with most humanoids for protracted periods. Some of them are true telepaths, to some extent. I was one of the first humanoid empaths to train solely with Tavs at the Academy. I started right away, first year. My first crush was on a person with four legs, dark fur, and very long fangs," he admitted softly, and he sighed. "I loved her deeply. Still do." He smiled down at Kimmer, and her face echoed understanding. She knew what the Tav connection meant to Dal. "Tavs are special," Dal continued. "I'd give anything to ship out with a Tav."

"Me too," Chief Rial mused. "I have a long-standing request for a Tav crew member, but I've never had a taker. I know some ships are manned with Tavs. Hmmn," he reflected, "should that be catted? Anyway, when I first put in that request, the Academy presented me with you, Dal."

Dal looked surprised and pleased. "Coincidence, of course. It would have been an honor, otherwise. I never knew."

"Speaking of honors," Kimmer said insistently, "register the G2 as Kellierin, Dal. Please?"

"So be it," Dal said, as he logged the name of the star.

Kimmer grabbed her medkit from a storage locker and headed to the aft cabin. "You coming?" she asked Dal.

"I'll be right along, Kimmi. Chief Rial wants to see me first," he answered. "I can feel his impatience," he added in a whisper, just loud enough so that everyone could hear.

Kimmer grinned, winked, and left. Dal was no telepath, but could often infer what others were thinking. It was an integral part of him, and she found it endearing. Koren had not.

White Team remained on watch. Rial came over and put his arm on Dal's shoulder. He leaned his head close, scanning the incoming data. Dal looked up briefly. As he did so, he asked in a voice just loud enough for the Chief to hear, "What's your sense on Cren?"

Rial sighed. "I don't know what to make of the boy, but I believe it won't be a crew member, unless something changes drastically. No matter how much his Poppa wants him out here. Something smells like a yorbu in all this."

"What if there are mitigating circumstances?"

"Such as?"

"Cren's a kid, Chief. Forget his papers. How old would you guess he *really* is?" Dal saw new light dawn in Rial's eyes, so he released his work station, point made.

Rial raised his eyebrows and cleared his throat as he sat down. "That colors the whole story."

"Cren's got possibilities, Chief," Dal continued in a low voice. "I know he sounds like a spoiled rich kid. He is. But he wants to contribute, and he needs to belong. Besides, he can actually *see* space. To me, that's a signature of other talents yet undeveloped. He's innovative. If you could feel his intent, well, you'd understand some of the complexity that drives him. But there's a wall inside him. A thick one. Something's very dark in there, Chief. He isn't ready to share that yet. Give him time. When it happens, I think I can convince him to level with us."

"And what do you think waits for us out there?" Rial asked, nodding at the viewscreen.

Dal shrugged. "You got me." He fiddled with the blue stone on his ring, the symbol of his responsibility as Blue Leader. "I feel strange about this place. I can't quite put a name to it. The feeling I have is tenuous, and I didn't want to mention it to the crew. High EM can affect me that way, and scatter my thoughts. Empathy is but a different type of EM, after all. I plan to do a complete electromagnetic survey of the star. Bounce a pulse off it. That should give us a better understanding of its relationship to the cloud."

Just before he left the cabin he added as an afterthought, "Chief,

I know I haven't made a planetary connection yet. But I sense that something is out there, waiting for me. Expecting me. I can't explain it. I have a feeling that this place is special. That somehow, this place is going to change us all."

Rial watched Dal depart. Thanks, m'boy, he thought. And just what did you mean by that?

Chapter

4

With a dismissive gesture, Dal turned his back on the small dot on the computer model. "One small world, too close to the star. Useful, someday, for a solar monitoring station. Two planets might already hold carbon-based life, and are potential colony sites. The one we're orbiting is cold, but I believe the Tagur folk wouldn't say no to it. Except for a few atmospheric layers, the planet we are orbiting is a sister planet to the one we have tentatively named Kellierin. That planet has a smaller axial tilt, as well as being closer to the sun, and may be more desirable for the colony. I feel that we should finish orbital survey here, and then move on to assess the inner planet. If all goes well, we'll land there first. Naui, what obvious stabilizing influence do we have on the inner planet that is missing on the outer one?

"There is a relatively large satellite?" Naui questioned more than answered.

"Good. Yes, that may mitigate other influences. Why?"

"Any outside force has to deal with an impact on the planetary system, not just on the planet. That could be good for life."

"True." Dal turned to Cren, who had begun to fidget as Naui spoke. "What do you have to add to that, Cren?"

"Well," Cren, glanced apologetically at Naui, "actually, for the EM fields, this specific satellite could complicate matters."

"How so?" Dal asked, but he was obviously pleased.

"It has its own EM fields. There'll be tidal effects, not just of bodies of water, but of electronic particles. These force fields will tend to interact. We can't tell what that will mean." He set his features and crossed his arms, expecting an argument.

"Very good, Cren!" Dal commended.

Naui looked pointedly at Cren and narrowed her bright eyes. "I need to know about this!" she demanded. Cren was startled, and his planned defenses went into meltdown. She wasn't angry, or even sarcastic.

"Yes you do," Dal agreed. "We need to go in as informed as possible concerning EM. Fill Naui in on electromagnetics as it may apply, Cren. If any of you need brushing up, feel free to attend the session."

Cren leaned back, eyes wide, slowly relaxing his tense shoulders. "I can't give specifics," he warned. "There are so many potential variables."

"That's ok, Cren," Naui piped. "I need background stuff. I need to know what to look for."

"The system itself will be our best teacher, Naui," Dal cautioned. "Cren will refresh you on the basics."

Cren blushed. He wasn't used to this. Nobody was playing games here.

"Chief," Dal continued, "You aren't partial to cool worlds, and I've not had any experience with cold habitables. Any comments?"

"Just from my old bones, Dal." Everyone laughed. The Chief could outlast most of them when it came to exploration. "I prefer warm worlds, but we won't be there forever. I have a lot to learn, like the rest of you."

"Anybody else?"

"Sensors indicate we won't see the birthing area from inside the cloud, Dal. How will this change our mission?"

"Melion, the atmosphere will effectively block that part of the mission until after ground surveys are done. Fortunately, any radioactive scatter from the birthing stars is also absent inside the ecosphere. There are strong EM fields *around* each planet, as well as the rather massive one spiraling about the whole of the Kellierin system itself. These fields appear to interact, and we can't be sure of all the ramifications of that. There is no sign that the fields are in any way harmful to life on the surface. We *will* have to protect ourselves against the cold, however. This planet may not offer much in the way of tempting foodstuffs, but let's not suck on any icicles just yet," he joked. "Wait until we're sure there's no residual sulfur before we do a taste test. That goes for you as well, Naui, even though sulfur isn't as harmful to Orelians as it is to us Metrowyl types."

"We can't penetrate the atmosphere too well with sensors alone. At least, not with *these* sensors. We're all aware that the ship is somewhat long in the tooth." He shot a meaningful look at Chief Rial, which the Chief ignored.

Dal pointed briefly at the milk glass planet on the screen. "We found a discrete layer of low albedo clouds. We don't understand why they don't reflect substantially greater amounts of light. These clouds take some of our beamed energy and scatter it in an unusual pattern. The mechanism by which they do this is unclear. They could do the same with a portion of the solar radiation as well. If so, this could be helpful for colonists."

"I have a question on the stability of the star?"

"Yes, Rennie?"

"Is it?"

They all laughed, except Cren.

"There's always a question of inherent instability," Dal agreed. "Especially in an anomalous situation such as this. This system seems to be in a stable phase at the present."

"Seems?" Cren said warily.

"To the best of my knowledge, the star is stable. Metrowyl Prime is a G1, Cren, and you've lived with it all of your life. There are no guarantees. Take it from there." Dal's voice had taken on a strained tone, and he leaned on the edge of a console. He was growing weary.

"Are we ready to go in?" Rial wanted to know.

"Just about. I want to send a scanning pulse, to bounce off the star."

"Then do that, please, Dal. And Good Guardian, sit down," Kimmer urged.

Dal complied. As he slipped into the console seat, he closed his eyes for a moment and sighed, swaying slightly. Suddenly, he straightened. When he opened his eyes, his tired look had been replaced with alert focus.

"I sensed something. Down, guys," he laughed, waving his arms briefly as everyone talked at once. "Not . . . intelligence. But something." He paused, groping for words. Then he gave up and smiled apologetically. "Nearly a presence. But not. I have no way to describe it. I've never felt its like before."

"*Meow, reawllrr,*" Rennie yowled softly. "You'll be spitting hairballs next," he teased.

Leh laughed. "Save on uniforms, if you turn Tav," she joked.

Dal shook his head. "If I were Tav, I'd identify it for you now. Maybe. Such as I am, I got the impression something recognizes that I'm here. And it was . . . confused about that. I can sense Katayan sleeping in the aft compartment. That is a clear presence. This other was quite undefined. I still miss the sense of the planet below. I can't make the connection. Odd, that."

"What do you mean, Dal?"

"This close, I should be aware of it, Cren. There's a distinctive rhythm, throbbing, pulsing, like a background to everything we will find later. If you drop me blindfolded on any planet I've surveyed, I could tell you which one it was. It's like a fingerprint, or a flavor, Cren. Unique. Once I attune to it, I sense all other impressions native to that planet much more easily."

"Planetary sentience?" Cren looked skeptical.

"I didn't say that. That belongs to your space vids, as far as I can tell. What I feel on each planet is a unique signature. Almost like tasting a melody. A harmonic, of sorts. Now that I've experienced it on the last ten or so worlds, once I connect with it, I can just about guarantee what we'll find on a planet, in general terms, at least. But I can't make the connection here, and I usually can do so from orbit. This time, I guess it'll have to wait. I suggest we finish securing for a break of orbit."

"How are you feeling today, Cren?" Kimmer asked while they worked.

"Oh, better, I guess. Cren sighed long and deep, glanced at the screen, and shook his head.

"Something's bothering you?"

"What Dal said, Kimmer. What could be aware of us all the way out here?" Crensed questioned, chewing on his lip.

"Dal said 'it recognizes *I'm* here', Cren," Kimmer explained. "I think he means it's sensitive to empathy. We know that the empathic function is highly reactive to EM forces. People say Tavs can manipulate EM radiation like the rest of us can braid a rope. Maybe that's all it is. Fields attracting fields. An astrophysical effect."

When Cren didn't respond to her words, Kimmer sighed.

"Dal, why not drop a relay buoy," Rial suggested. "With your summary of what we've gathered so far."

"Summary and buoy ready and waiting, Chief," Dal grinned. He pressed his console pad, and the familiar sounds of a dispatching buoy filled the cabin.

"Course plotted to the next planet and ready to go, Dal," Renzec called out from his console. "All the stations are zipped down."

"Wait for the pulse results," Dal ordered.

The Chief looked carefully at Cren. The boy stared with glazed eyes at an unidentified point somewhere in the cabin, seeing nothing. Rial's eyes met Kimmer's. He opened his mouth to suggest a meeting with Dal and Kimmer on Cren's behalf. Suddenly, alarm signals blurted from the sensors. With one exception, the crew strapped themselves securely to their stations.

"Massive EM wave front heading directly toward us," Renzec reported. "Initiating at the star."

"Radiation readings climbing," Koren called out. She stared intently at her monitor. "The star? She flared?"

"Not a flare, Korey," Renzec frowned. "At least, not a normal one. Look at the shift. The wave initiated right after the scanning pulse hit the edge of the heliosphere. It's strong, Dal. We can't break orbit without meeting it."

"Estimated time to wave front impact, Renzec?" Rial queried as he realigned the primary sensors and reinforced shielding where he could.

"Just long enough to get down far enough so we don't fry. Maybe," he said as he set final controls. "Have to get down fast. Dal?"

"I've got her, Ren," Dal said, taking the hint, and the controls. "Rennie's right. Whatever's waiting for us down there, it beats becoming crispy critters up here. All hands secure," he warned. "This could be a wild ride." He smiled grimly, but there was a faint sheen of sweat on his brow. He checked the console. One light remained off where it should have glowed violet. He glanced around briefly, wincing as his neck muscles screamed.

"Leh, take charge of Cren, will you? Make it fast, here? Katay?" he yelled to reinforce his thought aimed at the catabit. "Dig in back there!"

"I'm on to Cren, Dal," Leh released her net of emergency straps. Cren had remained rooted in place when the alarms went off. Leh hustled him into his station and strapped him down. She wasted no time getting into her own seat. "All secured," she cried.

Dal continued maneuvering the craft to bring them down in a steep arc on the side of the planet opposite the sun. The craft was already descending rapidly. The air grew hot. One by one the sensors started to crackle. Dal felt his skin crawl and prickle, and his hair lifted straight out. Every movement of his fingers caused a static display. He felt Katayan's mental complaints. That was one unhappy catabit, and whatever he was gripping would have permanent claw holes, and they would be deep. He couldn't take time to check the hull viewscreen, so he missed the riot of colors snaking across the outer skin of the small craft as the onrushing precursor of the massive wave front washed over the ship. Rial noted it briefly, and then activated and secured the remaining shields. All screens went dark. "Carry it through, and make it now," he warned Dal.

"Brace yourselves," Dal called, as they plunged at an angle far too steep into the swirling atmosphere below. The monitors screamed they were going way too fast. Fingers of blinding, blue-white arcs zapped across consoles. Gravitational force gripped them, and their velocity drove them back from their panels, except for Dal. Save for an instant of reflex withdrawal as the first arc spit across his controls, he concentrated every ounce of strength he owned keeping control of the ship. His hair surrounded his head like a blazing halo. The arcs halted abruptly as they were buffeted by their entry into the turbulent mesosphere. Somewhere behind him, Dal heard a crash and a yell. A sharp percussion rocked the small craft, and the cabin tilted perilously as the lights went out. There came an ominous, long scraping noise, and the shock of a muffled thud. And then, for what seemed an eternity, nothing.

Chapter

5

Kimmer opened eyelids that felt too heavy to lift. Her eyes smarted, but she saw nothing. After the sight of coruscating arcs ravaging the controls systems, the darkness almost felt welcome. Dal! She reached out with her mind, frantic, remembering her last sight of him glowing with strange light. She felt his presence, although it seemed fuzzy. His mind's touch was gentle, calming, reassuring. It "cleared" from the initial fuzzy feeling as he grew more alert. He had been able to channel the energy of descent. The process had opened painful, raw pathways through his psyche. His shields were transparent to her, so she could see he was unharmed. Like most of their psychic contacts, she received only concepts, but it was sufficient. She could feel the pathways already beginning to integrate and heal. He would come out of this experience unharmed.

If only she could link like that with the rest of the crew! It was so dark! She took a brief inventory of her own self, and found all parts accounted for and functioning as well as she could expect. The silence was profound. She called, "Is everyone ok?" and was surprised at the quaver in her voice. Equally shaky answers in the affirmative came from all stations, except from those of Dal and Cren. She jumped as a cold nose butted against her arm. Katayan! His mind pushed against hers, questing. She could feel his anxiety for the crew.

"Go on, KatKat. Check them out," she urged. She pushed her

headband over her forehead. She flicked on the small headlamp and saw the golden form carefully picking his way around the debris toward the nearest crew member. She started gingerly moving about the cabin, heading first to Dal. She activated her medikit and scanned him quickly, then sighed with relief as he opened his eyes. He inhaled deeply, and let the air out very slowly.

"Whew," he murmured, and gingerly reached out to Kimmer for a careful hug. "Rough ride." She embraced him gently, and then gave a close sweep of her medicorder to an area on his temple oozing a small amount of blood. She handed him a pressure pad. "It's cut, but not deeply. I'll be back," she said, and reluctantly parted from his arms.

"See to Cren, love," Dal whispered as she moved away. "He's stable, but he needs emotional balancing. Immediately. No other major emergencies." Kimmer nodded and moved off, deliberately picking her way across unfamiliar obstacles strewn across the path her headlight cut through the dark.

She found Cren free of physical wounds, but, as Dal had sensed, still in a dazed state. She promptly administered a hefty neurotransmitter stabilizer for his frazzled nervous system, and smiled a little smugly as she watched Cren's levels approach normal for the first time.

Her head lamp glowed and bounced, illuminating a small wedge in the darkness as she checked her crewmates to determine the extent of their injuries. As she moved, she spotted glimpses of a golden rump or slashing brown tail moving carefully about the cabin. She occasionally changed direction, as she received brief mental images of crewmates and blood or pain, distorted in a catabitly way. She moved from one companion to another, pausing only to share a brief touch and a few low words of comfort with each.

"We are all basically well, Chief, both mentally and physically" Dal reported, having completed a second empathic scan on everyone. "Which is more than I can say for our cabin interior," he added as he flicked on his headlamp. "There are, however, no broaches in the hull. I fear, though, that some of our electronics are the worst for wear," he added.

"How's the Matrix?" the Chief asked in a worried tone. "My board is out."

"Ragged, Chief. Nothing that we can't sort out in time."

"How did you weather that electrical storm, Dal? It looked violent, there for a while. I smelled something smoking."

"My ego is singed, Chief, that's all. I didn't anticipate that wave," Dal admitted with a shaky laugh. "Actually, my finger tips are still tingling, and the soles of my feet, but I'm ok." He picked a few pieces of paper off his uniform. "I do seem to be holding residual static. If there were any loose catabit hairs in my vicinity, they're attached to me now.

"Chief, I didn't expect the fireworks, and I missed them," he mourned. Too busy at the time. Totality Day came early this year, I guess. Without a picnic, which I regret."

"That last sort of shuddering noise, Dal?" Rial questioned, picking up on Dal's lighthearted banter, and the fact that the rest of the crew still weren't talking. "Dare I ask what we hit? I hope it wasn't alive when we struck it, because it surely isn't now. Perhaps we could roast it for that picnic you long for. Even Grandmother's cross-eyed yorbu wouldn't have survived such a crunch, and it was a most durable beast."

"Of that I have no doubt," Dal affirmed. "But we'll have to forgo the thing roast, Chief. The thump was a soil berm. Unless the soil here is as sentient as that cross-eyed yorbu you're always going on about, we haven't done a lot of harm."

Rial finally got his light working. "Dal, my boy," he grumbled as he looked around the cabin, "I realize now that I have failed in an important aspect of your training. You must do something about your landings. You definitely need more practice. Preferably without *me* in the ship. A whole planet to chose from, and you have to hit a hit a berm?" Rial chuckled softly, helping Dal to ease the tension.

"Unless I have erred drastically," Dal explained dryly, "that berm wasn't here before we landed, Chief. We left more than a vapor trail behind us."

"Let those Survey pilots in, the neighborhood goes down the exhaust tubes," Renzec muttered as he grappled with his panels in the spot lighting.

Dal laughed, albeit weakly. With every movement came a new ache, and even his brain cells felt bruised. He peered at the part of his console that was still operational. "Our initial endeavor on this planet appears to be the creation of a rift approximately a quarter mile long. Actually, it's more of a tunnel, except toward the end. The sides are fused from the friction of landing. Some lucky life forms will have a fine shelter, courtesy of the Survey Service! At least we finished up on the surface, mostly. No problem, really."

Katayan let out a low, warning yowl.

A shriek broke through the banter. "*Ahhaagh!* No problem? *NO PROBLEM!* We crashed! I can't see!" The hefty dose of tranquilizer finally broke through Cren's trance. "Somebody get over here!" he demanded. "I need help. *Now!* I can't see. Somebody get this damn animal *off my head!*"

"Katayan!" Dal ordered. There was an immediate sound of a catabit launching himself off Cren's head and on to the back of Dal's console. "Thank you, KatKat," Dal sighed, stroking the aggrieved animal, who was making irritated whirring noises. "I know you were only trying to help.

"We're down, Cren," Dal reassured. "We're in no immediate danger. Kimmer will be around again soon to help you. *VERY soon,*" he emphasized. Kimmer got the message. "I'm working on getting us some E-light, Cren, but it may take a little time." Dal began to address the panel in front of him with more speed. "Are you in any pain, Cren? Think carefully." Dal's voice was calm, but it held a strained quality. They had gone from null-grav to full just before the stress of rapid descent and added G forces. His body had no time to adjust, and it was beginning to clamor for immediate attention as the adrenalin wore off.

Even in his agitated state, Cren wasn't oblivious to the amplified pain. Especially as Katayan, in desperation, had tried a new tactic: bouncing the awareness of it to Cren. Along with the awareness that it was Dal's pain, and not Cren's. It had an immediate effect.

"Dal, I'm sorry. I guess I don't hurt. I feel funny, though. It's so dark! Why'd we land have to on the night side?"

"The wave was coming, Cren," Dal explained patiently as he worked. "We needed to have the planet between us and the wave front, for protection. The wave front was coming from the sun. It's dark because all our shields are up and our main cabin lights are out. The emergency lights aren't working yet. We're trying to remedy that situation as fast as we can. Turn on your head lamp, if you can find it."

"But Daaal," Naui whined, in parody of Cren, "if we landed on the day side, at least we could have watched ourselves ignite. And . . ." Her words were stopped abruptly by a furry tail swatting her across the mouth. *"Ukkk! Kat! Bletch!"*

"Smooth it out, Naui," Dal warned abruptly. He took another deep breath, and fought to maintain control over his own rebelling body. Every muscle was now part of a raucous chorus of complaints, and they threatened to drown out all else.

Suddenly remembering, he reached in a pocket for a hypospray, and pressed it to his neck. His head cleared almost instantly, although some of his muscles continued to spasm. He took off his headlamp and aimed it with one hand while he effected repairs with the other. He had to prop his hands to maintain position, but he could no longer endure the pressure of the head strap. More of his panels came to life, displaying a comprehensive story of the status of every major piece of equipment. Not too grim a tale. He moved his fingers lightly over the panels, and to his satisfaction, multicolored sensors glowed in response.

It *was* dark in the cabin, except for illumination from crew headlamps, and Kimmer's light bobbing about. She had finished her initial crew check and boosted Cren's meds. For once, he didn't argue, and she was relieved. Dal didn't need more grief from that sector, and neither did she.

A console light flicked on from Renzec's area. He was checking power on the life support system. Creaking sounds from the direction of the engineering console indicated that Chief Rial was busy. He was humming an alien, atonal melody.

"We'll have emergency lighting on in just a second. Don't know why it didn't . . . there," Dal said triumphantly as he made the last link. Muted E-lights cast a harsh, greenish-tinged glow on the disheveled crew. Dal glanced around for a quick inspection and winced as a hot wire of pain from an entrapped nerve shot up his neck. He clutched his console as a wave of dizziness swept him. He held his breath for a second, and then let it out slowly thorough his mouth, gaining some control over the pain. Then he took a slower reconnaissance of the cabin, guarding his muscles from sudden movement.

The place was a shambles. One panel had fallen out of the comm console. That must have been the big crash. Not much looked broken, though. The bulk of movable equipment had been secured. The craft was basically intact, though the landing had left it somewhat skewed. Dal reached for his outermost sensor panel, and was brought up short by another wave of pain. A brief hiss escaped his lips.

Kimmer looked up sharply and glanced at Dal. Concern clouded her face, but he waved her off. He used his last hypospray. Kimmer shook her head and looked reproachful, but she resumed scanning Naui. The diminutive xenologist was moaning softly. Maybe that was why she had been so irritable with Cren. Pain had that effect on everyone. Her enormous, turquoise eyes opened wider as Kim tended her bruises. Katayan hopped onto her lap and began to wash her neck. "I love you too," she murmured as she stroked the catabit with her left hand. Then she smiled weakly. "Does Dal always drive that badly?" she joked, and then she cried out as she tried to bring her right hand up. "Uh oh."

Kimmer played the medicorder over Naui's hand. "It's just sprained," she reassured her patient. "But rather badly." She unclipped a device from her belt and snapped it around Naui's wrist. "You'll have to go easy for a while," she cautioned. "Hold your hand still and let the electrostim work while I recheck the others. Then I'll wrap your wrist. It's going to need support for a while.

"Bumps and bruises, and a few cuts," she reported to Chief Rial. "Cren, well. . . . The extra grav stress on the trip down may show up later as muscle cramps and soreness, especially for Melion and Dal. The rest of us can be thankful our soreness will go away relatively quickly. We'll all feel like kneaded dough puffs tomorrow, though. Let's be grateful we weren't flash fried." She raised her eyes in Dal's direction, and he responded with a short laugh. Then she moved over and scanned him again carefully, fondly brushing his thick hair out of his eyes.

"You better take it easy," she warned in a low tone.

He gave her a reassuring wink. "I'm doing fine. Mind over matter. I used the hyposprays you insist that I carry."

She straightened up and rested her small hand on the generous curve of her hip. "You absorbed so much energy on that trip I wonder that we require extra lighting at all in here! What happened to that wave? Did you deflect it with a happy thought?" She gave her head a saucy shake, and turned to tend to Melion.

"Me? You think I stopped it, Kim? Not me. Honest."

"You felt that kick in the tail going through the mesosphere?" Renzec interjected. "That little beauty was the wave welcoming us to the Kellierin system. It almost sent us spinning. I think this lady's giving us notice. I'll keep my hands to myself."

"That'll be a first for you, Rennie," Koren gibed. Renzec just grimaced and ducked his head back under his console. The green glow of his laser melder cast intermittent halos about his hands as he resumed repairs.

"It *was* a strong wave," Dal said, as he picked at few more pieces of paper sticking to his uniform. "It was compact. Tight and dense. Almost as if it had been aimed . . ." He paused and thought a minute. "I guess 'focused' is more accurate. Then it spread out, attenuated by the atmosphere. There must have been some hell of a light show from the surface. Wish we could have seen it," he said wistfully.

"Be content, my boy," Chief Rial cautioned. "You were illuminated enough, from what I saw." Then he scratched his chin and added in a more somber tone, "We could as well have *been* the light show, you know."

"Actually", Dal commented as he scanned the few hard copies available, "once under the mesosphere, we were safe. Aaand, if I'm not mistaken," he said, fingering a few sensors, "there are some intense EM effects appearing in the atmosphere as we speak. Nothing dangerous. But fascinating." He frowned as he readjusted the controls. "They're moving around, and they're transient. I can't get a steady reading. Some kind of aurora, but I've never seen the like." Dal leaned back, content for a while to observe his panels. He began a series of slow, stretching exercises, but he remained sitting.

Chief Rial unstrapped and went over to Cren. The young man was sitting where he had been restrained, dazed but no longer complaining. He seemed oblivious to the others starting to pick their way about the cabin. His breathing was shallow, but regular.

"Are you functioning, lad?" he asked kindly, and put his hand on Cren's shoulder. He knew his medic. All the provocation in the worlds wouldn't cause her to over-medicate the boy.

Cren looked up and seemed surprised to see Chief Rial leaning down with a look of concern.

"Chief Rial! I'm ok. Why? Where are we?"

"Safe on the surface of the planet." The Chief checked him over and helped him unstrap. "You were talking to us, and then we lost you for a while. Kimmer was by to give you something light and balancing. Then I thought it best to let you be, but now it's time to get moving again."

"I thought we were going to die," Crensed admitted. His eyes got big. "Dal looked like he was on fire! This old bucket has patches on its patches. I expected it to burst at the seams. It was groaning something awful! Then everything went away. I feel better now, though. Just wondering how I let Father talk me into shipping out."

"That's something I've been meaning to find out myself, Cren," the Chief said with a sigh. He plunked himself down on some misplaced matting. "*Now* would be a good time for you to tell us your story. This E-light's good enough to chat by, but not great for much else. Cren, there's a whole world out there begging for us to interact with it. It's promising, lad."

"I think it's promising to kill us," Cren insisted, but he brushed himself off, managing a tentative smile.

"Would have done, if we all zorked like you did," Naui came over and accused. "Leh strapped you in after the alarms wert off. She could have been hurt because of you."

Cren looked apologetically at Naui, and back at the Chief. His shoulders slumped. "She's right, Chief," he admitted glumly. "I don't belong out here." Naui's eyes widened in amazement, and her jaw dropped. She flopped on a console seat, guarding her injured hand.

Cren's eyes flicked around the cabin, and finally focused on his objective. "I'm sorry, Dal. I'm a failure at this Survey stuff."

Renzec muttered, "Fardle barf."

Dal eased himself out of his console and moved deliberately across the cabin toward Chief Rial and Cren. Rial wadded up some of the loose matting, arranging it on top of some debris. Dal sat down carefully, and focused on the remorseful novice. "What makes you say that, Cren?"

"Everything out here is so. . . hostile. I really don't think I can take much more. What am I going to do?"

Dal looked at the big green eyes locked on to his, begging for help. He knew what was needed. He had waited long enough. But now, when he was so worn down!

"To get the answers, you first have to ask the right questions," he said in measured tones, rising slowly. "The question is, 'What are we going to do?' We are crewmates, Cren, and we're all in this together. We're a family.

"Cren, listen to me." Dal's voice compelled attention, and Cren found his eyes riveted to the deep, golden gaze. "The universe is neither hostile nor friendly. It wasn't designed for our comfort. Justice and fairness you can expect from your crewmates. Not from the universe. We're in this life to evolve. This trip has been torture for you. It will get worse, unless we make some changes now."

Cren looked miserable, but said nothing.

"Your father bent many rules to get you here," Dal accused

sternly. "Probably more than we know. Our lives may depend on what you can contribute. We signed on a specialist in electromagnetics and xenozoo. An Academy graduate, with honors. How long did you actually attend the Academy?"

"Only a year," Cren blurted. "Then I had to leave." He hung his head.

Chapter

6

Dal sighed, brushed his fingertips across his forehead, and glanced around at his teammates. Then he closed his eyes, and focused. He breathed deeply, rubbing palms together until he felt the tingle of energy. He slowly opened his eyes, no longer conscious of the others in the room. There was only Cren, and the need to balance and heal. The E-light cast an eerie glow, adding to his sense of other-worldliness.

"Come here, Cren," he commanded in a steady voice. He stood and stretched out his hands. "Come to me now." His eyes seemed to glow. Such was the strength of his presence that every eye on the ship fixed on him, wondering.

Cren stood. He moved slowly, eyes on Dal's. His eyes widened as Dal's smaller, slender hands clasped his angular ones firmly. The crew stood or sat close, observing breathlessly, except Koren. She gave a shudder and backed against the bulkhead, closing her eyes.

A faint, blue-white incandescence began to seep through Dal's hands, enveloping them. The glow spread, becoming stronger. It grew to encompass Cren's hands as well, and then, his whole body. Just as abruptly, the light vanished.

Surprise dawned on Cren's face like the first rays of a yellow sun on a summer morning. As the strain and fear fell away, so did the years. The crew watched in amazement, Kimmer's awe tempered with concern for Dal, as Cren's features relaxed and softened. His eyes took on a new focus and clarity.

Dal released Cren, and touched his shoulder gently. "You are whole again," he said softly. "It will be easier to tell your story now. I promise."

Cren's eyes lit up with a bemused joy, as he moved in silence to his previous seat. He appeared calm, which was more than could be said for the rest of the crew. They were all bewildered, yet didn't want to break the spell, if spell it was. Koren edged back warily into the circle of her crewmates, but as far from Dal as she could get.

"What in the name of the Guardian was that?" Renzec hissed to Kimmer.

"Tavs call it 'starfire of the hand' ", she whispered. "Dal mentioned it once. They teach higher order adepts and healers how to link with another's EM field to restore balance."

"I'm impressed. When did they teach him that?"

"They didn't. This is new."

Dal returned to his seat, outwardly serene, but he stepped very slowly and deliberately. Rial leaned over and whispered, "Dare I ask?"

"Later," Dal said wearily, his energy drained. He leaned forward, his arms resting on slender thighs. He addressed Cren in the same mild, even tones he had used before.

"Cren, we need to understand you before we can function as a team. You've had major obstacles in the way of that understanding, but they have been cleared. The Joriens have been in the thick of political maneuvering lately. Events are set up for a major clash. Is that why you're here?"

"Tell us, Cren," Naui prodded. "Your father wanted you out of reach. Who did you kill?"

Dal darted a reprimanding look at her, and then laughed lightly, shaking his head in mock dismay. "Naui, our queen of tact." He picked up a wadded ball of paper debris and threw it in her direction. She batted it down with her good hand, but kept silent, her eyes challenging Cren to reply. Cren did not react. He had looked inside, and was having trouble dealing with what he had seen.

"Through me, you've felt how we all feel, Cren," Dal continued. "You know something of what we are. The strength of the bonds that connect us. You are part of that now. If you seek fairness, you've found it. Blunt she may be, but Naui's right. Time to tell your story. We'll listen for as long as you want to talk."

Cren finally moved, looking at each of his crewmates with new eyes. It was true. He was part of them. At least for now. He sighed deeply. "Thanks. All of you. For the chance to explain." He took a deep breath, surprised at how good it felt. Katayan bounded over and jumped up on Cren's shoulder, nuzzling his neck. Cren laughed, and more strain fell away.

"I didn't kill anyone, Naui. Not yet," he amended. "Father was only trying to save me. It's all my fault, the crisis at home." He at looked intently at his crewmates. They all waited for him to continue, except Renzec. The engineer had his head buried under his console. He popped out briefly as Cren looked around. "I'm listening, Cren," he called out. "But we need light. Anyway, I think better when I'm fiddling, ok?"

"Ok, Rennie. I'm that way myself," Cren said. He breathed deeply. "Whew. It's hard to start. Father told me not to say anything. That was hard. I know I seemed dumb at times, and I'm not. Father says there's going to be war. It could take out the whole planet. It's all my fault."

"Cren," Kimmer said gently, "You keep saying that. You might be magnifying things. You've had a hefty dose of calmative, and you're not accustomed to medication."

"Just since I got on the ship, Kimmer," Cren admitted. " I tend to babble too much if I take meds, so I was afraid of them."

"Aaah, so that was it. I can relate to that," Dal reassured him. "We all talk more when the pressure's off." He raised his arms in a gesture that encompassed the cabin. "The immediate world has fallen around us, and we're not going to get it cleaned up any time soon. We'll listen." He settled down as comfortably as he could. Katayan hopped from Cren's shoulder into Dal's lap and purred softly, kneading with his paws.

"I've felt some kind of fracas building back home for some time,

Cren," Rial interjected, seeing Cren wasn't yet ready to talk. "I thought it would be a self-limiting thing. A posturing power struggle."

"I, too, was aware of the rumor-mongering along the space docks," Melion added. "It had increased dramatically."

"Every news brief sets it off," Rial said. "It's calculated. It drums up military support. How do you know it isn't a ploy?"

"This is real all right." Cren sighed. "It's hyperilon. I found a way to make it transparent."

"So," Renzec humpfed from under his console. "What d'you think our ports are made of, kid?" he snorted. But he pulled out from his work and leaned over a panel, moving a little closer. He understood the gist of Cren's revelation.

"You mean processed hyperilon, don't you?" Dal asked, and Cren nodded. Dal's face became grave. Hyperilon was the most valuable structural material in the known galaxy. It was versatile, light, strong, and able to withstand practically anything. It could be fabricated as opaque, translucent, or transparent. To be flexible, or not, depending on the process. Once it reached its end state, however, it couldn't be changed. What had so far been missing was the ability to distort light hitting a hull in such a way that the craft was, in essence, rendered invisible, merging with its background.

"How did this happen, son?" Rial asked patiently.

"At the Academy, I was almost three years younger than my classmates when I started. Then, as I said, I left after a year. Don't get me wrong," Cren explained hastily. "My grades were way up. There was this lab project. Just an extra thingy, sort of extra credit. With electromagnetics. They let me run with it. When I mentioned it in a comm home, Father wanted me to take over the application end right away.

"I'd been playing with acoustic transparency, you see. Using transparent hyperilon sandwiched with foam polythanics. I'd developed a material with the same density as water. Kind of an invisible fish blind." Cren said earnestly. "At the Academy, they thought it would be valuable on aquatic worlds. Father got all wound up about it. Got a government project, so we didn't need front money. The chance of a lifetime. I had to take it."

From the looks on his crewmates' faces, they didn't agree.

"How did you feel about leaving the Academy?" Dal asked.

"I wouldn't have lasted," Cren shrugged it off.

"Why did you go to the Academy in the first place then?" Naui said. She placed her small, square hand on his in support.

"Father thought going to the Academy would be good for me," Cren answered. "I enjoy the vids, you know. Space exploration vids. "Your Future Is Now," and all that. The plan was, I'd take a few years out to do school. The Academy classes would be leadership training. It was fun, even, compared to the tutoring I had before. I don't know if I could have done the whole thing. Father said I wouldn't make it all the way. Anyway, the paper I wrote had applications. One of our subsidiaries patented them all."

"Wait a . . . !" Renzec said, holding up a finger. "Oceanics! Yeah. I read a paper on that. We've been to ocean worlds. But hey, Jorien Enterprises wasn't involved in that research. They couldn't be! Conflict of interest, Cren. Didn't your father sit on the Committee that got them the grant. . . ." His jaw dropped as the light dawned. "So *that's* what happened! I could never get any follow-up on it. Come to think, I never saw 'Crensed Jorien' on the patents, or on the paper. I would have remembered the name when you came on. It was a good paper, but it left out all the details I needed before I could apply the science."

Melion spoke up suddenly. "That is true. That paper is in my files as well. It's good work. But it does seem," she looked at Cren suspiciously, "censored?"

Cren confirmed that with a nod.

"Cren is not the acknowledged author," Dal finished. He raised his hand, palm out, to stop comment as Naui started to speak. "I read the work as well. Yet," Dal continued, "Cren *is* telling the truth." He caught the Chief's eye and got a raised eyebrow. "He simply was not credited for his work."

"Father thought it better to keep our name out of the neo-hyperilon business. The paper Oceanics published was a watered down spin-off of the one I wrote. You see, it's only good business to keep more than a few subsidiaries of Jorien Enterprises like, separate. Without a paper connection. That's legitimate," Cren insisted.

"Yeah, we know," Renzec nodded, pointing at Cren with his melder for emphasis. "Daddy made a bundle, didn't he?"

Cren shrugged his thin shoulders. "The bottom line, Renzec," he said earnestly. "That's *got* to take priority." Even in the E-light, they could all tell that Cren believed this. "Once Oceanics got the contract, I developed EM induced transparency. I didn't think of the ramifications. I screwed up." He sank his head in his hands and gave a shuddering sigh.

A slow, grim smile spread across Chief Rial's face. "By Grandmother's cross-eyed yorbu, I believe we've got another genius among us. Son, we're damned sure not going to sit here and let you absorb all the guilt, just because your creativity was channeled inappropriately." He looked at Dal questioningly. "Am I reading this right?"

"I believe so, Chief. As far as it goes. Cren must take responsibility for allowing his father's manipulations. He signed on, knowing we'd rely on him, yet he was untrained. He didn't think about the consequences of his actions."

"Sometimes it's survival mode, Dal. Maybe he found himself in a corner, and didn't see any way out," Rial said.

"That does happen. Was it like that, Cren?"

"It felt like that." Cren looked bleak. "Dal's right, though. I knew better."

"All of us take the easy way at times, Cren," Dal admitted. "Sometimes it's the only way we see. The important thing is what you do with you life from now on."

"It's time to break the pattern," Rial agreed. "In the Survey, we go with what we've got. Right now, we've got you."

"If the Guardian were just, engineers would rule the galaxy. Politicians would be used primarily as landfill." Renzec muttered. "I'm going back to work," he continued, waving his laser melder for emphasis. Then he again pointed it theatrically at Cren. "And I want to see *you* later," he said as he bent to resume his labors. "Once you work this out, *we* have some projects to discuss."

"I haven't said the worst. Somebody in the company was dealing the technology to both sides."

"Good Guardian, Cren!" "Somebody?" "Both sides?" Groans and gasps predominated, as everybody tried to comment at once.

"Smooth it!" Dal's crisp but soft order somehow permeated the din. "Cren, continue," he directed.

"I don't know for sure who did it," Cren sighed. "I started following a paper trace, but before I got anywhere, I wound up here."

"Did your father know about your 'paper trace'?" Naui asked suspiciously.

"Father isn't like that, Naui." Cren pleaded. "He was just trying to get me to a safe place."

"Cren, your father has holdings all over," Koren said gently. "Surely, he could have found a safer haven for you?"

Cren shook his head. "Father said he wanted to protect me from blame. For the war, I mean. If word got out.

"The bottom line though, is that I know nothing about deep space exploration, except what I learned from the vids," Cren admitted flatly, "but I'm all there is to carry on the Jorien name and pick up the pieces, if it all goes boom back home. Please understand. It's not easy for anyone to say 'no' to Father. Even me."

That was too much for Naui. "Especially you," she said. "I think he wanted you out of the way before you found him out!"

"Enough of judging. How old are you, Cren?" Dal asked, shooting a mildly reproving look at Naui as he got up and headed for his station with Katayan on his arm.

"Almost 17."

"Well, kid, we're not losing that much, then. We got you before they gave you too many bad habits!" Renzec let out a loud bray, and ducked back under the control board.

"But I don't *know* Survey skills," Cren insisted.

"Don't fret," the Chief said firmly. "We can't put you on a transmuter strip back across the Freel-Omar with a ticket to the Academy. Now that we know what's what, Kimmer can put you on routine meds. Not much we can about what's happening on Metrowyl. But we'll find a way to utilize those energetic brain cells of yours, and worry about what to do with you when next we dock at HomePort. I may have some choice words for your father at that time. Until we hit HP, you're part of the crew. You've signed yourself up for some heavy-duty on-the-job training."

As the Chief helped Cren up he suggested, "Start your new job now, by assisting Kimmer. You had first year, and that means basic medic training. Put a support bandage on Naui's injury."

Crensed looked doubtful, and Naui's eyes narrowed. "Kimmer could do it faster and better," Cren objected.

"That's exactly why *you're* going to do it instead," Kimmer chimed in lightly. "Here." She threw the plasti-spray over in Cren's direction, and he caught it automatically.

"Just apply your knowledge, and the bandage," Kimmer encouraged. She returned to sealing the small wound on Melion's arm.

"Come on, genius," Naui teased. "See if you're bright enough to get the electrostim apparatus off and the bandage on. And tell me more about neo-hyperilon."

Abruptly, full lighting came on. A ragged cheer burst from the crew. Renzec raised his hands over the power console with a shout of victory. Then he looked around, and his triumph faded as he viewed the carnage. He whistled. "Who's next in line for cleanup detail?"

Just about everything that could have shifted in the craft had taken the opportunity. The Chief managed a wry smile as he picked his way through where Dal was working industriously at his station. He peered over Dal's shoulder. "What've we got?"

"Nothing we can't fix." Dal accessed the log. "As we passed through the low-albedo cloud layer, we hit an electrically quiet strata. Markedly lessened atmospheric static. I was able to bleed out some of our charge there. We got knocked around, though, by mesospheric storms. Then the wave came. Fortunately, it was significantly attenuated by the atmospheric layers we had already passed. I can't decipher the nature of that wave. A new kind of EM, possibly, on a carrier wave of some sort." Dal's eyes got the unfocused, dreamy look for a moment. "It had a new 'flavor' I didn't recognize. I don't have a name for it. But I am starting to get a resonance from the planet. When we slid in, we went subsurface briefly. Interesting," Dal said thoughtfully. "Never did that before," he mused.

"Let's not do it again any time soon, ok?" Renzec gibed.

Dal ignored the sarcastic comment and concentrated on his instrumentation. "Chief, these clouds absorbed rather than reflected the wave. See how the X-rays, gammas and some of the EM storm effects diffused throughout the layer. They took all we could bleed, too. Once we got below the clouds, we were in no danger.

"You have any thoughts on the wave, Rennie?" Dal asked as he turned toward the engineer.

"It's an oddie, Dal. Until our pulse hit the heliosphere, this star appeared as calm as toreg soup. Then wham! Chief, you ever heard of a solar wave like this, with no flare?"

Rial moved cautiously to Renzec's board and peered at the panels. "No flare at all? In any spectrum?"

"No flare, Chief."

Rial shook his head as he checked all the monitors. "From what I saw on Dal's screen, we're lucky the scanners weren't fried. If we had remained in orbit. . . . Can you sense anything at all out there, Dal? Any sign of intelligence?"

Dal shook his head. "Negative on intelligence. There *is* abundant animal and plant life on this world, however. It's scattered, mostly to our south, but it's here.

"We're on a major continent. It's not the locale I'd choose to place a future settlement. We're close to the edge of a fairly significant ice sheet. Just about a half foot of compacted snow on the ground outside our landing area. Many small subnivian life forms registering, but not in the immediate area. The berm we've created is confined to the nose of the ship. Our exit ports are safely above it. The wind is howling, though." He activated his personal sensor array, and gave a low whistle. "Guardian! What's that!"

"Perhaps we'd be able to answer more intelligently if you put it on the wide screens, so we could all see," Chief Rial suggested dryly. "Ours aren't working, remember?"

"Uh, sorry. There. It's to starboard."

They caught their first view of the alien sky.

"Look! Look at it! Look at the colors!" Naui cried with excitement. She rushed to the screen. Spread wide across the heavens were sheets of multicolored flame, hanging like curtains from the vault of the sky. They writhed and curled in an ever-changing design, dancing a mad frenzy to the tune of excited ionic dervishes.

The wind was indeed howling, judging by the swirls of loose snow and ice chips being whipped here and there across the ice sheet. For the most part, what they could see of the land, caught in the light from the sky, was empty of feature. Where visible, the thick, roiling mesospheric clouds formed a bizarre, dark purple backdrop to the celestial extravaganza.

Chief Rial came over to stand by Naui, followed by the rest of the crew. "So that's what's to starboard," he exclaimed in wonder. "Open audio frequencies, Dal," he whispered.

A soft "shhhssss" hissed at them from the sky. The wind not so much howled as replied with a high "khhheeee" as it moved smoothly over the ice.

Dal switched the large forward screen, now displaying berm, to target the area to port. The prismatic display of the sky reflected on the snow and ice, and illuminated a craggy range of mountains dominating the horizon in the distance. Glaciers rode their tops and winked with lurid gleams from the celestial light show. Close by, they could see some windblown, stubby trees strewn in clumps across the tundra. The crew clustered around the large screen in an effort to pick out details.

Cren gasped, and whispered, "Wow!" Dal tore his eyes from the screens to check out their young charge. Cren's face filled with so much delight and wonder it was transformed. He didn't even notice Dal's satisfied look, so mesmerized he was by his first close-up view of an alien world.

"Cren," Dal said softly, "some things cannot be explained. Only experienced. Each new planet can be a rebirth." Kimmer came up and clasped Dal's hand. The crew stood together, mesmerized.

Ten minutes later, the light show to starboard faded and the wind stilled. But the planet had another surprise in store for the explorers. On both sides, the short, stubby trees brightened the night with winking luminescence. By punching up the magnification on the closest one, they could see individual flexible filaments stretched out like wiry stems from thick, stubby branches. Miniature dots of light scattered at random intervals on the graceful, curving stems continued to blink.

Chief turned in amazement to Dal. "What do you make of that?"

Dal returned to his console and concentrated on the data coming over. He changed the settings to zero in on the trees. "The sensors show some life form, Chief. Insectoid, specifically. Now that the sky show is over, I'm getting EM readings from the trees! "

"Insectoid? In this climate?"

"That's what the sensors report."

Rial turned to the rest of his crew. They were still gawking at the screen. He clapped his hands together twice. "All right, gang. We could goggle endlessly, but we've got a job to do. It looks like we won't have much time to catch up on our reading matter here. Break into teams. Let's do it! Dal?"

Groans replied, as the crew moved away from the windows.

"Blue and Red Teams, off-duty," Dal directed. "I want as many of us rested tomorrow as possible. White Team gets to monitor the sensors." The team mentioned cheered. "And start the cleanup." It was Rial's turn, as White Team leader, to groan. "But first," Dal added, "we have a ceremony. Cren, come over here, please."

Cren came over to where Rial was leaning on the back of Dal's chair, and looked apprehensively from the Chief to Dal.

"Cren," the Chief explained, "there is a ritual we have whenever we land on a new planet. We raise a toast to the planet, not necessarily with drink, though we have done so, but with our minds and hearts. Things being what they are," he opened his arms to encompass all that surrounded them, "I believe we should make this one a spiritual salutation only.

"This is your first planetfall, Cren. Because of the unusual circumstances, the rest of us must expend extra effort to teach things to you as we go about our tasks. It will be a part of *all* our routine jobs," he glanced pointedly at Naui, and she nodded rapid agreement, "to supply any education that you need. It's my belief that our lives together are all made more enjoyable if each individual's life is made more enjoyable. Our crew is a unit, made up of three teams. We work together.

"Cren, for your part, you must learn. It is not only what you know that determines your quality of life but also your ability to control your attitude. Make it positive. Is that clear?"

Cren looked overwhelmed. "I'll try. Am I in a lot of trouble for what Father did? Back home, I mean."

"What your Father did?" Rial sighed. "Case in point. *You* did it, by your agreement. But the past is the past. We're powerless to deal with it. Guilt also is pointless. Let it go! From now on, accept accountability. Be grateful if it comes from your crewmates, and not from nature. Life out here is very unforgiving. Your only protection is to evolve.

"And now, crew, gather." The Chief moved to the center of the cabin, and held out his arms. The crew moved carefully around and joined to link arms in the rough form of a ring. Katayan sat on Dal's shoulder. Cren was grabbed by a beaming Naui, and he became one more link in the circle. He felt a spiritual link as well, different than anything he'd ever felt before.

The Chief smiled at them. "We look forward," he intoned quietly, and the others joined voices to the chant," to adventures which await, and questions to be answered. To the birth of knowledge. To this world, and the next, and the long journey after." There was silence for a space of time. Then the crew broke into teams.

"White Team, you have some house cleaning to attend to," Dal ordered. "Keep it quiet."

Moans ensued from Leh and Naui and they made their way to their stations. The Chief would have none of it. "The data is being recorded without you. Let's clean up this disarray first. My Grandmother had a cross-eyed yorbu that made a worse mess each and every time it ate. And the smell!"

Dal was heading into the aft cabin passageway when he felt a hand touch his arm. He turned to see Cren looking at him oddly.

"What is it, buddy?" Dal asked. "Something that you don't understand?"

"Yeah, Dal." Cren smiled. His face looked years younger than before the disclosures. "Just a couple of questions."

"Go for it."

"That ceremony. Do all Survey crews celebrate it?"

"Most do, Cren, in some way. Some party. Some have rituals. Some sing. The timing differs, also. But there is always affirmation and unification. It keeps us focused."

"I can understand. I really felt part of it all."

"You *are* a part of it all, Cren."

Cren grinned. "Well, then. Before we get any farther, there's one thing I gotta know. But it may be a dumb question."

"No such thing as a dumb question," Dal insisted firmly.

Cren looked even more relieved. "Ok, Dal," he asked with real concern, "what's a yorbu?"

Chapter

7

"Cren!" Renzec swept his binocs to his eyes and pointed north. "Up there, see that? What is it?" The ranging members of Red Team were out on survey.

"Uh, where, Ren?" Cren searched skyward, whirling around so fast he stumbled. "I don't see anything."

Renzec point out the disappearing dot in the distance. "It was some kind of raptor, Cren. Fast critters. You have to keep sharp, or you'll miss 'em. Tell me about raptors."

"We don't have them on Metrowyl."

Renzec groaned. "Raptors are birds of prey. This particular raptor looked like a hawk. Probably swooping down to crunch one of those subnivian voles. See how the vole runs are collapsing where the snow has gotten weak? Most of the snow's melted here, so the voles are out in the open. Hawks are happy about that. Good eating."

"Voles? That's a bird of prey?" Cren asked in childlike innocense.

"Oh, man!" Renzec rubbed his neck and tried to keep calm. "A vole is a rodent, not a bird. A bird of prey kills and eats other things."

"All birds eat other things, Rennie," Cren said, his head hanging.

Renzec closed his eyes, counting to ten. Then his brows furrowed. He looked at Cren suspiciously. The kid was grinning. "Hey, you're putting me on!"

Cren laughed. "Yeah. I know what you mean, Renzec. Raptors eat other birds and stuff. Not wiggly things, like insects."

"Not exactly, and not always correct, but it'll do," Renzec said, rubbing his jaw as he resumed scanning the surroundings while they walked. He had been ragging Cren, and it was a good sign that the kid was comfortable giving some of it back.

"Now about the subnivian thing," Cren said slowly. "I can get into that, you know? I never thought there would be a whole world living underneath the snow pack during the cold seasons." Then he frowned. "But I don't have the surface stuff straight yet." He kicked a bit of the ground as they walked. Then he glanced behind them. The weight of their flexorboots left wet footprints in their path. "Rennie, how can I ever learn it all?"

"You can't, Cren. That's the secret. None of us can. It's important to remember. Just when you think you know it all, a world will throw something at you that you weren't expecting. " Renzec shook his head. "Some would say I'm slower on the uptake than most. But no matter how long you're in this job, each world is going to teach you something new. It's easier once you get some background though. You're operating under quite a handicap out here. For now, Cren, concentrate on learning what you need. Problem is, you need to know an awful lot of stuff. But you're picking it up fast."

Cren kicked more at the rough earth, moist from runoff. Then he stooped to pick up a stone, and sent it hurtling off in the direction of one of the low, gnarly trees.

"Don't *do* that!" Renzec rubbed his brow with exasperation. "Good Guardian, why don't you *think* before you do something dumb like that!"

"I didn't hit anything, Rennie," Cren insisted.

"That isn't the point, Cren. Don't be so damn defensive. I'm trying to teach you something, so listen up. Think about the possible consequences of what you did. For example, you had no idea what was under that rock. You didn't do a sensor sweep, like I do, before I pick anything up. Maybe it wasn't even a rock! Even if it was, it could have been dangerous. On Corolis VII, that action could have got you killed. They have a growth that lives on the bottom of some rocks, a neurolichen. It waits for some unwary life form, like you, to feed on. You see, it's a parasite. It puts out a pseudopod and oozes a neurotoxin that paralyzes. It can then feed off its prey at leisure. When it finishes its meal, it spreads itself thin again, under the soil, until it finds more rocks, someplace away from the remains of what it just ate. Then it goes dormant and waits for another meal to come by. It preys mostly on medium-sized ungulates. It killed two Survey members before they figured it out."

"That's awful!" Cren backed away from a group of large stones by his feet.

"No, Cren, it isn't awful. It's just life. Survey life, anyway. Many planets have amorphous life forms."

"I'll try to be more careful. I guess my kind of life has always been too safe. They get rid of that thing on Corolis? The neurolichen?"

"Why, Cren?" Renzec asked as they resumed walking. "Once the team became aware of the nature of the problem, it ceased to be a problem. The colonists farm the stuff, actually. That same neurolichen produces a metabolite used to treat a rare but fatal disease on another world. It pays the way for the whole Corolis colony."

Cren shook his head. "I'll never understand this. Father always said things were either good or bad. If something bit you, you bit back twice as hard. This is a whole new way of thinking for me."

Renzec grinned. "It's called 'growing up'. Not difficult, kid. All you do is take note of everything you experience and fit it all together where it belongs." He laughed. "That's the key, actually. All of life works together. It's supposed to, anyway. Each planet's an ecosystem, made of a lot of little ecosystems. It's important not to disturb anything unnecessarily. It's kinda fun to try to figure where things fit, but that kind of thing is really the SiTeam's job. We're supposed to find out what is here in general, and report it. Then they try to explain it."

"Sometimes I think I don't understand anything very well."

"I guess we all feel like that sometimes. Don't let it get you down, kid. There's even something I don't understand, Cren, that maybe you can explain to me." Renzec stopped and scrutinized the boy.

"What's that?" Cren stopped too, and almost at once started rubbing his arms. "Let's keep going, ok? I get the shivers."

Renzec resumed walking. "We need that cold weather gear. It

was sunny when we left. My fault. I was waiting for you to ask about it, and then I forgot. Cren, you hardly ever ask questions, although I can tell by the look on your face that you want to. Why?"

Cren sighed. "Father said I had to find out things for myself. If I asked a question, he told me to look it up. He said asking questions made you look stupid."

"Unlearn that right now, Cren! Ask any question, any time. The question you don't ask is the one that could get you killed, and maybe your crewmates as well."

"Ok Renzec."

"Good. Because I like doing ranging tours with you."

"Me? Why?"

"There you go! Easy habit to get. Actually, your legs are nearly as long as mine. I get to walk at my normal stride. Everybody else on the ship's short stuff. We can cover a lot more ground."

Cren laughed.

"Now, what can you tell me about this area?" Renzec asked. He started climbing a knoll. "Careful, now," he warned. "This surface, when it gets melty from our weight, it's slippery." They reached the top and looked out over the land.

"It's all lumpy and ridgy."

"Lumpy and ridgy, huh? That's what I like. Scientific lingo. These lumps are called 'hummocks' Cren. The ground we are on is called tundra. The lumps are caused by alternate freezing and thawing. See how open it is. We're above the normal tree line, except for this one stumpy variety. They don't seem to know when to quit. The boulders scattered around here indicate glacial action. Maybe recently, geologically speaking."

"You seem to know everything."

Renzec laughed. "I'll tell you a secret, Cren. I spent most of my last two off-shifts reading up. Not an awful lot in the computer on cold worlds, though. Come on over here."

Cren followed the engineer to a rocky area a short distance on the other side of the knoll.

"Now, these boulders. What do they tell you?"

"Well," Cren peered at them closely. "They're big and they're grey."

"I'll give you that, though big is a relative term and doesn't mean a thing on its own. But there's a lot more to learn." Renzec checked his wrist comm. "It is getting cold, though, and it's getting late, too. Maybe the geology lesson better wait." He turned his back to the rocks, walking towards the camp, but turned abruptly as he heard a "plunk".

"Kid, I told you not to do that!"

"It wasn't me, Renzec! Honest!"

"Freeze!" Renzec hissed as he moved noiselessly toward Cren and the rocks. He moved his sensor to his right hand, and flipped out a stunner with his left. "It sounded like it came from you."

"Behind the rocks, Ren," Cren whispered. His face was white, and his eyes flicked nervously around the boulder area.

"We may have Dal's thing roast yet." Renzec touched Cren's arm once in reassurance as he passed. He scanned the area. "There's a critter behind the boulder to your right, but I get an odd reading between the boulders too. Whatever's behind them is small." He moved stealthily to the edge of the rocks. Carefully, slowly, he worked his way around.

"Keer! Keer!" A strange noise pierced the quiet. Cren scrambled up the nearest low boulder, forgetting to scan it first. "What is it?" he asked.

"Keer!"

"Come over here, nice and slow, Cren. See for yourself. I don't believe we're in for trouble. Or a thing roast, either."

"Keer!"

Cren crept over the boulders, stunner in hand. A two-foot high primate stood on a low outcrop. Its thick, shaggy fur bristled, and it brandished a stone.

"Keer!" It yelled. Its round eyes grew big and it hopped as it spotted Cren.

"Keer!" Cren yelled right back at it. The creature jumped, dropped the rock, and covered it's face with large paws. Cren laughed.

Renzec took his eyes off the primate for a second to glare at Cren. "What in the name of all that's new made you do that!"

"I don't know, Renzec. It seemed right. Look!"

The creature put it's hands down and was staring at Cren.

"Keer?" it asked in quieter tones.

"Keer," Cren said back at it.

"Well, look at that." Renzec grinned widely.

Sure enough, the fluffed red and gray fur softened. The primate looked about a third smaller.

"Not much bigger than a murdle," Renzec laughed. "Makes almost the same kind of noise, too, only a higher pitch. I get an EM reading on it. Its biochemistry is about the same as ours."

Cren scanned, and then sat on, a low boulder "Come over here, little guy. Keer. Keer."

The primate lumbered over on all fours. It clambered up the rocks and over to Cren. "Keer?" It reached out a short finger and thumb, and tentatively plucked at Cren's uniform.

"Keer," Cren repeated. "Hey, slow down, little guy," he said, as the being climbed up his arm to his shoulder.

"Looks like you found a new friend. I wish you hadn't let it climb on you like that, Cren. We don't know anything about it. Put it down, gently but firmly."

"It's ok, Ren. I'll call him "Murl," Cren said, as the being nestled close to him.

"Cren, it's not a pet. We don't know what it is."

"I know, Renzec, but I need the company." Cren reached up to pet the creature, and it made a soft, cooing noise. "Everyone's been working so hard, and I don't want to be a drag on you. Katayan stays with the others. This guy is red, anyway, and we're Red Team. We should bring him back."

"Can't do it Cren. Could be dangerous. Besides, it's not according to procedure."

"I had the feeling that procedure never stopped this crew."

"Only for a good reason. Dal would give me all kinds of hell on this."

"But he's cold. Look, he's shivering."

"We don't know that's from cold, Cren. He's part of this habitat, and . . ." The comm alarmed on Renzec's wrist, and he flipped open the transmitter.

"Hey, teammates! You're 10 minutes overdue for call in. You better have a good excuse. Problems?" Koren's melodious voice asked over the comm.

"Sorry, darlin'. Everything's fine. Just got sidetracked. We'll be right along," Renzec assured her. He heard Cren cooing at the little beast and added, "We'll bring in a surprise."

"Oh? What kind?"

"The surprising kind. See you in about 20 minutes." He flipped the comm closed. "Well, I've done it now."

Cren beamed and stood up. "I guess we better get back."

"Yeah. I guess. Cren, you know what we've been telling you about accepting the consequences of your actions?"

"Don't worry, he's light. I'll carry him."

"You still have no idea." The engineer shook his head. "Maybe insanity's catching," he mumbled to himself as the twosome, with a passenger, set off across the tundra.

The other team's rangers had already unloaded their samples and sensor records. Leh and Naui were setting up ship's perimeter sensor fields when the rangers of Red Team came in with their find.

"What *is* that?" Naui squealed, and she ran up to Cren and clapped her hands with excitement.

"Keer!" the creature cried, and it shied away from her, scrambling with agility to Cren's other shoulder. "Don't know," Renzec admitted. "It has a limited vocabulary."

Leh came up quietly and looked at the furry discovery. "It has an EM signature. It's trying to communicate where you can't hear. I can sense esper signals. You shouldn't have brought it in. You *know* better, Renzec. And you *will* know better, Cren. I feel curiosity, and friendliness, but it's shy. Don't make so much noise, Naui. You startled it," she advised. Leh got to within a foot of the creature and closed her eyes again, concentrating.

"Kira-loga-de-er?" the creature asked.

Leh smiled, reached up and scratched it's head. The being closed it's eyes in bliss, and rubbed against her hand. It cooed.

"Its sweet," Leh said. "But I mean it. You shouldn't have brought it in, guys," she chided. "Chief will throw a fit. Were there any more of them out there?"

"No. Not that sensors picked up. Besides, Dal's in charge this trip." Renzec looked down.

"That may make things worse," Leh warned. "He's had a bad day. He pushed himself too far, and his legs went out from under him. Had a tough fall. That didn't improve his mood. Kimmer has been at him for hours to stop work, and now this! He's on his way now." With her sensitivity heightened to scope out the alien, she could tell Dal's mind was already sizing up the new EM source. He arrived within seconds.

"Renzec, what's this?" Dal bit out. He looked fatigued and disgusted, and slightly battered, with a bruise coming out on the left side of his forehead. He ignored Cren totally, turning his back on him.

"It's my fault, Dal," Cren said quickly, putting a hand on Dal's arm before Renzec had a chance to marshal his defenses. "I brought the little guy along. He's friendly, really. Don't be mad at Renzec."

Dal turned carefully, trying not to move his neck muscles more than necessary. "When I want your opinion, *novice*, I'll ask for it," Dal snapped. "Stay put, and be quiet."

Cren backed off, hurt.

"Your responsibility is to *observe and to learn*, Crensed. Do so. *You*, on the other hand, are *Renzec's* responsibility." Dal flicked open his comm. "Kimmer, report please. We need xenoscans." He stood in weary resignation until the medic appeared. He gestured at Cren's burden.

"Check them out, Kimmer." He pushed sweat-dampened hair back off his forehead with a weary hand. "When you clear them, take the alien into the lab and we'll do a thorough check."

While Kimmer quietly began a fast sweep of Renzec, Dal turned to Cren. "When Kimmer clears you, I want you in the ship. Deliver the alien to the lab. Then hit the books, Crensed. Procedures 46 through 52, dealing with alien contact. Generate a report on what you did wrong and what procedures you violated. Then give me at least five scenarios where your action could have had serious consequences, at least three of them possible fatalities. When you're finished, find Renzec. He'll review the procedures and your report with you, and write an evaluation. I'll check it all later. Now move!"

Cren's eyes got big, but he kept his silence and obeyed at once. Dal turned and addressed the engineer.

"Renzec, I'm thoroughly disappointed. You know the procedures, and the reasons behind them, and yet you ignored them. What does this kind of irresponsible action tell Cren? The alien could have parasites, its EM contact could have short circuited ship components, it could have disease. . . . Agh!" He dismissed the engineer with a wave. "Damn it, Rennie, you're Red Team Leader. I need to be able to trust you. When Kimmer clears you, *provided* you check out, head for the lab. We need to talk more about this, and what we should do about it."

Renzec nodded. Dal was right. He let out a long breath, and went over to where Kimmer was waiting.

"Over here," the medic ordered, pointing.

"Yes, ma'am," Renzec said sheepishly. He looked out at the quickly gathering darkness. It looked like it was going to be a long night.

Chapter

8

Koren and Cren worked across the tundra, colorful incongruities against the drab terrain. They wore standard colors, but cold weather gear was metallic hyperilon with jagged contrasting geometrics. Prompt rescue could depend on ease of sighting.

Koren walked ahead. Her jumpsuit fit like a second skin, as her slender legs moved her effortlessly over the glacial rubble. Cren stumbled behind carrying the native "murlota".

"Cren," Koren asked as she glanced back at him briefly, "do you want to talk?"

A wash of blood rushed to Cren's face. "No."

Koren stopped, turned, and flipped off her 'corder.

"Listen." She flipped her hood down, unconscious of the effect of her thick, wavy hair cascading down her shoulders. "It was no big deal. Talk to me." Koren waited in vain for a reply. "Cren," she said firmly, "we have no nudity taboos out here. Get use to it." She flipped open her corder, scanned the area, and plunked down on a reasonably flat, reasonably dry boulder.

"I wanted advice, Koren. I did *not* expect to be stripped naked!" Cren objected. The murlota riding his shoulders squeaked in alarm, and Cren reached back absently to comfort it.

"Demonstration is the best way to teach.

"Once you showed me how to fit the insulator over my feet, the rest was easy. I'm just not comfortable with the intimacy you guys take for granted," he flushed. "It did itch something awful at first. Before it sort of melted on."

"It reacts with your body oils," Koren explained. "It does melt, and seeks out your skin. It breathes. I'm sorry about the itch, Cren. You should have said something. Survey folk are the most communicating people in the galaxy, because we never know what information will turn out to be important. Rub lotion on your skin the night before you plan to go out, Cren. That will prevent the itch. Your insulator is permeable, and will react to body secretions. Have you been able to urinate ok?"

Cren's face flared again.

"Can it, Cren. Maybe modesty works on Metrowyl. Here, it's a luxury we can't afford. We live too close to the edge. We *define* the edge."

"But why is the insulator transparent?"

"Skin color might need to be monitored quickly in case of an emergency, Cren," Koren said. "Besides," she teased, "you have a cute bod. A bit on the skinny side, maybe. You'll fill out, once you stop growing." She smiled and resumed the survey.

Cren thought about it a moment, digested the thought, shifted the murlota, and then moved up to walk along beside her.

Koren continued her lesson, "The insulator, double thickness stretchsuit, and hooded vest should protect you sufficiently in this location at this time. Empty your vest pockets after each trip. Make it a habit. We stash samples and articles we need in these pockets-that's why there are so many. Ask, if you can't figure out the function of something. It could be important.

"Replenish whatever you've used on a trip *before* you store your vest in the locker. There's a check list on the locker door. By the way, if you think of a better way to do something, speak up. We're forever rewriting Standard Operating Protocols.

"Always keep your boot liners dry. There are several pair your size in storage. Mittens, too. They have liners also, but we haven't needed them here." She shook her thick hair off her shoulders, where it fell in a bright mass collected by her hood.

Cren groaned. "I'm catching this information with my 'corder,

Korey, so I can review it later. Otherwise, I'd never remember it all. There's too much. Can we rest now?"

"For a little, Cren. There's a lot to learn at first, I know," Koren said sympathetically as she scanned the rocks. Then she sat. "How are you acclimating yourself otherwise?"

Cren looked around at the generally flat, glacial moraine, juxtaposed with low growing vegetation and the occasional clump of boulders. The air was quiet, with a light wind. "I'm doing ok," he acknowledged. "I feel guilty, though." He sat down on another boulder and adjusted the murlota.

"Why so?"

"In the Protocol, it says that only two members of a team can leave the ship for exploration, except in emergencies."

"True. The person at the ship has to be able to rescue the rangers in case of need."

"I don't know how to handle a rescue, so I'm always ranging. I bet Dal would have made other arrangements if it we didn't bring back the murlota. Rennie's grounded, stuck with maintenance. I'm sorry that he had to pay for my bad idea."

"Renzec knew better, Cren. Consequences, remember? And Dal was the one who really paid for Renzec's error. Because you brought the murlota in, he was up late.

"It's my own observation that the murlota's preferred method of travel is to ride draped about a human's neck and shoulder." She laughed, low and musical. "So Cren, you bear that burden. Don't worry about Renzec.

"Perimeter surveillance is one of our most basic duties. We all cut our teeth on it. Any but the most superficial reconnaissance requires footwork, and we need some detail. It's the part of Survey most glamorized by your space vids."

"Yeah," Cren nodded. "I loved Survey vids. Never knew what would happen next. This is different. It's boring."

"Be grateful, Cren," Koren warned. "Foot surveillance can be boring, or it can be fun, but it can also be dangerous. You have to be ready for anything. Lose your focus, and you could lose your life."

"If you say so, Koren. I still feel bad that Ren is stuck at the ship. You two have something going."

Koren smiled. "Don't be concerned. Rennie needs his space. He gets moody."

"So I've noticed," Cren laughed.

"Besides, we're supposed to have three working groundhoppers. One should always be waiting shipside. In practice, that's not always the case. On our ship, even maintenance can be exciting at times," she said with a laugh.

"Weren't you and Dal together for a time?"

"For a time, Cren," Koren said in a wistful voice.

"If you don't mind my asking, what happened?"

"It's a long story. Cren. Basically, Dal is changing, and I'm not comfortable with what he's changing into."

"But isn't that what we're about, Koren? Investigating new life forms?"

"We aren't supposed to *become* new life forms!" Koren smiled sadly. "What's human and what's not? Where do you draw the line?"

"I wouldn't know," Cren grumped, feeling sorry for himself. "I'm having enough trouble myself. I'm a misfit."

"Of course you are," Koren agreed amiably.

Cren looked shocked.

"Cren, you've taken the place of a trained specialist. Sure, you're a misfit. Our objective, and *yours*, is to change that status. Maybe you're expecting too much of yourself right now."

Cren looked unconvinced.

"What do you want?" Koren asked him.

Cren looked confused. "What do you mean?"

"The Chief says the first question we need to answer in life is, 'What do I want?' What would make you happy right now?"

"I don't even know what I am, much less what I want."

"Cren, Dal says that the secret of life is finding the right questions. Then the answers aren't so hard to find."

"Dal's given me lots of good advice," Cren said. "Chronic pain can make anybody irritable, but the only time I've ever seen him angry was the night we brought in Murl. Dal's shown a lot of patience with me, but he doesn't seem to have much for himself."

Koren looked at Cren thoughtfully. "You're very perceptive, Cren. Tell him your observations. He works too hard. He had a tough Change. Sometimes I think Dal should have been born Tav. "Our Season of Change is unique in the galaxy, so far. How much do you know about it, Cren?"

"The rudimentary stuff in medic training. Some kids wind up in the hospital, don't they?"

"Sometimes, Cren, during a Crisis. Radically changing biochemistry can cause a variety of aggravations as the body and mind fight to bring new forces into balance. Those with even limited empathic skills have the addition of learning to handle raw emotional input from others. At best, there are energy disturbances and shifts. Each Crisis is followed by a period of relative quiet, as the body and mind balance. It's called integration entrainment. A Crisis can be precipitated by mental, emotional, or physical stressors. Most Survey crew spend their Season of Change at HomePort."

"And the military grabs the espers."

"You got it," Koren said. "But they haven't found many lately." Koren patted Cren's knee. "I'm glad they didn't get Dal. For all his strangeness, you'll never find a better person, heart and soul. Come on now, Cren, it's time we started back."

Cren tried to imitate the rhythmic way Koren moved her body in an automatic pattern as she walked, scanning from side to side, up and down, so she could observe as many things as possible with minimum effort. He felt miserably clumsy.

In the distance to their north, there glinted reflections from a long reaching tongue of the ice shelf. Farther still the tops of ice-covered peaks winked mysteriously. The high clouds bent light in alien ways, causing strange shadows to play across the ground.

"I can't believe we're leaving already," Cren said as he stopped momentarily to shift the murlota clinging to his back. The animal wound long, hairy arms around Cren as it craned its head to check out the boulders surrounding them.

"It's time," Koren said simply. She stopped and scrutinized the lichenous strands of vegetation hanging from the side of the boulders, away from the prevailing wind. She wrinkled her nose, and ran the 'corder over its surface.

"Why, Koren?" Cren continued. "There's so much that could be done to make this place livable. Even profitable." His toe scuffed one of the strange tufts of low mossy growth arranged in colorful patches scattered across the terrain.

"Leave it for the SiTeams. The other planet may be better for the colony. We're only here first because of the wave." Koren swung around and resumed her ground-eating stride. As they approached the ship, she stopped and sniffed the air. She took off her mitten, and squatted to feel the cool, rough soil melt with the warmth and pressure of her bare fingers. Her eyes closed, and she attended to the presence of the world.

Cren remained silent and waited, watching her. There was a light breeze, carrying the scent of something undefinable but pleasant.

Koren stood and opened her eyes to the milky blue-white sky, raising her hand to shield them from the formidable glare.

Cren stopped the murlota from pulling at his hair, gently disengaging the five fingers and two opposable thumbs. "I want to know where this guy came from. I can't see a whole tribe of them living in the peat bogs, or on those stubby light trees. Dal says there's a 'bo-real' nearby."

"That's bo-re-al. As in 'boreal forest'. Not just 'boreal'. It's a descriptive term for a biome. A habitat."

"Bo-re-al. Dal believes that's where the murlota came from."

"We might check out the trees before we leave. That may be full of surprises. They may not all be as gentle as your little friend."

Cren was silent for a space, musing. He started searching for something. After a while he found it. "See that big rock over there? The upright one? I want to do something."

Curious, Koren acquiesced. Cren fumbled around in his pack, and took out one of Renzec's tools he had borrowed. Koren inspected the tool carefully and raised her eyebrows. "Go ahead, Cren, you might just learn something." As she scanned the area, Cren carved the name 'Jorien' in block letters, deep into the rock face. Then he started to write 'Crensed' above it. He finished the first three letters when he ran out of power. He gave a cry of frustration, and the murlota yelped.

"You ran out of power. I thought you might. What if you needed that tool to save your life? Don't ever go out with an uncharged tool, Cren! Remember this lesson. It was cheaply taught."

"I'm sorry. There's been so much to for me to learn."

"It's hard to change a lifetime of habits overnight. But keep trying," Koren advised.

As they walked toward the ship, Cren asked, "Koren, has anyone ever come across a murlota this close to an ice pack?"

Koren burst into laughter. "Oh Cren. Nobody's ever come across a murlota *anywhere!*"

"Then how do you know it's a murlota, huh? Did Dal tell you?"

"Dal never saw a murlota before, either. None of us did. The Chief *named* it. He said it looked like a cross between a pet murdle and his Aunt Lota, only without a moustache and fangs. So he called it a murlota," she smiled.

Cren looked disgusted. "I may be new," he said as he picked at his pale-colored sleeve ruefully, "but I know murdles don't have moustaches and fangs."

"Ah," Koren's smile melted the snow," but you've not met Aunt Lota!" Her laughter peeled across the tundra as they walked into camp. Most of the crew were outside the ship, discussing plans.

Renzec was a short distance away, involved in the repair of the recalcitrant groundhopper. From the disheveled appearance of his clothes and his sour expression, it was not going well.

Cren swung the murlota down to the ground. It ambled over and promptly climbed Renzec's leg.

Renzec grinned and assisted in the climb to shoulder level. "Hey, guy, I have to fix this heap. You want to help?" he asked as he scratched its chin. It jutted its lower jaw out to enhance the effect.

"Just like a murdle," Cren remarked.

"What you forget," Renzec said soberly as he detached the murlota and resumed straightening the landing stanchion,"is that this here *isn't* a murdle," he insisted as he disengaged a murlota hand from a spanner. "Although I'll give it credit for trying." Then he grunted with the effort of trying to finish the job without the proper tool.

At that very moment, Dal came around the edge of the craft, limping slightly. He handed Renzec a long cylindrical gadget with a curved-claw end. "Is this what you need, Renzec?"

Renzec grinned. "Where was that! I looked all over the ship!"

A long-suffering look came over Dal's face. "I just tripped over it in the aft compartment," he said evenly.

Renzec winced. "Uh-oh! Yeah. Right. Sorry. Now I remember. My compartment closure sticks."

"Get it fixed, Ren. After you're done here. Then put your tools in their proper place."

Renzec hooted. "After I'm *done* here. Right. May be a while." He shooed the murlota away, brandishing the tool in mock anger. It squealed and scampered over to Cren.

"Dal, can't we stay a few more days?" Cren asked.

"Not now, Cren!" Dal warned.

"We could build something here. We could make this great."

Dal sighed and sat gingerly on an untidy pile of containers. He rubbed his right thigh distractedly. "Build? Make? Do you think this planet *needs* anything we can provide her?" He spread his arms as if to embrace to whole area. "Look around you. Really look. This place is doing fine without us. We're not here to upset the balance of nature. The SiTeams will decide what's to be done, if anything. Learn your job."

Cren felt crushed. "That's not fair, Dal. I only want to contribute something," he said defensively. "There's a place in the universe for builders, too, you know."

"Of course there is, Cren," Dal said softly. "We're all walking the path of life. It's only when we cease to struggle against the flow that we resonate with the true path. You are struggling.

"You speak of being fair. Cren, the universe is rarely fair. But when it's in our power, *we* must strive to be fair." He shifted position slightly and grimaced. "For example, the murlota. If you took the murlota off planet, like you've asked so many times, it wouldn't have the comfort of its own kind. Perhaps it needs trace elements we can't provide. Maybe it was searching for a mate when you found it." Dal sighed wearily. "It belongs here. We don't."

Koren had been watching the interaction unfold from a perch on a nearby rock. Things were getting heavy. "Dal's right, Cren," she said lightly, putting her arm around the lad's shoulders. "We know very little about the murlota's needs."

Cren mumbled something unintelligible and got up. The murlota held up its arms to be carried, and Cren swung it up on his shoulder. Meeting no eyes, he went into the ship.

Dal raised his eyes skyward and sighed. "People," he said, "we have to find a way to make things easier for Cren."

"He isn't doing much work now," Renzec observed.

"That's my point," Dal explained. "Cren is part of our crew. He's had too much time on his hands lately. He's not using it to study. My fault. I've felt so jangly. The EM fields, maybe. *Everything* here seems to have its own EM field. Leh and Katayan feel it too. We have had to filter our sensitivity because of it. Maybe I haven't been sensitive enough to Cren's needs."

"Maybe you're not being sensitive enough to your own needs," Koren mused.

"That's not the point," Dal said. "You and Rennie have borne the brunt of Cren's training so far, because you're his teammates. He needs all of us to teach him. He needs responsibility."

"You're asking for it," Renzec laughed.

"That's precisely what I am doing, Renzec. Tomorrow, somebody has to check out that ice-sheet edge and light trees we spotted on the flyover. There's a lot of EM readings. Should be fun to investigate. Why don't you two go off and see what you can find." Whoops of enthusiasm greeted his suggestion. "We'll make other arrangements for ship coverage. And for Cren. See if you can find out what causes the intermittent luminescence on the light trees."

"I'd like that. But we'd have to be out over night to do a good job on the luminescence," Koren said, with hope.

"Let's schedule an overnight for all the ranging teams. None of the projects are more than an hour's 'hopper flight away. There *are* large life forms in that vicinity," he cautioned. "I'm uneasy about that. Use protective fields around your camp, and stay together. Follow SSP/SOP."

"How will you deal with Cren shipside, Dal?" Koren asked.

"He's seen too many Survey vids. I'll start him unlearning," Dal promised. He stood up stiffly. "Oh boy. I've got to do more physical therapy. Or remember my medications."

"Maybe both," Koren suggested.

"You sound like Kimmer," Dal groaned. "Let's go over plans for tomorrow with the others. Get them please, Renzec. And don't leave the murlota in the ship alone. I have no desire to find out what kinds of trouble those agile little fingers can get into."

Renzec fetched the others, and Dal outlined his plans. After explaining Red Team's mission to the crew, he asked, "Are you comfortable with this, Cren? It could be a very important responsibility."

Cren straightened his shoulders. "I know how to fly a hopper, and I've read emergency procedures. I'll do all right."

Dal smiled. "Good man. Two experienced people will be in or near the ship at all times to advise you. Review any protocols you might need before you turn in tonight. Give a yell if you have any questions. I'll be glad to answer them.

"Leh, that sticks you shipside. You haven't been out much. Is that ok with you?"

Leh nodded her head in agreement. "I've had that jangly feeling too. I find it hard to deal with, so I don't care to go out. I'd like to practice my empathic skills on Cren, with his permission." she said. "And I could use another ear for a tale I'm working up. I've been intrigued with a builder's view of a virgin world. It could make a great story. Cren could be a help in developing it." She turned to Cren and favored him with a bright smile. Cren beamed.

Naui's eyes lit up. "Hey! I get to wear the shiny stuff!" She had acquired a love of bright colors from her Orelian relatives.

"We all sleep come nightfall. The sensors are rigged to alert us if the need should arise. We have a few hours of sunlight yet, so let's not waste them." He began to rise, and then froze suddenly. The blood drained from his face.

Kimmer came up and looked searchingly in his eyes. "Are you ok?" she whispered as her hand rested lightly on his arm.

Dal gave her hand a reassuring squeeze. "I'm fine. Just moved too fast. I forgot my meds, that's all. Cren's a trained medic. Get him to bug me about it. What could go wrong?"

Kimmer rolled her eyes sarcastically. "You know the answer to that. Especially when you're pushing yourself this way."

"We all put up with a little extra pain now and then. It is part of life," Dal said firmly. He turned to Cren, who was watching Dal and Kimmer with total absorption.

"Cren," he explained gently, "The murlota should travel with Blue Team to the boreal area. That mission has the best chance of encountering others of its kind."

The animation left Cren's face. He swallowed hard. Then he said in a small voice, "Ok, Dal.

As Cren handed the fuzzy creature over, he made a promise to himself. He would try to focus on what could be learned from every experience. No more wasting time brooding over things lost. He had no way of knowing how much his resolve would be tested in the next few days.

Chapter

9

Kimmer woke with the vague feeling of a summons disturbing her dream-fogged mind. For a few moments she remained motionless in the dark, listening to the quiet, regular sounds of Dal's breathing beside her. A dream? Then the comm flashed, giving mute witness to reality. She sat and hunched over close to the comm, and depressed the pad. "Kimmer here," she acknowledged softly.

"Kimmi, help," Melion's voice strained through the comm.

"What's happening, Mel?" Kimmer felt the bed cushion move as Dal activated the compartment light.

"My muscles are so tight I can't stand it," said the weak voice from the wall.

Kimmer checked her wrist comm. Nearly dawn. "I'll be right there, Mel." She closed the link.

She grabbed her stretch suit and started to wiggle into it. "Sorry, love."

Dal gave her a sleepy smile and rubbed his eyes. "If not you, then me. Somebody's always needing something. Those meds kept me sleeping longer than I should have. Besides," he said, poking her gently in the ribs, "the benefits are worth the costs. Katay is already waiting. Don't fret, Kimmi. We both have round-the-clock responsibilities. It's part of the deal."

The aft cabin sleeping area was divided into four sets of three compartments, each with a roll-down, sealable outer wall. A compartment was comfortable privacy for one. Or even two, if they were very, very friendly and didn't require a lot of lateral movement.

Kimmer spared a second for a longing look at Dal, from the tousled, tawny hair to the slim, muscular body still half hidden by covers. Her mind flashed to things she'd rather be doing.

Dal grinned and his eyebrow raised suggestively, reminding her that he could feel her powerful emotions.

"Empaths," she muttered, and Dal chuckled as she grabbed her medpak.

Kimmer freed the wall panel of the compartment, and it swung up and out of sight. "Kimmer," Dal called softly as she swung her barefoot legs over the side, "if Mel can't make it, I'll shuffle the scheduling."

Kimmer stood on the decking as the anxious catabit stropped his sides on her legs. She shook a finger at Dal. "No! I know what you're thinking, Dalrion Darnel."

"Just let me know," Dal insisted.

Kim sighed as she swooped Katayan up and moved over to Mel's compartment. One problem at a time. She touched the circular depression in the lower right corner of Mel's outer "wall", and it rolled up into the space between compartments. Kimmer leaned in and flicked the overhead lamp on.

Dark purple shadows hung under Mel's half-closed, unfocused eyes. Sometime during the night she had kicked off her covers. They were bunched around her now, damp with sweat. The smell of that sweat, pungent and sour, foretold coming Crisis. Kimmer settled the mewing catabit close to Mel. She immediately began receiving impressions from Katayan. They were not good.

"When did you take meds?"

"Two hours ago, on schedule. They aren't doing it, Kimmer. My skin feels sore if I touch it. Every cell feels like it's gritting its teeth."

Kimmer checked the 'corder closely. "Chills on and off?"

"All night. When I wasn't sweating." Melion moved fitfully, trying to find a comfortable position.

Kimmer sighed. "Mel," she decided, "you're grounded 'til you get some sleep." She put her palm up to quash a developing debate, and

Melion shut her mouth obediently. Disappointed showed on her weary face.

Kim pressed a hypospray into Mel's neck. "That's to attune and relax your muscle sarcomeres. Those are the areas causing the tightness. There's a med to calm down the electrical discharge, with a little extra something to get you off to dreamland. Wish you had twoed. Even a temporary arrangement. Sex realigns the body's electrical system."

"Your avocation as matchmaker is hampered in the limited environs of a Survey craft, Kimmer." Melion said slowly. "I'm too analytical to two. I would like company though. Can Katayan stay?"

The catabit purred loudly and nestled in the rumpled coverlet. Then he put his dark brown nose on his front paws and closed his eyes in contentment.

"There's your answer! When you let the pain get intense, it's harder to control. You know better," Kimmer said. As they chatted, she could see Mel's muscles begin to lose their rigidity. Katayan had already drifted into sleep after linking with Melion, pulling her along.

"Will I be able to work shipside?" Mel murmured drowsily.

"Not much. Your mind is apt to be foggy, even after sleep. Don't worry. You've trained Naui so well, you won't even be missed," Kimmer exaggerated.

"Thanks ever so much," Melion said wryly, fading. "I may just sleep through the rest of the Change."

"Fat chance," Kimmer said softly. "We need you, and you'd be bored." She remained, watching, until the pale golden eyes were covered by heavy lids, and the 'corder indicated she'd achieved a deep, restorative sleep.

Kimmer looked down at the pretty face, now soothed, but marked with the testimony of a long night of pain. If only Mel had called her earlier. Dal set a bad example at times. She checked to see that the wall comm was activated, and that Mel's wrist comm was on medimonitor continuous mode. Then she pulled the outer compartment wall down over the two in shared slumber. Kat would do his best to guarantee sweet dreams for Mel. Time and rest were

Mel's best medic now. She went to her own compartment and changed into a fresh stretchsuit and soft boots. Then she walked briskly to the front cabin.

Dal was at his station, running down a checklist. He glanced up as she passed through the doorway. "How bad is she?" he asked in a voice heavy with compassion.

"She can't range, Dal. Katayan is with her. We'll probably make the next planetfall before she goes into Crisis. You should still stay here," Kimmer urged as she walked over. "Your compensating systems could break down under the stress, and I don't want you in the field if you flare into Crisis."

Dal took her hands in his and looked up at her somberly. "Maybe we can compromise. I'm through with the Change, anyway."

"There will be residuals, Dal. Maybe for always. I think your talents have just begun to develop. Like with Cren after the crash. That was something out of legends. It certainly unnerved Koren. I wish you'd explain it."

Dal grinned ruefully. "The Chief's been at me too, Kimmer. I can only tell you what I've told him. There's a kind of power, Kimmi. An energy. Tavs call it 'the force which connects'. I tried to channel it. They call that use 'starfire of the hand'. Some day I'll learn how to really manipulate it. It is not a passive process, and it is not generated from within. The wielder has to deliberately reach for the energy, attune to it, and then transform it. Somehow it connects with that which needs healing, and creates the proper resonance there." He looked troubled. "I'm flying blind on this. I can feel new EM paths developing, but I still don't understand what they are or how to use them. During that landing, I could feel the EM forces wrapping themselves around me. I haven't had time to sort it all out. I've been in constant sensory overload ever since."

"I know. Exposure to unknown electromagnetics could cause all kinds of complications." Kimmer frowned.

"Or unexpected benefits. I promise to take better care of myself on this trip. You'll see." He smiled encouragingly. "Think of it, Kimmi. We could be together. *Alone.* For the better part of two days."

Kimmer nodded assent, and smiled. "Be good with Koren and Renzec paired off, too. Give them time to work some things out."

"Renzec's been more temperamental than usual," Dal agreed. "Koren deserves better than that."

Kimmer leaned over and kissed Dal's forehead gently. "She had the very best, love. She couldn't handle it."

Dal smiled sadly. "We didn't fill each other's needs any longer. Our paths went in different directions." His face brightened. "Then I got lucky," he said gratefully.

"We both did," Kimmer amended, basking in the glow of his palpable affection.

Dal consulted his day plan, looked up and smiled resolutely. "Cren is going to get his responsibility. Can I safely put Mel in his hands?"

"He knows the basics. Melion is a methodical, responsible person. *She* listens to her medic. You, on the other hand, seem to need a full-time keeper."

Chief Rial walked into the cabin and nodded to them. "Why are you expressing obviosities, Kimmer?" he asked as he winked.

"Melion is ill. She needs to stay here and sleep."

Rial frowned, and looked at Dal expectantly. "And?"

"I've modified the schedule. I'm going out."

The Chief raised his eyebrows and turned to Kimmer.

"If we didn't stay in team structure, Dal could stay shipside, or I could stay," she said with little hope.

Rial looked dubious. "Survey works best in teams. They shouldn't split up, except for emergencies. This doesn't qualify. I don't want Cren going out, and Leh can help Mel. If you feel strong enough that Dal needs to stay put, Kimmer, I'd rather scrub the foothills mission. There are enough tasks to keep us busy at the ship. Especially with Mel down."

"Chief," Dal interjected, glancing apologetically at Kimmer, "we only have three planned missions. They're easy and flexible. I'm fine. A little stiff, that's all. Kimmer will attest that most of my current problems are my own doing, or overdoing. She'll be with me.

If Renzec drops us off, he can swing back and pick up Koren. We don't need a 'hopper."

Chief Rial turned to Kimmer. "How is Mel?"

"She's hurting. Her vital signs are stable. Katayan is with her. Symptoms are mostly peripheral. I'd guess ten days or less to Crisis. I'd like Dal to verify that, however."

Dal nodded, pushed back from his station, and went to do a depth scan on Melion. For that, he needed physical contact.

Rial waited until Dal left. Then he asked, "Kimmer, can Dal range?"

"Yes." She sighed. "If he takes it easy." Kimmer sounded tentative.

"Make him behave, hear?" Rial ordered.

"He won't like it." She ticked off her fingers. "No climbing. Minimal physical exertion. Careful attention to meds and nutrition. Rest. He's already overtired. That makes his symptoms worse. Empaths have trouble integrating the physical and mental portions of their development. Dal's no exception."

"Can Cren handle Mel?"

"If Dal agrees with my prognosis. I'd like to keep KatKat here. He can help balance moods, and he's very protective. When Mel wakes up, she may be able to handle light duties."

Rial scratched his chin. "Leh's a good stabilizing influence. What she shouldn't have to handle is a sick patient plus a moody Cren. If an emergency comes up at a field camp. . . Still, Cren surprised me with the 'hopper. Boy flies like a raptor. Maybe knowing he's needed will be just the ticket. He's improving his coping skills.

"One more thing." The Chief looked closely at his medic. "Is there any chance that Dal's judgement is being affected by Change residuals? Or by his medications?"

"There's always a chance, Chief," Kim qualified, "but I haven't noticed anything. When he's gone too light on his meds, pain interrupts his concentration. None of his meds impair cognitive action. Have you seen something?"

"Not at all, Kimmer. I just needed your confirmation. How did he sleep?"

"He could have used a few more hours," Kimmer said contritely. Then she colored lightly as she saw the look on Rial's face.

"How's he managing, otherwise?"

"Dal's functioning fine," she said evenly. Sexual dysfunction was an early symptom of the lack of EM integration.

"If that status should ever change. . . ."

Kim nodded as Dal entered the cabin. " Kimmer's right about Mel," he reported. "We should make it to the inner planet before she hits Crisis."

"No hunches lately?"

Dal was quiet for a minute. "I'm not saying that."

"Specify."

"Wish I could, Chief."

"Something's bothering you."

"Yes. It could be the EM fields. I don't know."

"Carry it through, then," Rial agreed. "But Dal," he warned, "cut down on activity hours. Simple observation. We'll stay on null-grav once we're spaceside. Agreeable?" He looked at Kimmer, and she nodded.

"But you may not be sound in your theories concerning the murlota, Dal," the Chief continued. "I've been thinking about what you said last night. Perhaps the primates do travel alone at certain times of their life cycle. . . ."

Kimmer left them to their debate. She checked the time as she entered the aft cabin. The others were waking up and starting to move about, gathering their gear. She hid her smile when she noticed Cren and Naui bashfully exiting the same compartment. They shared a lot of interests. Cren was way too young for anything else to be going on, and Orelians matured even later. Neither had shown signs of approaching Change. Still, it was a sign that things were moving in that direction. She prayed the Guardian would deliver her from having more crew in Change right now. She composed a list of Procedures for Leh to review with Cren. Only then did she allowed herself the anticipation of spending the next few days-and nights-alone with Dal.

Chapter
10

"This doesn't make sense! These are all female too!" Naui turned her head to regard the herd of 40-some dainty korets. Velvety dark muzzles were buried deep in the fragrant green grass emerging through patches of dwindling snow. The tangy but pleasant smell of the herd carried up on the brisk, clean air, with the occasional rich scent of dirt flung from sharp hooves as they dug in exposed turf. Remnants of dingy white hung in odd clumps from their coats, but here and there a peek of tan and cream-striped hide glistened where the fur had sloughed off. Soon they would resemble the sleek animals grazing in meadows further to the south. Spring had come.

"All female but him, that is," Naui amended. Her brightly mittened hand made a iridescent arc against the background of milky sky as she pointed to the regal stag some distance apart from the herd.

"Chief Rial, every herd we've checked has only one male. What if something happened to the male? They'd die off."

"Naui," Chief Rial admonished, "we don't have all of their story by any means. Observe them. What do they tell you?"

Naui concentrated for a few moments. "There are no birds on these korets. There were birds on the other ones."

"True, but the insects aren't out yet up here, thank the Guardian! The birds eat the insects. The insects must arrive first, or the birds would have nothing to eat. So that relationship is probably not relevant to the lack of balance in the genders. What else?"

"About one third of the females are pregnant. If they're like the other herds, the foals will be female, too." She rubbed her nose, sniffling in the cool air. "Where are the rest of the males?" she insisted.

"I don't know, Nau," Rial replied. "Probably, there is a short summer, or else the females wouldn't all be gestating together. Must make for a busy breeding season for the male." He watched the feeding herd with satisfaction. Even as they shed remnants of their winter coats, the small-boned animals had the self-assured elegance and grace of their namesake.

"All we can be sure of is this." He paused, waiting for Naui to turn her head back to him. "If we observe them long enough, they'll tell us what we need to know. The mechanisms of nature are often slow to unfold, but they are always logical. The logic is not always obvious after brief observation, so exploration teams often have to wait until the SiTeams do a more thorough evaluation. We can deduce other things though.

"Notice, Naui, how the herds don't spook, as long as they can smell us. When we landed, after a moment's uneasiness, they settled down. Then we could make our way up here. That stag's keeping an eye on us, but he's not losing feeding time. I get the impression that it's more of a mild curiosity he's feeling toward us than anything else.

"But," Rial raised one finger of his outstretched hand for effect-totally nullified by his shiny, black mitten-"when we tried to approach other herds, if they couldn't smell us, they spooked. Why?"

Naui screwed her face up in concentration. She chewed once on her lower lip, but her eyes remained blank. "I don't know," she said finally. "It should be the other way around."

"Why?"

"We're bigger. We have weapons. We smell strange. The stag has horns and sharp hooves, but he's no match for stunners."

"How would he know? And how do you know we smell strange?" Rial asked patiently.

"Oh." Naui thought a bit more. "Well, we eat protein. Shouldn't they smell that? We share similar cellular structures, but we're alien. That should scare them."

"Why?"

Naui looked nonplused. "It's always been that way."

Rial laughed softly. "That's never an acceptable answer, Naui. And it's not true. Many animals must learn to fear."

"They have no reason to fear us."

"True. Can they know this?"

Naui sighed. "No." Her tiny snub nose twitched, and her brow furrowed, but she came up with no answers.

Rial smiled. "Hypothesis: What if there are bipeds on this planet about our size that smell like us? Things that pose no threat to them, because they can't move as fast?" Rial queried.

Naui's open face lit up like dawn. "That must be it!"

"That *could* be it," Rial corrected. "So why do they run when they *can't* smell us?"

"I know!" Naui cried gleefully. "There *could* be something here, a predator, something 'about our size' ", she quoted carefully, "that *does* attack them. It smells different. If they can smell us, they don't worry."

The Chief beamed. "Possibly," he chuckled. "See, youngling. You can often reason the possibilities of Nature. But she does give us surprises. We must be cautious and alert for them. And for those 'large predators', as well."

They were standing on a modest bluff, with the lake to their north. Their 'hopper nestled at the bottom of a long, gentle, snow-free slope to their south, hidden from the herd. The far side of the lake was rimmed by the steep side of a brilliant, blue-white glacier.

"Magnificent world, this," Rial said with contentment.

Naui stepped over to the edge of the bluff. The cool wind from the glacier riffled through the tops of the grasses covering the slope. She could see evidence of recent grazing nearby. "The grass looks richer over here. I bet the herd would be here, if we weren't."

"Maybe so," Rial agreed, and he walked over to her and gazed down the bluff.

The blue 'hopper resembled an ornament in a sea of green and white. Naui stifled a giggle. This pastoral scene brought to mind a childhood visit to Orelia, away from the confines of the city-world Metrowyl. She felt a powerful urge to spread her arms wide and run shouting down the hill. Maybe if the Chief weren't here. He would think her childish and undignified if she. . . ."

"*Yaaaaaaa*. . . ." Her reverie was interrupted by a muted cry beside her, and she turned in amazement to see Chief Rial open his arms and run laughing down the slope, toning down his joyful exuberance so as not to disturb the korets.

Naui stood speechless. She turned and caught the stag as he jerked his head up, eyes alert. Short blades of deep green protruded from both sides of his muzzle. After a moment, he gave a snort, and puffs of frosty air emerged from his flared nostrils as he again dismissed them as a threat. He plunged his head back into the succulent feast.

The young explorer giggled as she saw her Chief wave and beckon her to follow his lead. Naui drew in a deep breath. She threw her small arms out wide and raced down the slope, laughing out loud, abandoning herself to the moment.

Rial was lying on a patch of dry grass, catching his breath. Naui plopped down beside him, panting.

"Ah, Naui, child," Rial puffed, "if there's only one thing you ever learn from me, let it be this: *You are never too old to play.* Don't hesitate if the chance presents itself. It often costs little, and will profoundly effect your attitude toward life itself.

"You looked like a bright little kite, flying on a sky of grass." He smiled fondly at his young student. "Most of us are in the Survey because we love it, Naui. There's nothing in the universe that we'd rather be doing. That keeps us going, sometimes day and night. Our job is our hobby, and our great love, and it's so varied and wonderful that we never cease being entertained by it. Don't ever allow yourself to feel guilty about having fun. How do you feel, after that run?"

Naui grinned. "Alive!"

"Remember that. It will give you energy for the rest of the day.

We have lost nothing by that run, and gained a great deal." Rial sat up. "Let's check in. See how Melion is doing. Then lunch. Then what do you say about an overflight of those spires? Track down those EM emanations."

"Can we eat while we fly, Chief? I want to scan the lake before we plan tomorrow's work."

"Good idea on the food, Nau. But I'm of two minds about the lake," Rial said cautiously. He paused to run the 'corder over the grass. He grunted approvingly, broke off a tender blade and stuck it into his mouth, chewing thoughtfully. He took it out and examined the chewed end. "I don't recommend this as an appetizer, Nau. Tastes blah and green.

"Now, about the lake. I wish you and Cren had that underwater viewer rig built. Cren showed me the rough design. Impressive. How do you like working with him?"

"He has no self-esteem! I didn't expect that. No one has given him the respect he deserves. I expected he'd be spoiled, and poor in survey skills, with emphasis on material gain. He's all those things." Then she brightened. "But I like him, Chief. He is brilliant. I can't wait to put that rig together. We could go underwater and be practically invisible."

"So your interest in Cren is purely technological?"

Naui giggled "I'm not ready for that other stuff, Chief. It may be something to think about some day." Her mercurial face changed as she sombered. "He has a different point of view than the rest of us, you know?"

Rail nodded. "That's what makes him so valuable. We have to teach him to think on his feet. Once he applies that brain to Survey work, I think he could give Rennie a challenge in engineering, too. Keep an eye on the boy, and let me know if he needs anything."

"Yes, I'd be glad to do that, Chief. I was hard on him. Now I understand him better. He will be a good resource."

"But we'll have to work on the lake without his help. I'm a little concerned about using the 'hopper there. If we hover, we'll disturb the water below. Mess up testing. I don't want to land the hopper on the lake. Why not, Naui?"

"It takes us longer to power up from water mode. If danger occurs, we might not be able to move in time."

"That's correct. What would you decide?"

"The float boat."

"Exactly what I was thinking. The float's only big enough for one, but it has instant hover capability. There's a precaution we can take to add even more safety." He waited expectantly.

Naui thought. "If we took an overflight with the hopper today and scanned carefully? If there's something dangerous down there, we'll know all about it."

"We won't know *all* about it, Naui." Rial picked himself up and offered his team mate a hand. "But we'll know more." Naui reached over with her uninjured one and accepted the help up. "How goes your structural damage," Rial nodded at her guarded hand. The sparkling, light blue mitten shouted with orange and yellow triangles and squares.

"It aches at times," Naui admitted, "I have to keep the support on, but it's healing well." She looked shyly at the Chief. "I have to say something."

Chief Rial looked at her curiously.

Naui chewed on her lip. "Last year, when I came on board, I didn't want assignments with you," she confessed. "They were one long test, and I usually didn't know the answers. I'd get back and study so I wouldn't feel so stupid. Now I see Cren cycling through the same thing. I learned more from you on those trips than I did at the Academy. I was the only one putting pressure on me. You were helping me to learn. Like my pop did. I was his "little student". Now I like going out with you. I *have* to think."

Chief Rial smiled and gave Naui's good hand a squeeze. "Good for you. I'll tell you a secret. Some of that early push is by design. There are so many new things you need to absorb at first, you can't take it all in. So you learn to rely on your teammates. A little pressure also gives new scouts something to think about, besides homesickness."

Naui laughed. "*Now* you tell me," she said.

Rial turned to her as they took off. "Let me know if your hand begins to ache. It could distract you at a critical time. Don't be a martyr. We have a lot of ground to cover this afternoon, but the world won't end if we don't do it all."

"Yes, Pop," Naui said, trying in vain to stifle a giggle.

Rial laughed. "That's my little student!" Laughing together, they strapped in and took off for the heights.

Chapter
11

"This is absolutely gorgeous! No signs of the large creatures the other teams picked up during overflights," Kimmer commented as she activated the last perimeter monitor. "Maybe we're too far from the ice sheet here. That's a blessing." She sighed contentedly and gazed at the woodlands surrounding them. "It seems safe and peaceful. What do your interior sensors say?"

Dal adjusted the murlota clinging to his shoulder and wrinkled his nose at its musty odor. Then he closed his eyes and put out his psychic "feelers". "I sense abundant life in the immediate vicinity, Kimmer," he answered slowly as he opened his eyes, "but nothing large or threatening. There's something broadcasting EM from the trees in front of us. Maybe murlotas. I'm picking up anticipation from this guy. Even recognition, perhaps. I'm no Tav, Kimmer. I'm not catching everything. Just vague impressions." Dal sighed, and tried to stretch his muscles without jostling the murlota. It was getting heavier by the minute. "I feel the planetary pulse. Very powerful now. But there are so many fields I can't attune to it."

"Maybe it's not to be." Kimmer stretched her arms and yawned. "Can you believe how great this place smells?" Then she laughed playfully and winked. "As long as you're not downwind of the murlota, that is. Ready for the forest?"

"Sound's good." Dal reached into a vest pocket and brought out a hydrator and a small container. He shook out two capsules and swallowed them quickly. "Notice," he pointed out, "I'm not waiting until the going gets difficult before I take my meds. I'm being good," he grinned.

"That's a minimum regimen," Kimmer said, suddenly all business. "How's it working?"

"Good enough, Kimmer."

"Good enough? Let me know if you notice any muscle rigidity, or other sign of imbalance, promise?"

"I promise." Dal stretched his head and neck and winced. "I wish Cren hadn't carried this guy all the time."

The murlota pursed its lips and fluted a lilting note. It reached a nimble, grey hand to rub Dal's cheek affectionately, leaving a dusty smear. Dal smiled and clucked at it tolerantly.

"Let's see if it we can get it to walk," Kimmer suggested.

Dal swung the primate down gently. The murlota looked at Dal expectantly, and held up long hairy arms. Its big eyes looked entreatingly at Dal.

"Not this time," Dal said firmly. He took one wide grey hand in his.

The creature blinked a few times, pursed his lips again, and then twisted its neck around to look in question at Kimmer. She laughed and reached for the other leathery-palmed hand. "Let's try something different, ok Murl?" she coaxed. She turned and took a step toward the forest. Dal matched strides with her, gently encouraging the animal to take a few steps towards the forest. The murlota got the idea, and the three of them made their way across the meadow to the trees beyond.

As they drew near the forest, Kimmer paused and inhaled deeply. "Dal, that scent. Isn't it glorious!"

Dal nodded, closing his eyes and breathing in slowly, savoring. "Yes. A round mellowness, with overtones of pungency. Something regal there," he said eagerly. "Spicy. Is that what you mean?"

Kimmer chuckled. "I just meant the smell of the forest, Dal. I'm not up to all those nuances." She looked down at the little animal between them. "If that's your home, it smells great." The murlota responded with happy, chattering.

An eruption of noise echoed from the woods. The teammates looked at each other, grins widening, as the murlota gave an excited hop. It made for the trees, pulling them along. They scanned the woodlands, noting nothing of apparent danger. The murlota chattered impatiently. Laughing, they followed the creature to a worn path, leading under the canopy of stately trees.

Red Team settled their 'hopper on a flat plain, convenient to a small stand of the stocky trees. Nearby lay a shallow pond, still partly hooded with ice and fed by melting snow. The leading fingers of an ice field beckoned a half-hour's walk away, glowing pink and gold with the fading light.

Renzec swore as he checked the control panel.

"What now?" Koren asked. "The landing gear functioned fine this time," she said diplomatically. "For a change."

"Yeah. Now the frabling stabilizer's off."

"You need to have another talk with Chief Rial," Koren said. She leaned against the 'hopper wall, arms crossed.

"Not this time, Korey," Renzec muttered. He slapped the stabilizer with disgust. "This baby's had it. It just died"

"Just what I need to hear. Can you get us back?"

"Don't know. Have to take her apart. Again." Renzec sighed with resignation as he pulled out the tool kit. "Call the ship, Korey. Let them know we're down and out."

Koren grimaced, and hit the ship comm.

"How's it going, mighty explorers?" Leh answered cheerfully.

Koren groaned. "Not so mighty. Maybe not even explorers, Leh. The stabilizer's not working."

A burst of static came over the comm. Leh's voice resumed ". . . ting dark soon anyway. Can Renzec fix it?"

"Don't know yet. He's running the diagnostic. How's Mel?"

"She's rested and fed, and. . . ." Another burst of static interrupted. ". . . mospheric EM activity picking up fast. May not be able to keep in touch. If we don't hear from you by noon tomorrow, I'll send Cren with the 'hopper. He's itching to fly."

"Renzec usually can fix anything, even if he grumbles about it. If he has the parts."

"If not, call us," Leh admonished. "White Team is investigating those spires near the lake. Blue Team is in the boreal region. They found more murlotas."

"Great! Cren will feel better about that," Koren said, and signed off. "And Red Team sits on their butts, trying to get their 'hopper working," she grumbled. Then she shrugged off disappointment and got to work.

Cren entered the cabin, shepherding Melion with one arm and balancing Katayan on the other. Mel looked ragged, but was functioning. He saw her safely seated, and carefully positioned a gelcooler around her neck and the catabit in her arms, as Leh filled them in on news from the ranging teams.

Leh smiled appreciatively at the quality of care Cren was delivering. Mel patted Cren's hand in gratitude.

"Do either of you have any idea what's causing this uproar?," Leh asked as the comm began spitting static. "It's messing up transmissions. The sensors are frizzled, too. Even our site perimeter signals are fuzzy."

Cren shook his head. "I couldn't begin to guess. Nothing much has changed that I can see."

Melion looked at her panel and slowly called up some charts. Only after she had pondered the data did she speak.

"I can see a pattern. I believe. Not thinking as well as usual. The EM flux from the planetary field has been relatively quiescent during the day, generally speaking, for the duration of our presence. We've not been here long enough to know if this is the norm. At night, the EM interaction between the planetary field and the flora and fauna intensifies. I want to discuss this with Dal, before I say much more on that." Melion petted the catabit absentmindedly.

"According to our charts," Melion continued, "the EM noise increases during the evening. More so some nights than others. We have insufficient data to suggest a causal mechanism. Tonight we may experience an EM 'storm', such as happened when we landed. If this is true, we are witnessing the buildup." Melion's shoulders sagged visibly. Even this little effort exhausted her.

Cren glanced at the screen displaying the darkening sky. "Are you saying we have no reliable communications with our guys out there?"

"Probably not for tonight," Melion affirmed. She lifted Katayan off her lap, stood up gingerly and limped to the view screen. "They might see another light show, close up. Nothing dangerous, if the last one is any example." She peered at the screen, as if trying to spot her crew mates, and folded her arms across her chest. "Dal will love it." she said pensively.

Leh turned her attention from the screen to Melion. She could sense a plaintive note in her friend that was both surprising and disturbing. "Are you ok, Mel?" she asked.

"I ache all over. And I'm cold. I think I'll go to my compartment and lie down," Melion replied evenly. "Cren," she asked, "please scan me again. I need something, but I don't know what."

Cren complied. The medicorder reported her values drifting off, but not by alarming amounts. He checked with Leh, and dispensed the needed medication. After Melion retired to her compartment with the catabit, Cren turned to Leh.

"What's going on? Mel seemed to be doing well, and then all of a sudden she just got, well, down, I guess."

Leh beckoned him over. "Sit down, boy. I'm about to fill you in on the facts of life."

Cren popped into a seat next to Leh. "What do you mean?"

"I believe there's some carryover going on here. It can happen when an empath helps stabilize someone going through the Change. Guards are down. Sometimes emotional transfer occurs."

"I don't follow."

Leh propped her elbows on the console and leaned her chin in her hands. "It's like this. When Dal is stabilizing Mel, he opens his mind to her. The transfer goes both ways. She feels his compassion. His ability as healer. She gets this overwhelming flood of powerful positive imagery. She's reinforced and harmonized and all at once she feels much better. That's what stabilization is. Subconsciously, it amounts to a feel-good boost that her mind connects with Dal."

"Are you telling me Melion is in love with Dal?"

"No. Not really." Leh leaned back and smiled sadly, shaking her dark head. "I'm no psychologist. And I'm just getting a feel for this empathic thing." She scratched her head. "I never had *any* formal training. Didn't ask for this kind of talent. But my Grandma had it too. And I've felt the force of Dal's mind." Her grin widened. "Amazing. He's also a special guy in his own right. The combination can be overwhelming.

"I guess what I'm trying to say is that, subconsciously, Melion wants to be in love. With somebody *like* Dal. She's aware of the bond between Dal and Kimmer. She'll meet the right person. Someday. She knows that. But she feels the lack now."

Cren sighed. "I can't help Mel more than I have. I can't help the ranging teams at all. It's frustrating."

"Welcome to the world of the shipside, Cren. When things get touchy for the rangers, it's tough on us back here. More so when communications are cut off. This time, we know why. Our guys out there are knowledgeable and experienced, Cren. Trust them. Communications will resume in the morning." Then she brightened. "You *can* do something to help me. I'd like to try to broadcast some emotions, Cren. See if you can feel them. I'm new at this, so any feedback you can give me will be great. We're inside the ship fields, so the EM rise shouldn't be a bother. Maybe you will be able to sense Katayan. See if you can sense what I send. If we get tired of that, I can use your help on the Saga of Tagur."

Cren nodded. "Ok by me. Let's get on it."

Twilight was encroaching, and Dal and Kimmer still lingered with the murlotas in the forest edge. These primates were of slightly different color than Murl, and the scanner indicated that they broadcast on a lower EM frequency. After only a short time in their midst, however, Murl's EM signature changed to a near match with the others. The murlotas were still taking turns investigating clothes, hair, backpacks-anything having to do with their new found relative's strange looking friends.

Dal finally deposited the young primate he had been cuddling into the waiting arms of an adult. Then he stood up and adjusted his pack, making altogether too much noise.

"Let me guess. It's time to go," Kimmer called out from a pack of fur. She was lying on her stomach, inspecting something on the ground. She got to her knees, disengaging murlotas.

Dal came over and reached his hand down. "Past time," he agreed. Kimmer pulled herself up, grinning. Then she brushed off mosses, grasses, and not a few murlota hairs.

"What were you doing down there?" Dal asked.

"The root system of these conifers is complex," Kimmer explained.

Dal nodded. "Yes. It's a fascinating world." He reached over to the one reddish murlota in a sea of pink, touching Murl's fur one last time. "You're going to stay here with your new family," he said, trying to broadcast the idea. "We have to get back to our camp before it gets dark."

"Do you think you're getting through" Kimmer asked.

"I have no idea. I'm not getting anything from them, beyond a sense of activity."

Kimmer looked at the bouncing creatures clustered around them. "If Murl weren't a different color, I wouldn't know which one it was. Especially now. They all showing up on the 'corder, broadcasting the same EM."

"Not quite the same, Kimmer. I think I could tell the difference," Dal mused.

"Is his pattern that distinctive?"

"A little. It feels familiar, and the others don't."

"That's interesting."

"Yes, it is. I wish I had more training. I don't know what to expect."

"Sort of like having a complicated computer program installed, without a training module?".

"Sort of."

Kimmer stepped over to the closest conifer and rubbed her fingers over the deep grooves in the bark. She was delighting in the rough feel of it when her skin stuck suddenly. She gave a cry of surprise. "Oh, look, Dal!"

Dal bent to inspect a cluster of pale yellow globules, oozing along where Kimmer had broken off some bark. He sniffed. "That's where the spicy smell is coming from. It isn't on the younger trees. The tree is crying tears of gold."

"My poet!" Kimmer scraped off some older, non-sticky globules and held the mass up to the fading light. "They match the color of your eyes!"

Dal laughed.

"I'll run an analysis when we get back." Kimmer said with satisfaction. "All I can tell from the 'corder is that it's harmless. It's certainly aromatic."

"The sap aroma is distinct from the needle scent," Dal remarked.

"We have lots of needle samples," Kimmer said, patting her vest pocket. "I'd love to synthesize both. Lovely fragrances."

"Cren will have us marketing them all over the known galaxy before you know it." He reached out his hand. "Come on. Our packs are stuffed, and our 'corders are full. We made a start."

"Enough to tantalize the SiTeams," Kimmer agreed, taking his hand.

"Ikk! Kimmer. Are you afraid you'll lose me?" Dal laughed, and rubbed his hand where the resin had stuck them together.

"Cren will want to market a glue as well," Kimmer giggled. They hiked about halfway back to camp when their reverie was broken by the faint, fluting call of a single murlota. Dal stopped and looked back. "Good-bye, Murl," he called softly.

As they reached the camp, Kimmer felt a cold shiver down her back. "Let's sleep in the 'hopper tonight, Dal," she suggested.

"Any special reason?" Dal asked. "The sensor's say nothing obviously dangerous is around. What's bothering you?"

"I don't know. No reason to feel this way. I feel suddenly vulnerable. I felt perfectly safe in the forest." Then she laughed and held her arms out to Dal. "I don't know what's come over me."

"Hey. I do the empath stuff around here," Dal joked, as he gave her a reassuring hug.

"Maybe it's catching." She laughed again, but this time it sounded forced. "I wish we had Katayan here. I know Mel needed him, but all at once, something feels wrong. Let's check on the others. We might be able to get through on a boosted signal."

"You certainly are radiating anxiety, my lady love. Besides that, all I feel is a build up of atmospheric EM. Maybe that's what's got you feeling buggy. I get wired on that kind of thing if I don't consciously diffuse its effects. In fact, maybe that's what the murlotas were doing, with their low level broadcasting. Kind of a dampening field. Either that, or they were communicating something I missed. Maybe both. The EM is getting to the point where I can't diffuse it all. I haven't felt this wired since the first landing." He shrugged. "Maybe we'll have a light show tonight. We'll put the 'corders on recharge, in case. We may never see this sort of thing again. I could watch it forever."

They arranged the insulator padding on the floor to a setting conducive to slumber. Dal set up the air mat his hypersensitive body demanded. "You know," he hinted, "we could do more than sleep in this configuration."

"Oh? What did you have in mind? Better do your stretches first while I fix dinner. After dinner we can, ah, pursue our options. Take your meds as well. A muscle cramp at the wrong time could certainly ruin the mood."

Kimmer activated the fields that formed a secure shelter over and around the camp. As the fields strengthened and merged, she felt as if a weight had been removed from her heart. Bursts of static from the comm interrupted her contemplation.

"No luck?" she asked.

"Nothing." Dal was sitting by the comm unit, staring out at the night sky. As soon as the fields had gone up, he had shed first his mittens, and then his jacket. "I can't reach the ship, or any of the ranging teams," he said thoughtfully. "An EM storm's starting."

Kimmer pulled out two meal packets and sat next to Dal. "Eat," she ordered. "Take your meds. Maybe we'll get a lift from watching the sky."

Dal took both meal packets from her hand and set them aside. "Kimmer, why wait for the sky?"

Kimmer's eyes sparkled. "Are you asking for a special consultation?" she questioned with mock severity as she started rubbing Dal's shoulders and neck gently.

"A very special consultation," Dal said carefully, as he gently pulled her around and kissed her. "May I touch your mind?" he asked softly.

"Always," she replied in a breathless voice.

Ever so slowly, Kimmer felt the light brush of Dal's mind caress the edges of her inner self. His desire melted into hers, and she returned the kiss with increasing abandon, as their minds, and later their bodies, became one.

Very much later, Kimmer once again rubbed Dal's shoulders. "It's unfair," she commented, "how your muscles can feel so good to me, and yet cause you so much pain."

"They feel pretty good right now," Dal replied in a sleepy voice. "Say, you've been working hard all day too. Let me rub your shoulders for a while." As he opened his eyes, he cried out, "Kimmer! Look up!"

She raised her eyes to the vault of the heavens. Varied shades of blue and green formed luminous streamers dancing across the cosmic amphitheater, arrayed in changing patterns. The translucent top of the hopper seemed to glow with it. As they watched, the colors snaked and twisted, developing a lower edge of gold, and then drifting into red, moving constantly. She forced her eyes away until she found the dinner packets.

"Dal, you have to eat something *now*. Meds first."

She looked over at her lover, now totally entranced as he gazed at the writhing sky in wonder. The little boy in him, often hidden but never far from the surface, had taken over. Dal was totally mesmerized.

They shared a silent dinner under the moving curtains of color. Then they crawled under the covers to watch the dance of the heavens until they both fell asleep.

"Chief Rial! What was that?" Naui's tremulous voice pierced the dark.

Rial sat up abruptly. "I heard it, Naui. I can't figure out what's causing it."

Minutes passed as they waited in the stillness. Then a muffled groaning rent the air.

"Good Guardian! Sounds as if the planet's giving birth," Rial exclaimed. He moved from his sleeping mat and activated the light, and then checked the sensors.

"That's strange. Nothing large out there. No animals at all for quite a distance."

"I can't sleep," Naui said. She sat up. Her bowl-cut blue-black hair framed her tiny, gamin face, and her eyes were the size of night.

"I fell asleep watching the sky. I'm surprised I drifted off. Must be the good air," Rial said, as he examined the monitors. "Everything looks shipshape, my dear. Don't fret."

Naui had remained motionless on her mat. "I'm not comfortable out here with that noise," she said.

"I don't wonder," Rial said. "Our fields are as strong as I can make them, child. What would help you feel better?"

"I want to be in the 'hopper."

"We can move inside if it will help you feel better."

The alien groan shook the night again. When the reverberations died, Chief Rial heard Naui sniffle back tears. He walked over and knelt by her mat, where she sat with her knees drawn up under her shift. She came crying into his arms and he patted her back gently.

"There, there, child. It's perfectly admissible to be afraid. It can be a valuable survival trait. I'm scared out of my thoughts, myself," he admitted, looking around at the night.

Naui sniffed and looked up at him. "Really?" she said in near disbelief.

"Really. If there's only one thing you ever learn from me," he cautioned, "it's that you're never too old to be afraid. Being afraid is ok. More than ok. It can save your life."

Naui sniffed again, and managed a weak smile. "Now I understand better how Cren felt when we took to space."

"See! There's always some good from every experience. Cren's only a few years younger than you, anyway."

Rial checked his wrist comm. "We have half the night left. The aurora might have activated something, causing that noise. What do you think about that?"

Naui inhaled deeply. "That could be."

"Here. I'll help you get your mat into the 'hopper. You were telling me how your father took you on camping trips? Why don't you mind travel. Pretend you're back on one of those trips. Try to get some rest. We've a busy day tomorrow."

"How about you, Chief?"

"I think I'll stay up and keep the sensor screens company for a while, Nau. I need to do a little thinking. I've not dusted off my parka for ages. I want to think on cold weather planets. Maybe put a name to this noise." He moved over to the field controls and changed a few settings. The protective fields opaqued. He also muted the audio.

"Now we have visible evidence of our molecular shielding. Psychological security. I feel better, anyway. You sleep well, Naui. Tomorrow, you may have to keep me awake. I'll call you if anything interesting happens."

"Thanks, Chief." Naui went inside, and shortly there were soft, gentle snoring sounds coming from the 'hopper. The Chief smiled, and deactivated the outer lights, except for those on his sensor board. He put the remote audio monitor into his ear, and listened to the deep, tearing groans for the remainder of the night.

Chapter

12

"I thought we lost them," Koren reported, "but early this morning they were still there, attached to the trees. We blinked our lights at them last night, after the storm, and they responded, synchronizing their blinking rate with ours. This morning I tried to approach them, but they all took off. We're calling them flutterbys for now." Koren giggled over the revitalized comm unit. "That's how they attract mates. By blinking. We think. And the stubby trees really aren't bare. I think there are tiny buds under the skin."

"What's the status on the stabilizer?"

"Rennie's still swearing at it. He says he can fix it temporarily, though. Enough to get us back to base."

"Renzec says he can fix *everything*. Is he being realistic?"

"I don't know, Leh. He sweetened up last night for a few hours, but he was 'Mr. Mood' again this morning."

"He can be real sweet when he wants something, Korey. Don't let him get to you, girl."

"I'll try, Leh. How are the others doing?"

"Haven't called them yet."

"I'm glad Mel is ok. And that Cren's been such a help."

"I think he has latent esper talent. KatKat has been awful fidgety this morning, so take care out there. Nothing shows on the sensors. I'll call back later."

"Talk to you then." Koren broke contact and looked out the 'hopper window. The light crust of frost, formed the night before, had not yet melted. The morning mist had burned off, and the ground looked like a powdered confection. The odor of burnt connectors and acrid static repellant spoiled the illusion. Koren wrinkled her nose as she grabbed her hooded vest.

Outside, Renzec was sitting on an insulated pad. Assorted pieces of stabilizer were strewn in an arc around him. His uniform was smeared with lubricants and grime, and his face was marked with them as well. He was decidedly unhappy. It was not good to be around Renzec when he was unhappy.

"How goes it?" Koren asked hesitantly.

"How does it look like it goes?" Renzec snapped, not bothering to look up.

"Can I help?"

"Yeah, if you do miracles." Renzec said glumly. "Turgling piece of daff!" he exclaimed, and threw the part he held at the 'hopper hull in frustration. "I have to make a whole new restrainer for this conduit," he complained, "and there's not a thing that I can make it from," he said, stretching his hands out helplessly. Then he glared up at her. "Do you have to stand there, hovering?"

Koren inhaled deeply. "I only wanted to help," she explained softly. "Shall I call for a pick up? Maybe there's something on the ship you could use."

"Look, I'll think of something, ok? Give me some time!" He pushed himself up off the mat angrily. "What I don't need is a supervisor. Give me room to work," he growled as he reached for a sonic welder.

Koren backed off. She could understand his misery, but it wasn't *her* fault. From past experience, she knew Renzec would stay in this contrary mood until he fixed the thing, or found an alternative. Then he'd fall all over himself making amends.

Well, since Renzec didn't want her help, she'd make herself useful elsewhere. Check the light trees again. It was against Protocol, but she needed to accomplish something. Maybe she could find out where the insects went in the daytime.

She pulled out a 'corder and her pack, and hooked a stunner on her belt. Then, always thoughtful, she scrawled a message to Renzec. Maybe he'd fix the thing. Miracles did happen.

She left the ship. As she expected, Renzec didn't even notice. She walked briskly under the alien sun, breathing the fresh, crisp air deeply. In a short while, she felt invigorated again. Here she was, with the freedom to explore, and a whole new world awaiting. She laughed out loud with the joy of it. From somewhere up above, an unknown bird sounded a raucous call. It seemed as though it were laughing right back at her. Koren searched carefully in the direction of the noise, but saw nothing in the odd, milky sky. She had the sound in the 'corder. Another mystery for the SiTeam. A laughing bird!

About an hour later, she was wrapping up her inspection of the trees. A mysterious smile played across her lips. "You thought you'd fool me," she accused the trees, shaking a long, elegant finger at them. "You and your flutterbys! They live inside you, during the day, under the bark! Those things weren't buds after all! Nobody's going to guess this one. Except maybe Dal. He's no fun."

Then she noticed a series of regular, roundish depressions leading away from the trees, toward the ice shelf. Funny she hadn't seen them before. All at once she was overcome by a strange sensation, as if there were an itch inside her brain. She had difficulty thinking clearly. She felt as if she were moving in slow motion. She bent down and took off a mitten, running her finger around the rim of one of the imprint. She felt a chill trickle down her spine. She straightened up and gazed toward the ice shelf, wondering what secrets it held. Her hand flew to her head as a blinding flash hit her. Then she gave a gasp as something massive smashed into her left shoulder.

Chapter

13

"I have no idea, Dal. It scared us out of our boots last night," Rial confessed. "It seemed to come from all directions. Nothing showed on the scanners. The korets all left before the EM storm. Do you recognize it on the tape?"

"It's new to me. I felt uneasy when I heard it. I have no scientific reason for that feeling, though."

"Give me your hunch then, Dalrion."

"There's a natural force at work. Maybe some geological configuration that would magnify and distort the noises of large lake creatures, and yet block the scanners? I'm just guessing, Chief." Dal sounded worried.

"A close scan of the lake showed smalls only. We thought we had something big on overflight, but it was a school of fish. We found a marvelous bioluminescent ray yesterday, but it was hand sized. Today, lake life has disappeared. The ice has an odd property here. Nearly opaque to scanning. Maybe there's something under it."

"The noise stopped?"

"Not a sound this morning."

"A hollow under the glacier might amplify sounds."

"We need to access glacier data when next we get to HomePort."

"I've read somewhere about settling earth causing a sound like that. Not on tundra though. We're finished here. Just need a pick

up. Renzec is still fighting that stabilizer. He's going through unset-
tled times," Dal added carefully.

"Poor Koren!" Rial said. "Renzec is a whiz with machines, but has yet
to learn people. He's been bent out of shape about the equipment."

"Justifiably so," Dal said.

"That it may be. Just the same, I think I'll pass on contacting Red
Team, for now"

"There's no rush getting us out, Chief. Everything's stable at the
ship. We just signed off with them when you called."

"You don't sense anything else?"

"My nerves have been tingling since planetfall, Chief. Kimmer's
jumpy too, and I'm picking up on that as well. I can't sense much
else."

"Things are progressing well here. Naui dropped me off at the
spires. They're sedimentary, Dal. There are signs of periodic flood-
ing down closer to the lake. Maybe summers are warmer than we
expect. Naui is taking water and ice samples via flatboat. We'll keep
our comms on."

"What does Naui think of the lake so far?"

"She loves it," Rial chuckled. "She's forming a theory. Says it could
be important, but she won't give me a hint. She wants to figure it
out for herself. She's got the makings of a fine explorer."

Dal smiled. "Sounds good, Chief. Walk safely. See you later," Dal
said, breaking contact. Things were going well, yet there was that
undercurrent of apprehension. The Chief was uneasy. Katayan was
twitchy. And Kimmer. . . . He sent out a mental tendril her way and
stroked her mind lightly. She looked up from her outdoor duties and
smiled in his direction. Only this morning, they had decided to bond
as a permanent two. He hoped the glow lasted. He was sure the
bond would.

Dal left the 'hopper and called out, "Things are going well at
White Camp. I was thinking about calling Cren for a pick up. Renzec hasn't made any progress on the stabilizer."

"Maybe we shouldn't rush it", Kimmer suggested, giving him a
sultry look. "Why don't you come over here and we'll talk."

Dal laughed and hurried down to accept the invitation. He was about to touch Kimmer with his outstretched arm when a startled look flashed across his face. Shock and pain wracked his body. He gasped, jerked to a stop and dropped his comm pad. His shuddered and grasped his head. He took one more faltering step toward Kimmer and his eyes glazed. Kimmer recognized the look. Dal was in mind-link trance. He cried out and grabbed his left shoulder, crumpling to the ground.

Kimmer whipped out her medicorder and scanned him. The 'corder indicated no physical damage, but the muscles were tight, guarding against trauma. Brain activity seemed strangely slowed, and his pupils were dilated and fixed. Breathing was shallow, and his skin felt cold and clammy. Dal was reacting to someone else's trauma.

Kimmer made Dal as comfortable as possible. Then she snatched up the comm pad. It was dead. Her wrist comm was still in the 'hopper! She raced into the 'hopper and put in a frantic call to the ship. She could barely make out Cren's answer over the din.

"Cren!" Kimmer interrupted his greeting, "What's going on! Is Mel ok?"

"Sure, Kimmer. She's right here, helping Leh control Katayan. He just started this weird, low howling. He won't shut up, and he's trying to claw through the comm controls. He's broadcasting panic. We feel like climbing the walls."

Kimmer let out the breath she had been holding. "Dal's reacting to something too. We're ok, but *somebody's* in trouble out here. Cren, listen carefully. Don't tranquilize Kat if you can help it. We may need him awake. I need you to pick us up. But check with the other teams first."

"Will do. But he's tearing up the place. Hang on a moment, Kimmer. I got a call incoming."

Kimmer grabbed her wrist comm hanging on her station and fastened it, then chewed on her lip as she waited, with her eyes on the still form of Dal outside.

Leh's low voice came over the comm. "Kimmi, can your pickup wait? Cren is taking an emergency call. Koren is missing."

"Hold a second, Leh. Let me check Dal. He's trance-linked. It could be Koren." Kimmer sprinted outside. Dal was groaning and holding his head.

Kimmer stooped next to him and touched his face gently. "Dal," she entreated, "is it Korey? Can you tell?"

Dal groaned. "Yes. Korey," he hissed through tight lips. "Pain. Bad at first. Now numb. Katay's in the link. I can feel him. He's . . . angry? Wants to fight. And Korey . . . she's so cold! Got to do something. Can't think right, Kimmi."

Kimmer scanned him quickly, and activated her wrist comm to trigger a relay through the 'hopper.

"Cren, Dal's picking up an empathic read from Koren. Severe pain, sudden in onset. Shock protocol."

"Leh here, Kimmer. Cren's in the 'hopper. He's listening. Is Dal going to be all right?"

"Now that we know what's happening, Dal will be able to filter empathic sensations," Kimmer said briskly. "When did Koren go missing?"

"We don't know," Leh said worriedly as she signaled Cren to take off to Red camp. "Koren took off to the light trees while Ren dealt with the stabilizer. When he went into the 'hopper he saw her note and went to get her, but she wasn't there. Cren's taking off now."

Dal was struggling to get up. Kimmer put her hand on his shoulder and firmly ordered, "Don't you *dare* get move! I've got Leh on the phone. Koren's missing."

Dal moaned, and rolled over onto his right side. "Head injury," he mumbled. "And left shoulder. Never felt anything like this. Mind won't work. Felt like knives. In my shoulder."

"Dal says head and shoulder injury, Leh," Kimmer relayed. "Tell Cren. Does the Chief know?"

"Mel's filling him in as we speak. He's still up by the spires. They'll return as soon as possible."

"Anything else we need to know?" Kimmer asked, her voice tight. One corner of her mind was already reviewing hypothermia treatment.

"No. Katayan's freaking. Tearing up the place. I've got to give him something to blunt his sensitivity. I'll call if we get more news."

Kimmer broke contact and bent to tend to Dal. He would have to stay sensitive to monitor what was happening. She reached out hesitantly with her mind, but could only tell that Dal was confused and traumatized. She sat down and cradled his head in her lap, offering what comfort she could.

Chapter
14

Rial frowned as he signed off the comm link. He leaned against one of the tall sandstone formations and called Naui. "I'll explain later why we have to wrap up. Complete any tests in progress and meet me at the hopper ASAP. Find any rays?"

"Not a one, Chief," Naui replied cheerfully. "There's a thriving ecosystem, but the animal life disappeared overnight."

"Fill in more of your theory?"

"Not yet, Chief. May have to leave it for the SiTeam. See you shortly." She signed off.

Rial walked around the spire he'd been analyzing when the ship call came. From this high on the slope he had a magnificent view of the lake panorama. Naui was a tiny figure sitting in the boat, moored on the north side, adjacent to the sheer glacier. She saw him and held up one small arm in a colorful wave. He waved back, and started to pick his way carefully down the steep talus.

Suddenly, an earth-wrenching groan tore from the depths of the ice. His head jerked up as he covered his ears with mittened hands. He saw Naui do the same as she stood in the floatboat, turning her head to look up and over her shoulder at the glacier's edge. Helpless, Rial Jennery witnessed the whole face of the glacier peel away. The calving ice crashed into the lake, almost directly on top of the small boat. Icy water splashed up in violence, followed by a wave so huge it almost reached Rial. When the wave subsided, all traces of the boat, and of Naui, had vanished, and the 'hopper was half buried by rubble and ice.

Dal looked at his two with misery in his eyes. "I'm afraid for her, Kimmi. Really afraid." The magnitude of the problem sunk in as Kimmer lost herself momentarily in his thoughts. They helped each other up, then held each other tightly under the alien sky. And they waited. Then, abruptly, Dal shuddered.

"Dal!" Kimmer cried, but his fingers touched her lips lightly. "Shhhh. It's over, Kimmi."

"Koren? Is she unconscious?" Kimmer looked up into Dal's eyes, straining for some sign of hope.

Dal stared through her, his eyes focused on another realm. "She's gone, Kimmer. It's over," he repeated in a hoarse whisper.

As the meaning of Dal's words hit Kimmer, she buried her head in his chest and sobbed. They clung to each other tightly, grasping for comfort where there was none to be had.

Cren raced the 'hopper low to the ground. He was approaching Red Camp when he received the second call.

"Chief says there's nothing he could do," Leh said. Her voice sounded flat and strained.

"But Leh," Cren protested, "we just went over hypothermia yesterday. People can live a long time in cold water."

"It's over, Cren," Leh interrupted, unconsciously echoing Dal's words to Kimmer. "Half the glacier face landed on the boat. There's no way Naui survived."

Cren felt the bottom drop out of his stomach and begin a slow slide to the planet's core. Death had always been an abstract. Now it slammed him in the face, and there was no denial, and no release. Cren shoved the pain to the back of his mind, and tried to focus. One thing at a time, Dal said. Forget the whole situation when it got too big. It became a litany he chanted as he flew. His face was wet with sweat in spite of the cold, and he thought he could smell his fear like sharp edges, biting into the air of the 'hopper. For the first time in his life, the fear was not for himself.

He flew over Red Camp. His scanner indicated it was deserted. He turned the craft toward the nearby trees where the sensors picked up someone, or some thing.

"Cren, are you there?" Leh's anxious voice was heavy with strain.

"I guess I'd better be," Cren said in a strange, quavery tone. "This is our last working 'hopper."

"Only the back half of the 'hopper was crushed."

"It'll never fly," Cren muttered.

"Cren! Think!" Leh ordered sharply. Then she continued in a softer tone, "The stabilizer's in the front end."

"Oh. Right. Renzec can piece 'em."

"Chief Rial's salvaging it now."

Silence.

"Cren, you still there?"

More silence. Finally, "What does Dal say, Leh? About Korey?"

Now it was Leh's silence filling up the comm link. Then she sighed heavily. "Not good, Cren. He felt pain. Katayan started keening. That was before, ah, the lake. He doesn't feel it anymore."

"Koren's unconscious then," Cren said softly. Leh did not reply.

"She won't be hurting then," he said, trying to reassure himself. This couldn't be happening. Not to them. Not to him.

"Where are you, Cren?"

"Ready to set down by the light trees, Leh," Cren said in a more normal tone. "I can see Renzec. Right beyond the trees. He's holding something. Leh, I'm going to land now."

"Cren, call me as soon as you get to him."

"Right." Cren broke the connection.

As soon as Cren cracked the door of the 'hopper, he could see Renzec sitting on the ground. Tears left streaks in the craggy mask of his face, but he took no notice of Cren, and made no sound. As Cren moved closer to Renzec, his already strained mind identified the object cradled in the engineer's lap. It was the torn remnants of a bloody arm, clad in metallic blue.

Cren's eyes took in the enormous footprints leading away from the light trees. In the afternoon light, it was all too easy to spot the blood trail leading to the ice sheet. He was peripherally aware of smears, composed of what his scanner identified as brain matter. His conscious mind refused to accept the grisly details. One task at a time. Almost wordlessly, he bundled the semi-coherent Renzec into the back of the 'hopper and took off in the direction of White Camp at screaming speed.

He was near his destination when it registered that the silence of his comm panel shouldn't be matching his blanked-out mind. Not only had he forgotten to call the ship in an attempt to attenuate sensory overload, he had kept the comm off to incoming! One task at a time. He quickly flipped it on, and heard a frantic voice calling him.

"Cren! Please answer! Come in Cren!"

"Cren here. Sorry."

"Cren! Where are you? Where's Renzec?"

"Mel! Is that you?"

"Yes, it's me. Leh's here too."

"Mel, Leh, Renzec's with me. We're coming up on White Camp. There was a predator at Red Camp. It got Koren. Didn't see it, but it left prints. When I got to the site, there were no life forms close by on the scanner. It took her onto the ice sheet." He paused and swallowed hard.

"Can I talk to Renzec? Do we search?"

"Let him be, Mel. Dal was right. About Koren."

"I'll notify Blue Team," Leh answered, her voice husky. Cren heard Mel weeping in the background.

"I'm going to pick up the Chief. Be ready to receive us. Then I'll get Blue team. Ok?"

"Sure Cren. Blue Team is packed and ready."

"And tell them to stay inside, ok? You guys stay in, too."

"Sure Cren. We'll stay inside the shields."

"No, Leh. You guys stay *in the ship*. Both of you, hear?"

"We hear, Cren."

"And I'm leaving the comm link open, 'cause I forgot last time. But I don't want to talk any more right now. Ok?"

"Ok, Cren," Leh said in measured tones. "One of us will be monitoring you at all times," she promised. Mel was already filling in Dal and Kimmer.

Cren pulled the 'hopper in at White Camp. He glanced back at Renzec. The engineer looked up and met his anxious gaze with dull eyes, then looked away. He didn't want to talk, either.

Cren opened the 'hopper door to more pain. Rial stood silently, waiting for him. In one arm he cradled a dented stabilizer. His other arm was folded, holding something tight to his chest. As Cren helped the Chief secure the battered but serviceable stabilizer to the 'hopper floor, Cren couldn't help but recognize the lonely, battered, light blue mitten Rial was clutching. Even though he tried.

Cren later had no recollection of the time he spent at the ship. Chief Rial helped Renzec out of the 'hopper, and gently parted the shocky crewman from his gruesome burden. Cren was handed a hot drink, and he consumed it. Or so he was later told. Then he took off. He was a better pilot than Leh at the best of times, and the psychic battering her unschooled empathic talents had picked up had left her shaky on her feet. Mel had been sedated and helped to bed, Katayan at her side. So Cren flew.

He was startled out of his fugue state when he reached Blue Camp. Dal and Kimmer were standing quietly, holding hands. They greeted him and quickly stowed their gear, moving efficiently. They appeared weary but serene.

Cren leaned against the 'hopper hull and watched them for as long as he could. Then he reached out and grabbed Dal's arm.

"Hold it, Dal!" he cried. "Don't you understand? They're dead! Korey. Naui. They're gone!" His shrill voice sounded alien to his own ears. He wanted nothing more than to grab Dal and Kimmer and shake them out of their composure.

Dal dropped his bundles and grasped the young man's shoulders firmly but gently, while Kimmer watched them both with concern.

"We *do* understand, Cren," Dal said softly. His calm golden eyes met Cren's troubled ones. Dal saw anger, fear and confusion, as well as the remnants of shock that was quickly melting into raw pain.

"I *felt* their trauma, Cren," Dal reminded gently as he continued to search Cren's eyes. "It's like I was part of them when they died. With Korey it was . . . not easy." The young empath closed his eyes against the remembered pain. Then he dealt with it. He looked at Cren with compassion. "It was different with Naui. Just a shutting off. I don't think she felt any pain. But I experienced their deaths, and Kimmi felt some of that too. Strange paths opened up inside me today, and I had to deal with the experience as much as I could. I'm not sure what it all means yet. I had to process other information too. I'm not done with that process, by any means, and neither is Kimmi, but we can't let it cripple us.

"It's going to be hard for you to understand right now, Cren, but we have ways of dealing with death in the Survey. You haven't learned them yet. Hospice training is part of the last Academy year, because death travels with every Survey ship, and they want that knowledge fresh in our minds when we go into space. No one can graduate without that training. You will never feel that lack more than you do today. Think on something for a minute.

"You were able to provide help on the spot today. You served a need. You could act. Kimmer and I had nothing to do but work through our grief and try to process it. Our love for Koren and Naui is not diminished by our coping mechanisms. Neither will either of us diminish their memories by negative actions or emotions.

"Don't take my words wrong," he said in a voice heavy with grief. "Kimmer and I cried a lot today. We will cry again, but we'll all cry together, as a family."

Cren dropped his gaze, crestfallen. "I don't understand," he whispered.

"You will," Dal promised again. He put his arm around Cren's shoulders and walked with him to the 'hopper door. "Do you want me to fly us back? You've done your share."

Cren closed his eyes. Something inside of him began to fold, and threatened to crumble. He *had* done his part. He could sit in the back with Kimmer, and Dal could fly them home. Cren suddenly felt on the verge of collapse.

Dal noticed, and tightened his grasp of Cren's shoulders. He concentrated, willing his own waning strength to flow to his younger crewmate. "You're going to be ok, Cren," he promised.

The strength that had begun to disintegrate inside of Cren hesitated, and then began the process of reassembling itself. Cren felt energy flow into him, and with it, a new resolve. He took a deep breath.

"I *am* ok, Dal. I'll take us back," he insisted. "It will help me deal with it."

"You're right, Cren. It will," Dal agreed. Cren helped Dal retrieve the remaining parcels, and they strapped into the 'hopper. Kimmer started singing a soothing song of comfort, a child's song that Naui used to hum when she worked. Dal joined his tenor voice in harmony. Cren vaguely remembered the haunting melody and words, but he hadn't the heart to sing. They took off against the darkening sky.

Chapter

15

If life had been going well, Norian Killain Duvou would be in her private meditation garden enjoying a pleasant hour of contemplation. Life hadn't been going well. Not for a long, long time.

The Coordinator for the Unified Peoples, late of Tagur, was worn down, weary, and greatly in need of solace. Relinquishing the world her people had won with such courage, hardship and blood had aged her far beyond her considerable years.

Her work-roughened hands struggled for purchase on the smooth surface of the packing container beneath her bony thighs. She finally gave up, and floated weightless among secured bins and storage drums. Just this once, she had felt the need for a sitting meditation. The Guardian could keep null-grav! She was sick to death of it.

"Guardian, can't we be done with this!" she prayed aloud. "You say to watch and wait. I've been watching and waiting forever! Forgive me for being heartily sick of this ship and everyone and everything within it! I know you've set the laws of your creation. We must abide by them. But so few of us remain, and many of those are tiny, sick and helpless. Don't let our babies die without a world to call their own. We've done our part. Now it's your turn. Give us a home!"

Her voice rose in pitch as well as in volume. "What joy do *you* get out of making life so painful, anyway?" Her voice caught, and she clenched her short, thin fingers together in front of her chest in supplication. "Lord, please deliver us from the clutches of our enemies," she pleaded solemnly.

After a respectful silence, she opened her eyes. With glaring insolence, she shook a knobby fist at the storage compartment ceiling. "I do everything you want, but you never listen to me! We've run out of time! *DO SOMETHING!*"

Bitterness coated her thoughts as her shaking fist sent her moving. Then she straightened out to her full five foot height and composed herself. "We need gravity in this tub," she muttered. She kicked off the first solid surface her feet touched, and glided to the door. So much for serenity. Carefully securing a hold on the strategically placed U-shaped grapple, she activated the door release and floated through. Her anger fled as she caught sight of her young assistant, Tisa.

"So," Duvou growled in mock reproof, "found me again! Don't I get a moment's peace?"

"I know you wanted time to meditate, Coordinator. But I couldn't wait. We have a planet!"

Years drained from Duvou's face. Then a grin spread so wide and so fast on her ruddy cheeks they looked to split with the effort. Then a shadow flickered. "They're willing to give *us* a planet," Duvou said warily. "What's the catch?"

Tisa's grin faded. "They haven't exactly *given* us the planet," she admitted wryly. "It *is* there. Waiting. Really it is! Caught a Tav narrow beam. Must have been sent to HomePort, although it didn't specify, and it was off target, and I intercepted it."

"That's illegal, child! How did. . . . Never mind," the Coordinator amended. "Don't want to know. What did you get?"

"The preliminary report. It's a system out on the edge of nowhere. With a habitable planet. Maybe two! We'd have to make it across Kreel-Omar. But I don't see anyone else waiting for it." She wrinkled her nose. "Coordinator, the Survey called the system 'Kellierin!'"

"Hot damn! We have that message from Queen K herself, promising us the next available planet. Kellierin, is it? A sign from the Guardian, that's what it is. We have a home!"

Duvou grabbed Tisa in a hearty hug that belied the elderly woman's seeming fragility, and they whirled about in null-grav. Tisa was as abruptly let go, as the Coordinator flung her hands and gaze upward. "You listened!" she cried triumphantly.

"Hand me that sealant, kid," Renzec called to Cren. The day was brisk, and in spite of the trauma of the day past, or maybe because of it, packing was completed in record time.

Cren wasn't ready to go. "We still don't know what killed Koren, Renzec," Cren complained as he handed over the flow container of gel sealant.

"You still don't get it, do you kid?" Renzec asked as he finished installing the functional stabilizer. He stood up and handed the container back to Cren. As he wiped his hands on his thighs, he studied Cren through sun-slitted eyes.

"Get it? Hell no, I don't get it!" Cren felt his frustration rise like pressure in a volcano. "The Chief *thinks* he knows what happened to Naui. And *something* came out of nowhere and grabbed Koren. We're taking off on schedule, like nothing happened! I don't think I want to be a part of this."

Renzec measured Cren slowly. Then he picked up his tool kit deliberately and went up the ramp of the 'hopper. As he hit the entrance, he looked back and asked bluntly, "Part of what, Cren? Our crew? Survey? Or life in general?"

Cren swore to himself as he gathered up the last supplies and threw them into the 'hopper. Renzec watched silently. The boy had to get the anger and frustration out. Then he asked Cren, "Can you calm down enough to pilot the other 'hopper, or shall I come back with Dal."

"That's not funny, Renzec!" Cren fumed.

"Not trying to be," Renzec insisted. He twisted around to look at Cren, silhouetted in the 'hopper entrance. "People make choices. We don't have control over all the consequences. We try to make the best of what we've got. There are predators here. The glaciers calve. So we leave warnings for the SiTeam, just like we left a buoy before we came down. We have to get to the next planet soonest for Mel.

"Cren, as soon as we get space side we'll gather. We'll talk about what happened. There's no more evolution on this plane for Koren and Naui. There is for us.

"I've been the 'bad boy' on this crew for too long, Cren. This morning, I promised myself, and Koren, no more. Maybe you can help me with that. Doesn't mean the slot is open. We're down two, and you're light in knowledge. We have to pull together.

"Now, let's get the 'hoppers back and stowed, and we can quit this place."

Cren muttered something under his breath, but secured the 'hopper door. If the closure was a little on the forceful side, Renzec let it pass.

In free fall, the blood pools more evenly, and the muscles relax. The lessening of gravitational pressures not only gave relief to Melion and Dal, it supplied psychological relief from the loss weighing down the whole crew. It seemed easier for them to share their feelings. Having an empath smoothed the process immeasurably.

The rehash of the previous day's devastating events began with the newest crew member. By the time it was Rial's turn to speak, even Cren felt more at peace. He held Katayan in his lap and petted the calmed catabit.

". . . and I can't help thinking, Rial continued, "that if I hadn't encouraged Koren to be more independent, she might not have gone to the light trees alone."

"Are you saying it's wrong to cultivate self-reliance?" Dal probed gently.

"No," admitted Rial. He thought for a moment. "I guess I feel responsible. I know it's unsound logic, but I feel guilty."

"It should be some comfort to know that we all share that feeling, to some degree. None of us can take the blame for what happened. You've taught us to live in the now, Chief. We do whatever we are doing as well as we can do it. No one in fairness can expect

more. Koren and Naui lived well, taking responsibility for their actions, and for their lives. They were doing their chosen jobs as they
thought best.

"But if I hadn't crabbed at Korey . . ." Renzec began.

"She might not have left the site," Dal finished the thought.
"Maybe the predator would have come to the 'hopper. Renzec, it
wasn't the walk that killed Koren. It wasn't you. It was the predator."

Dal glanced around the group. He sensed that healing had begun for each of them, and for the group as a whole.

"Speaking of the predator, what did you discover, Kimmer?" he
asked.

Kimmer looked up from her musing. She had been lost in times
shared with Koren and Naui. "It's probably a biped. Bigger than we
are, I'd guess seven to nine feet tall. It could be related to the murlotas, judging from the hairs and prints. At least part of it had white
hair four inches long. It was probably carnivorous, not omnivorous,
and had at least four sets of fangs. It's claws were long. I have no
way to tell how something so big could sneak up on Koren. It may
have the ability to go fairly silently. Dal had that time of muddled
thinking. It may be able to affect brain waves in proximity. All the
creatures we've seen here use EM to some extent. It probably lives
on the ice pack this time of year. That's all."

"We'll need to report to HomePort soonest on that," Chief Rial
noted, "and send the buoy data. This planet is habitable, whatever
we find on the next one. It deserves a SiTeam review. The Tagur folk
need a home."

It was just that moment that a 'ping' from the master control
panel notified them of incoming data.

Dal raised a hand palm out, halting any movement toward the
panel. "After we've finished the gather," he ordered softly.

Rial looked at Cren. "Anything to add, son? This is your first experience with death out here, and it won't be your last. We've covered a lot of space since you spoke. Questions or comments?"

Cren thought a moment. "This helped a lot, being together like
this. I still have to live with the fact that I'm not the specialist you

need. Maybe that specialist could have prevented these deaths. You say we should search for positive aspects in our experiences. What could be positive about this?"

Quiet followed his question, and the silence loomed large after a while. Finally Rial spoke. "It seems to me you learned a lot yesterday. About death. About life. About yourself. You did all that was asked of you, and more."

"At what cost? If that's learning, I don't want it. I want Naui and Koren back!"

"Cren, there are always some things you can't have," Dal said sadly. "The cost of yesterday would have been paid, regardless of any gain. I can't ignore the extra paths that opened up in my mind during that experience, just because they were forced by pain and loss. I will learn what they are, and what they will allow me to do. We can honor our friends by using their deaths to learn. It's part of life to feel broken and incomplete at times. If we recognize that we all share these sensations, we won't feel so alone and empty."

"I had awful dreams last night," Cren confessed. "I dreamt I was arguing with Naui and Koren. Shouting at them. I don't want those dreams again. I'm almost afraid to go to sleep." He reconsidered, and amended, "I *am* afraid to go to sleep."

"It's normal to feel angry at them, Cren, because they left you" Leh commented. "I had those dreams myself. They disturbed me too. Sometimes we work out our anger in our dreams, and learn from them. But I had happy dreams about them as well."

"I had some good dreams also," Cren reflected. "But they were about things that never happened! I didn't know either of them long enough to have many memories."

"Your arguments with Koren and Naui never happened either, Cren," Dal pointed out.

"I had both kinds of dreams also, Cren," Rial commented. "Walks we never took. Talks we never had. Only after someone's death do you realize you never spent enough time with them." He gave a slight push and drifted over to Cren. "Don't let the angry dreams be more real to your mind than the pleasant ones."

"Maybe we can use these dreams to help cope with our loss.

That virtual dreaming you taught us, Dal. It works. If I start day-dreaming about what I want to dream *before* I fall asleep. I can often program my dreams. Maybe that way we can say things we wished we'd said to them while they were here," Kimmer suggested.

"Sound idea," Dal commented. Time to break this up. They were covering surveyed space. "Why don't you check that relay now, Leh. If anything comes up about our loss that any of you want to discuss later, we'll set up another gathering. Healing is a process. All we've done today is dress the wounds. Take it easy on yourselves for a while." He looked in Melion's direction, and she smiled wanly. Her ride up to orbit had been done under sedation. It was only a matter of days until Crisis. The stress of the dual tragedy had accelerated her symptoms.

Leh heard the message, and swore to herself. Then she pressed for a hard copy, which she handed to Dal. "Can you explain this?"

He scanned it and whistled. "Time hasn't been standing still while we've been planet side. Somebody must have been here and checked our placement buoy. Only the Tavs knew where we were. I think we'd better scratch any message to HomePort. Things are going bad there. It looks like they'll soon be worse here, too."

"Out with it, Dalrion!" Chief Rial ordered.

"It's from the Tagur colonists. "They're on their way."

"What?" "They can't be!" Exclamations of disbelief filled the air.

"It is," Dal affirmed. "Docking permission still denied them at HomePort. Martial Law declared on Metrowyl. The Tagur ship intercepted a Tav report about us on a bootlegged relay. They sent this message the same way, before they left HomePort."

"What set off Martial Law?" Cren wanted to know.

"Nothing here to signify," Dal answered. "Just a notification to expect the Tagur people. They've named their ship, like the Tavs. 'Guardian's Reprieve'. Conditions must be bad on the ship to risk the trip. Or on Metrowyl."

"Or both," Rial agreed.

"How many on the ship, Dal?" Kimmer asked.

"Don't know."

"I don't understand," Cren said, mystified. "I thought they needed a Scientific Team to certify habitability."

"That's standard. Can you blame them, though? What choice did they have?" Melion asked. "We have two planets in the habitability zone. They only need one. But which one?"

"Planet II looks like it doesn't have the atmospheric problems of III. It should be warmer," Dal remarked. "We owe it to the colonists to check it out as quickly as possible. We'll orbit. If it looks promising, we'll land."

"I thought the EM phenomena were stronger there."

"Definitely, Mel," Dal affirmed. "But they're different. They cause scatter, but in a pattern. They don't bounce our signals right back. Maybe we can work with that. Any objections?"

There were none.

"Renzec, break us out of orbit. Set up an orbital sweep of Kelli II. Grab all the data we can from up here. We need the best possible settlement site, and fast, in case they do make it out here." He looked thoughtful. "Maybe they have Tav help too," he mused.

Renzec went to his console and began to plot a course, muttering, "Colony prep is *not* what I signed up for."

"Shut it off, Renzec," Dal ordered, and turned to Leh, who was poised for action. "Leh, what stories have you heard about the Unified Sect?"

"Nothing cohesive. I've kept up with their plight. It's great material for an epic saga," she explained. The role of storyteller held importance as educator and entertainer, and Leh was one of the best.

"We've got to ensure they don't bring in stock contaminated with whip snake larva," Kimmer cautioned.

"I don't think they have much in the way of stock left. Except maybe embryos. What they do have, though, is an amazing leader. If she's still around. She kept the colony together by force of will," Leh grinned and flicked a glance in Rial's direction. "She's used to being Boss Lady," she warned. "You might have a problem getting her to listen to you."

Chief Rial humpfed, not at all happy with the prospect.

"Blue Team better catch some sleep, if we. . . ." Dal looked up abruptly, and his eyes focused on nothingness for some moments. Then he spoke in a dreamy tone. "I felt something! That 'presence' I felt before. I couldn't feel it on the planet. It's out *here* though. I can't quite focus on it." He sighed, and noticed most eyes were focused on him. "I still don't think it's sentient."

"I have a suggestion, Dal, but it might sound crazy," Cren said hesitantly. "It's something Mel and Naui and I discussed."

"Say on."

"Am I right in thinking that you'll want to pulse the sun again, just before we go down to Kelli II?"

"We're going down anyway. We'll be ready this time, if we get another wave. I think we should," Dal said.

"What if we modify our pulse? Modulate it, so that it resembles the EM wave pattern the Kellierin sun threw at us, but not exactly."

"Why, Cren?" Dal asked. He thought he knew, but he wanted Cren to explain it to the others.

"If we modify the pulse, and the same thing happens, it could be a response. If nothing happens, it could mean quite a few things. But if it modifies the response to match ours. . . ."

"Perhaps the source recognized our modification," Melion added. "Then again, it may mean nothing at all."

"That's right, Dal" Cren continued. "What I'm hoping is that we get a return signal modulated to ours, and subdued."

"Then we'd have to check . . ." Dal began, but his train of thought was interrupted by Renzec.

"We have company." He leaned close to his monitor. "Ship breaking Matrix. Heading our way."

"Not the Tagur ship!" Kimmer cried.

"Not the Tagur ship," Renzec confirmed. "It's Survey!"

Dal hugged his console, and magnified the view screen. "A scout ship! But its lines. More rounded." He brightened, and then quickly frowned. "Looks like heavy phaser scoring on the aft hull. Sending standard contact signal"

Cren floated over Dal's shoulder. "Look's like it's been through a war." he observed.

"Perhaps it has," Dal said somberly.

Kimmer gave herself a gentle push, gliding next to Cren. She anchored herself with a handhold on Dal's station.

Chief Rial inspected his own monitor carefully. "Can you raise them, Leh?" he asked.

Leh's long fingers worked diligently. "Got it. On an odd frequency though, Chief," she reported.

"Put it on speaker," Rial ordered.

Layers of static and buzzing noises came over audio as Leh worked to capture the transmission. Finally, a voice.

". . . can hearr yourr signal, Surrvey craft. Apprrooaching Surrvey crraft, Chief Awrr'Koof commanding. Orrbiting crraft, say again. What faction arre *youu*?" The voice was gruff and tense, with an unfamiliar quality and a strange accent.

Leh glanced at Dal in consternation. "Faction?" she asked in a whisper. "What's he want?"

Dal had a strange look on his face, a sort of half-smile, and his eyes gleamed. "See if you can get interior video, Leh. At least, see if you can clean it up."

Leh made further adjustments, and the audio cleared. But the video remained exterior only.

"Approaching craft, we are *Survey* Scout Ship 192, of the planet Metrowyl, Chief Rial Jennery commanding. We do not, repeat *do not*, understand your query regards to 'faction'. We have completed survey of planet III and are about to continue our inspection of this system." Leh said in a clear, calm voice. Then she looked at Dal, questioning.

"You appear damaged. We have a medic and empath on board. We offer assistance." Dal added, choosing his words carefully.

"Injurred we arre, indeed," the voice replied. "*Doo not* apprroach," the voice warned. "Warr has been declarred! Forr the lasst time. *What is yourr faction*?" The screen blurred as it switched to interior view. The reason behind the unusual timbre of voice coming over the audio was instantly obvious. Intense blue eyes with slit pupils glared at them from a face covered with thick, dark grey fur. The finely chiseled, bewhiskered muzzle was cornered by inch-long gleaming fangs. Velvety ears, one slightly torn, rotated like cupped isosceles triangles, the better to catch the slightest sound. The commander of the approaching craft was Tav!

Chapter
16

Dal glanced at Rial, waiting to see if the Chief wanted to take over the comm. Rial merely nodded for Dal to proceed.

Dal could feel the tension radiating from his crew mates, especially Cren. He pushed those feelings from his mind, and reached out mentally to make contact with the Tav, only to meet an impermeable block. Switch to Plan B.

"Are you Chief Awr'Koof?" Dal asked politely.

"Yesss."

"Chief Awr'Koof, we arrived here before hostilities began at home," Dal said evenly. "Due to the unusual EM forces and the birthing-star field in the immediate vicinity, we approached the system with caution. That took time.

"We are unarmed, except for hand-held, defensive weapons." Dal heard Cren gasp. Hidden from the video screen, Kimmer took a determined grip of Cren's arm with one hand and placed two upraised fingers of the other over his mouth. Her lips pressed tightly together, and her eyes blazed a threat at Cren. Then her fingers moved from his mouth to form a small, tightly clenched fist, which she shook in front of his eyes in case he hadn't gotten the message. He got it.

"We have refused many HomePort systems upgrades because of their militaristic nature," Dal continued in a calm tone. "You can scan us for confirmation. We *have* no 'faction'. We are motivated only by a desire for knowledge."

The feline face regarded them with slit-eyed caution. "So youu say. And youu arre. . . . ?"

"I am called Dalrion Darnel, second in command. I am an empath, trained by Tavs at the Academy. Your news was the first we've heard of declared war, and we request more knowledge. We invite you to inspect our ship. We speak the truth."

"Dalrrion Darrnel." The felinoid paused, searching Dal's face for something, but Dal felt no mind probing his. "This star system. What is *it* called?" the felinoid asked.

"We call it 'Kellierin'."

The blue eyes regarded Dal thoughtfully. "Preferrable, it would be, Dalrrion Darrnel," he finally said in his rumbling tone, "if youu come herre. We must be cerrtain that youu still walk the Path of Light. Youu would allaow mind-link?"

Dal glanced at Rial, who shrugged. Up to Dal.

"I will come," Dal said to the Tav. Then his eyes lit up and a slow smile crept across his face. "May I bring someone?"

The slit eyes narrowed, and a low growl issued from the furry throat. "Is that one also empath? Orr perrhaps yourr commanderr?"

"No, Chief Awr'Koof. We have a new crewman. He has little knowledge of other races. This is a chance for him to learn."

The felinoid lifted his dark lips back, showing more fang. He bobbed his head once. "Knowledge must be sought. It is agrreed. We await yourr prresence." The face vanished from the screen, to be replaced by the exterior of the battered craft.

"Good touch, Dal," Rial acknowledged. "Tavs believe that there are two reasons for living. Teaching and being taught. I can't say I disagree. But Cren," he warned, "keep your mouth shut and your mind open."

Cren, still hovering next to Kimmer, nodded apprehensively.

Dal turned and grinned. "Don't fret, Cren," he said. "You survived Tav contact before, although it was peripheral. Their love of peace is as strong as their love of knowledge."

He looked to the Chief. "I plan to use the 'hopper Renzec pieced together. It may help reassure those of the crew not in mind link."

Dal glided toward the suit locker, and Cren, with a nervous glance at the rest of the crew, hurried to follow.

"Anything else I should know? About Tavs, I mean." Cren looked doubtful as he watched the scout craft expand on the view screen as they drew closer. The vessel had just missed destruction. The sear along the hull came perilously close to the power converters.

"Sorry, Cren. I've been reviewing the first time I met a Tav, and I got lost in memories. They're an honest, just and interesting race. I'm sure there are some bad formba fruits in the basket, but they must be rare. They revere integrity.

"They strive to master infinity's mind. They follow the Lord of Light-the positive vital force that runs throughout the universe. That is their name for the Guardian, Cren. They are tolerant, except of intolerance. Don't get their ruff up. They make awesome adversaries. Be careful what you say.

"Their fur is exquisitely soft. Don't touch it, unless you're invited. You probably won't be, although they are very tactile. Their scent is quite pleasant. Like citrus, with a hint of exotic spice. They are born teachers," Dal emphasized. "You will be expected to learn."

"I thought you wanted me as backup."

Dal smiled, and shook his head. "Don't need any. My empathic talents are nothing compared with theirs. Once we're in mind-link, he'll *know* what I say is true. Tavs aren't all telepathic, but this one had a formidable mind-block. It may have worked both ways. What are you worried about, Cren?"

Cren narrowed his eyes and ran his fingers through his tousled mop. "I don't know if I can take mind-link, Dal. Not yet, anyway."

"What are you hiding now, Cren?" Dal teased. He laughed. "I'm joking, Cren. There will be no need for that. My mind will give him all the information he needs."

"Doesn't it bother you? Having somebody strange invade your mind? I mean, I know you can sense our feelings, and you've done some weird things since I've been here, but this is a different thing entirely," Cren said anxiously.

"He won't 'invade', Cren. Positive mind touch, with a willing partner, is not unpleasant. It can be enjoyable. It can even be one of the best parts of sex. The pleasure centers are in the brain, after all."

Cren's jaw dropped. Dal seemed totally serious, so he decided now would be a good time to start being more careful about what he said.

The docking went uneventfully. Once they opened to the other ship's air, however, Cren knew he was in trouble. As soon as they cracked their helmets, they were assailed by a heavy, obnoxious odor. Cren didn't say a word, but he breathed as shallowly as possible. Citrus? Spice? No way! Cren's watering, anguished eyes spoke volumes, telling Dal what his mouth did not.

Dal only had time to mutter, "That's *not* Tav," as the inner hatch opened, and the pungent odor became overpowering.

Cren was perplexed. "Dal?" he whispered.

"Quiet. Follow my lead."

The stench permeated everywhere. No one was at the lock, but the door to the control cabin had been left open. As they entered, Cren felt the offending odor coat his tongue. Dal had assumed a composed demeanor. Cren mustered his limited ability to do likewise.

Though battle scarred, the craft had its gravity mechanisms intact. The Tav sat on his back legs, using his tail for balance. He was alone in the cabin. He beckoned them in with a large paw. There was something regal about him, although the room was the worse for wear. Items were strewn about the floor. Time, or some other consideration, had not allowed the crew to put the cabin to rights. Cren glanced around nervously. Visions of a clawed, fanged legion, waiting for him in the aft compartment, filled his mind.

Awr'Koof gave the impression of controlled power, compact and ready for action. The shaggy fur on his right hip was frizzled and singed, and he wore a bandage on part of his thick tail. Around his neck was a broad black band with silver trim, signifying Survey Chief Master status. Crensed tried to imagine Awr'Koof in a black uniform. He failed.

Awr'Koof approached them and bowed his head gravely. Dal

bowed likewise, and Cren followed suit. Now that they were in close proximity, Cren could detect an underlying citrus spice fragrance coming from the Tav. Unfortunately, the other odor prevailed.

"Again, greetings, Chief Awr'Koof," Dal said clearly. "It is good to meet face to face. Where would you prefer to link?"

"Please," the Tav said gravely, "sit herre beforre me. We will walk the path as one forr a time." Awr'Koof turned his head to regard Cren somberly. "And youu arre called?"

"Cren, Chief Awr'Koof." Cren was surprised to find his fear was transmuting to awe. He thought of Rial Jennery, and he realized that anyone in Survey black, even if relegated to a mere band, held his great respect. Against that tradition, the configuration of the wearer wasn't so important.

Dal touched Cren's forearm lightly to indicate that he stay put. Then the empath settled in a soft, rounded, cushiony seat. A seat designed for feline comfort. Cren took a step back toward the bulkhead, and leaned his weight carefully against a console.

The Tav sunk on his muscular haunches directly in front of Dal. His head canted to one side, and the blue slit-eyes looked into Dal's golden ones. Awr'Koof waited a moment, and then yawned widely, closing his eyes and displaying even rows of pointed, gleaming teeth, sharp as a reprimand. As the fanged jaws snapped together, Cren drew up to his full height, sharply alert. His alarm interrupted Dal's concentration. The empath raised one hand in supplication to Awr'Koof.

Awr'Koof again bobbed his head and yawned even wider. Dal turned to flash a quick, reassuring smile in Cren's direction. He explained quickly, "The yawn indicates there is no rush for this examination. By closing his eyes, the Chief let me know he already trusts us. The link will be confirmation of his impressions, and a way to gain a great deal of information as fast as possible." Dal turned once again to the task at hand.

Cren sighed. They weren't about to be eaten, then. Aliens have alien ways. Another of the Chief's axioms. Dal and the Tav seemed motionless, gazing behind each other's eyes. He let his own eyes roam the cabin, trying to ascertain where the bad smell originated.

The cabin's layout was the same as his ship, with a few exceptions. It was a newer ship, and the bulkheads were more round. Dal had told him that even Tav philosophy of life had no sharp edges, whatever that meant. Two stations were equipped with Tav seats, but the others were standard. Mixed crew? Only three stations were activated. There was a conspicuous absence of movable items on surfaces. Stuff was all over the floor. Had they gone to null-grav abruptly, and then, just as suddenly, resumed gravity? He smiled. He was learning to observe. Cren's inspection was interrupted by a noise. His eyes flashed to Dal, but he and Awr'Koof remained linked and motionless, although their features had changed. The door to the aft cabin was opening. Two young women in Survey uniforms entered, both sporting bandages. They regarded him briefly, nodded in silent acknowledgment of his presence, and then turned their full attention to the mind-linked tableau.

Cren straightened. Not what he'd expected. The woman closest to Cren was the smaller of the two, with short blond hair. She was dressed in deep navy blue. High ranking then. The other looked younger. Her uniform was only a shade darker than his, like Naui's. He felt a moment's pang. This woman was dark and slim, and her long black hair was disheveled. He realized that she was regarding him with the same candid curiosity. He blushed, and ordered his eyes back to the mind-linked pair just as Awr'Koof raised his head. Dal let out a long sigh.

"We arre as youu see us," Chief Awr'Koof nodded to Cren, waving a large but well formed grey paw, claws sheathed, in the direction of his crew. "Only Tadrria and Arranda surrvive. And I."

The blond came up and stood by her Chief. "The Survey craft that fired on us had been conscripted by one faction or another," she said in a clear, vibrant voice. "We never found out which. When we refused to surrender, they opened fire. We engaged the Matrix. Still, we lost three crew. We were already down one," she grimaced. "That was *one* of the reasons we were in the Metrowyl System."

The Tav appraised his visitors thoughtfully. "It is as youu susspect, Dalrrion. We had a message too deliverr. So youu see," he said in his deep voice, "we had too be surre that the warr had not prreceded us herre. Otherr Tavs know of yourr voyage, and one could have been taken and mind prrobed. They arre using empaths *forr thisss!*" His jowls quivered, and the front of his muzzle peeled back to show the entirety of his fangs, and the ruff around his neck stood up briefly. "Warr is an aberration of the Forrces of Light. We will *not* take parrt. Ourr lives arre devoted too constrructive ends, not destrructive ends."

"In actuality, Chief Awr'Koof, we could use your help in something *very* constructive." Dal briefly outlined the problem with the coming refugees. "Are you free to assist us, or have you a more pressing mission?"

"We doo have a mission, Dalrrion. One that may well mesh with yourrs," the grey felinoid answered. Please too call me "Koof". His eye ridge whiskers lifted. "Ourr prresent mission was too confirrm this planetarry system, Kellierrin, and the Surrvey crrew explorring it. The name youu chose forr this system did not go unnoticed.

"As youu, Dalrion Darrnel, arre awarre, ourr Queen Kellierrin founded a special school forr the empathic adept. She prrocurred the besst teacherrs in the galaxy." The blue eyes twinkled. "Specifically, Tavs. When Herr Majesty saw that warr was inevitable, she secured a crraft, ostensibly designed as a school ship. Ourr surrvices werre rrequested in the efforrt to see them too safety."

"Is this not odd, my friend," Dal questioned gently, "that the Queen was able to take this ship out?"

Koof breathed out a near sigh. "The King has been kept unawarre of the Matrrix drrive rretrrofit. He has bent his mind too the militarry, which he builds strrongerr each day. He does not yet see the full value of empaths. Queen Kellierrin has been wise in the face she shows too him, in spite of prrovocation."

"My life-mate is a Masterr Teacherr, Coorrdinatorr of Knowledge forr this school. We have hidden the ship. HomePorrt, as yet, knows nothing of Kellerrin system. Expect arrrival of fifty scholarrs, too arrrive by indirrect means, so that they will not be followed. With verrry few staff, mostly Tav."

"Why few staff?"

"Only those absolutely needed remained," the blond crew member interjected. "The other Tavs returned to their home. They wanted to fit as many children as possible onto the ship."

"How young are these students of whom you speak?"

"Most but half the age of yourr crrewman, herre," Koof nodded at Cren, "the rrest youngerr. They will be safe herre. The Lady of Light has told usss. She will come too Kellierrin."

Dal's eyes widened. "I felt some presence. . . ." Dal stopped, not sure how to proceed.

"Prresence?" Koof looked startled. "Therre is no Prresence of Light herre naow, except that which is always with us. The forrce which connects. No sentience yet herre. I would know."

The Tav peered intently at Dal, and then seemed to grin as he pulled his fine grey lips back to expose shiny teeth. "Ah. Youu sense the rraw essence. It will evolve. Youu will see."

Dal looked perplexed.

"Youu will underrstand. In time. Much trraining youu need, too become awarre of *yourr* parrt." The Tav turned to Cren.

"And *youu*, Quiet One?" Chief Koof cocked his head to the side and focused his attention in Cren's direction. His eyes seemed to twinkle. "Doo *youu* not have a question on yourr firrst visit too another Surrvey crraft? Youu rremained in quarrters in the otherr Tavian ship. With grreat fearr, I have been told. Fearr remains no morre. Youu obserrve, and listen. Youu know Forrces of Light. Youu measurre, but don't yet trreasure. Have youu no question?"

Cren reddened, but said nothing.

"I feel unease. What is it youu wish too ask?"

Cren shook his head, unconsciously wrinkling his nose. "Nothing, Sir," he insisted.

The Tav huffed a hearty laugh. "Come," he purred. "The question has burrned in yourr mind since youu opened yourr helmet. We arre, all but youu, empaths herre. You must verrbalize, orr it is impolite forr us too rrespond."

"All empaths! But I thought. . . ." Cren was confused, and he looked at the young women with new eyes.

The senior scout raised her eyebrows, and the younger women smothered a giggle. Cren blushed crimson, and he looked at Dal with pleading eyes. Dal seemed amused, and shrugged. "Don't look at me. Ask Koof, Cren."

"Ah, Sir, I *am* curious," Cren began apprehensively. The Tav waited patiently. "Ah, what is that, ah, strange . . . smell?"

The Tav and his two young crew looked at each other, and at Dal. Then, slowly, they started laughing. The laughter grew, and the Tav clutched at his belly with a front paw, leaning against a bulkhead as he huffed. Even Dal shook with helpless waves of mirth. The older scout weakly grabbed on to a support. "Forgive us, Cren. We've become accustomed. It may seem impossible to you, but it does happen."

"Tadrria," Koof gestured with his free paw, "fetch TwikTwik. Enlighten Crren."

The young, dark haired women walked to the aft compartment. When she returned, she carried a fearsome looking thing in her arms. The creature was about a foot high, and a foot and half long, and was obviously the source of the odor. It's face was totally covered by its rough, long brown fur, except for glimpses of three-inch long fangs. It made an alien, creaking noise. She handled it gently, and gazed at it fondly, in spite of the reek.

"TwikTwik may not seem a being one wants in a small ship, but it is exceedingly valuable in the field. It looks frightful, and smells worse, but it's harmless." She smiled encouragingly.

Cren studied it suspiciously, and made no attempt to touch it. "What is it?" he asked.

Dal took one look at Cren's face and shook his head weakly, wiping tears of laughter from his eyes. "That, my friend," he gasped, "is a yorbu!"

Chapter

17

For two days, both craft swung in surveillance orbit around Kelli II, monitoring the planet. Koof made one last visit to 192 and addressed her crew, promising to return as soon as his duties allowed, and advising each of them as best he could, working up the chain of command.

"Dalrrion, youu have grreat need of guidance in the use of yourr gifts. If the Lady wills, spend time with my mate. Youu have needs beforre youu become whole. Doo not get too settled." He closed his eyes slowly at the empath. "Youu belong on the empath school ship."

"Nothing could give me more happinoss," Dal replied, and the look on his face gave evidence even to non-empaths that he was not just being polite. Kimmer bit her lip, and Koof regarded her with a solemn gaze. "Youu will neverr be alone," he promised her. He had foretold she would be a great healer. But her mind was filled with his words for Dal, and they troubled her deeply.

"Rrial, doo youu know Norrian Duvou, she whoo commands the Tagurr surrvivorrs?" the Tav asked.

"No. I've heard she's a . . . formidable woman."

Koof rumbled Tavian laughter deep in his throat. "Betterr, Rrial, too think of herr as a forrmidable *leaderr*. Woman she is, yess. She lost herr childrren and theirr offsprring on Tagurr. Naow, the whole colony is herr child. Rrememberr thiss. Go gently with herr, Rrial. Youu will learrn much from each otherr. She drrops herr wisdom intoo stagnant pools, stirrring the waterrs and rrefrreshing them. She is a good frriend."

"As are you, Koof," Rial nodded. "I will take your words to heart. Go carefully. Return soon. We, too, have had our losses. We need you. Meanwhile, we'll do our best to get ready for what's coming."

Koof nodded. "That's all one can doo. Put one paw in frront of the otherr and go as farr as youu can."

After the other craft Matrixed out, Dal switched on full-grav and addressed the crew.

"All of you have studied the readouts and maps of Kellierin. It shows promise."

"Let's hope she keeps her promises," Renzec said thoughtfully.

Dal caught Kimmer's eye, and her leading glance to Melion. Her skin had developed a grey undercast, and her auburn hair hung damp and limp. Her hand shook slightly with the negligible weight of the map she held.

"We all hope that, Renzec," Dal said. "Mel, I know grav is tough, but better than going from null to deceleration."

Melion nodded wearily. "Kimmer explained it, but I keep forgetting. The brain fog. You know."

Dal nodded. "You'll be able to weather Crisis in comfort, anyway. We'll be closer to the equator this time."

"We'd better," Leh snorted. "Closer to the sun, and what do we find? More ice!"

"Up north of where we'll land there's ice, Leh," Dal said. "There is a greater axial tilt here, with an absence of those unusual cloud layers the last world had. We have a cooler core temperature too, with less volcanic action. That adds up to relatively cooler temperatures in general."

"Have you decided on a landing site?" Rial asked.

"Yes. You may not be happy with it. In the comfort range, there are only two large land masses. The smaller one is desert. The other is more northerly. Half of it is snow-covered for a substantial part of the year."

Groans resounded.

"There's enough time for crops on the lower two-thirds of the continent, which is where we'll set down. There's a large lake, nearly in the center of the land mass. It's surrounded by lush valleys. Mid-Spring has come already. The colonists need to get their crops in soon. I've selected this area to land," he pointed to a location midway up the western lake side.

"But those gorges? A colony means children. There's a safety issue."

"I know, Leh, but gorges are scattered all over. We can't avoid them. There are even more to the south. This site is mixed grassland and forest. It isn't far from the mountains. There are two radiation belts circling the planet, but they're fairly well defined. We'll go in polar." Dal leaned back at his console. He seemed to be on the verge of saying something else.

"What is it, Dal?" Kimmer pried.

"I did reach something on the planet. Something sentient. Non-mammalian." He half-closed his eyes, shutting out the excitement his announcement caused, trying to recapture his sensing. "I can't be sure. I think there are many small beings. For want of a better term, I have to say they feel 'bright". He laughed.

"Is it the same presence you felt before, Dal?"

"No, Chief. This is distinctly different."

"Dangerous?" Rial asked.

"Not that I can tell. They feel very positive. We may have more grief from the refugees than from the native life forms."

"I agree. Koof said the refugees are in a post-traumatic state."

"I never read the news clips, Chief Rial," Cren said. "I thought Survey prevented things like Tagur."

"We cut the risk, Cren. No more," Rial said sadly. "Leh, tell us the tale, please. We can only spare a few minutes, so keep it short. We need it fresh in our minds."

Leh smiled. "I thought you'd never ask, Chief. Ok, without embellishments.

"The Unifieds turned toward the Tavs for guidance. They adapted an underlying philosophy of peace and oneness with nature. They disapproved of the excesses of Klev and his court. Vocally. Klev began to take notice when their support grew.

"When the leaders of Unified sect expressed a desire to leave Metrowyl and return to a natural way of living, Klev seized on it as a way rid himself of troublesome dissenters, and perhaps exploit them at the same time. The Survey had found a likely planet for them. Tagur Four.

"The Unifieds could only buy one ship outright, and it was antique. Others were leased for the voyage. By then, the SiTeams cleared Tagur as close to paradise. So it proved to be for the first three years of the colony's existence. Rich, deep soil begged to be turned into farmland. The climate was benevolent, though a little cool. Then came the fourth year, and the rains.

"The colonists weren't surprised. They had seen evidence of periodic deluge. But the waters brought more than moisture. When the rains ceased, leaving pools of water all over the muddy earth, tiny red flutterbys flickered everywhere. Cocoons deeply buried had waited patiently for the floods to end their dormancy.

"Later, the survivors would discover an eight year cycle. The Survey scouts and SiTeams came at the wrong time. They had no warning. Flutterby eggs wintered over, high in the trees.

"Larval forms came on the winds of spring. Thread-like worms drifted through the air, barely visible. Structures were coated with them, as they crawled to ground. The colonists thought they might be a threat to crops. The people gathered, and voted not to destroy the life form, but to study it instead. They wished to avoid upsetting the balance of nature. Noble, but that was their undoing.

"Small animals begin to take sick. The colonists noticed itchy white spots on their own skins. The windworms burrowed deep into muscles, gorging themselves on their hosts. At the same time, they secreted anti-clotting factors so that they could feed more readily. The hosts died, and the worms moved on, or dug deep into the earth, to await the coming of the rains in eight years' time.

The farmers eventually discovered they could prevent whipworm infestation by covering their skin with hyperilon fabric. The worms could also be surgically removed from muscle tissues, if it was done early. Many colonists died by the time the land dried up and the worms completed their cycle. The farm animals were decimated. Now the colonists knew why native herds bred so rapidly.

"The colony paused to reassess and lick its wounds. Then they received the second blow, in the form of whipsnakes. Scientists believe that the whipsnakes of Tagur Four have a life cycle linked to windworms. The snakes slithered up trees with amazing speed. Once in high branches, they whipped their bodies from tree to tree, finally dropping on their prey. Their wiry muscles constricted the throats of animals, and people, weakened by windworms. They fed well.

"Of more than ten thousand colonists, less than three thousand remained. One was their leader, an elderly woman by the name of Norian Killain Duvou. She had watched helpless as her family died, and her friends. She endured multiple surgeries for infested windworms. And she persevered.

"In desperation, the survivors shuttled to their one remaining hope-the battered vessel they had originally purchased. With grim determination, Duvou brought her people back to Metrowyl, only to be refused entry. They orbited the satellite of HomePort, as rumors of war grew. Then, somehow, they heard of Kellierin."

Leh looked up at her audience, which remained spellbound. "That's all I've got so far. The saga continues."

"If it's to have a happy ending, we'd better get moving. You're doing a great job with that story, Leh," Dal remarked. "Thank you for helping us put our work into perspective."

"I ache for them, Dal," Leh said. "Their losses were overwhelming."

"Dal," Cren asked as the group headed for their stations, "speaking of losses, is it ok if we name something on Kellierin for Naui and Koren? Something beautiful, and something substantial?"

"Of course. Good idea We'll find something appropriate, Cren. Something that reminds us of them. I think it would be a positive action, and we will have need of that. We're facing more unknowns than just this world holds. The refugees. No SiTeam. Time constraints. . . ." He sighed.

"We could be in for more than you know," Renzec said. "This Du-vou lady's coming here with experience in running things, but this is an unsurveyed world. Chief, you could be in a real uncomfortable position."

"Can't say as I look forward to it," Rial remarked ruefully.

"Chief," Cren asked as he strapped into his station, "if yorbus are so great on survey, why didn't we take TwikTwik with us. It smells bad, but we're going to need all the help we can get."

"Yorbot, lad," Rial explained. "The plural is yorbot. They as-suredly do have their uses on survey. Better than scanners, at times. Psychic, even. *If* you can interpret their sensing. But each yorbu bonds with one or two humans only, or at most, a family or clan. Koof says they work well with empaths. That yorbu was secondar-ily linked with Tadria. She could communicate with it, but barely. It had been bonded with her two, you see, and was still grieving for her. Some people have a way with yorbot, Cren. I learned a lot from the one my grandmother kept. But it took a lot of time and patience on my part. And I must admit, I never quite got use to the smell. That cross-eyed yorbu was a peculiar beast."

"But Chief," Cren objected, "Tadria told me yorbot *have* no eyes!"

"Ah," Rial said triumphantly, eyes twinkling, "You see! It was *most* peculiar, even for a yorbu!"

Tisa checked the sensors. "Ku'Fenn. We've reached Ku'Fenn," she said with excitement. Beneath them, the bustling satellite of the outermost planet carried on business as usual. "Thank the Guardian! I can't believe we're finally going to see the last of this system!"

"We had no choice, Tisa." Norian Duvou grimaced at the star chart in front of her. "No choice but to ship out. War's at our heels. Now, though, we may have to pay for that choice." The command center of 'Guardian's Reprieve' was barren, except for the Coordi-nator, her first assistant, and a small quantity of patched and worn equipment.

"What do you mean?"

"This jury-rigged Matrix might not get us across the Freel-Omar. There's nobody left to fiddle with it proper. If it conks in the middle, we're done for." Duvou grumped.

"Do we set the course?" Tisa asked patiently. She looked at her commander with concern. The lack of gravity could not compensate for the stress etching the aged face.

"Set the course? Where to?"

"Kellierin," Tisa said cautiously. "Where else?"

"So where's Kellierin? I know, I know," Duvou waved her assistant's protests off. "I know the coordinates where the Tav ship broke Matrix. That's *all* they gave us. That might be enough. Maybe. If we had a hot-shot pilot. And a decent ship. And didn't have odd EM stuff at the target. Or a protostar field. We're *not* rigged for a long hop. We'll have to break out of Matrix and recalibrate, target, and hop again, over and over. Each time it's going to strain this bucket. And we don't know the conditions in the nebula. You know what *our* conditions are!"

"Your orders, Coordinator?" Tisa prodded.

"Guardian protect us," Duvou said finally, sighing. "Set her up for the longest hop we can make in the general direction of those coordinates, and then we pray. Open a channel to Ku'Fenn Central, Tisa. I want to. . . ." Duvou's words stopped suddenly as a sleek grey craft appeared on the viewscreen, heading toward the "Guardian's Reprieve". Their comm crackled.

"Ship Registry Metrowyl 29441, out of HomePort from Tagur Four, we have you on our sensors. Please confirm identity."

Duvou breathed in deeply, held the air in her lungs for a long moment, and let it out all at once. Her shoulders slumped. Then her jaw jutted firm and her eyes got hard. She nodded at Tisa, and her assistant opened the comm channel.

"This is Norian Killain Duvou, of the *private* vessel "Guardian's Reprieve", she said crisply. "We require no assistance, thank you."

"Stand by to be boarded, "Guardian's Reprieve"."

"Repeat, we require no assistance." She flicked off the comm. "Get us the hell out of here, Tisa!" she hissed.

Tisa's fingers flew, but the view screen filled with the seal of the Royalist Forces. The comm cracked again. The seal faded, to be replaced by the stern visage of a man in a crisp dark uniform.

"I am Colonel Lar, special envoy of His Most August Majesty, King Klev of Metrowyl," the man said officiously. "Coordinator Duvou, your ship *will* be boarded for inspection at this time. Any failure to comply will be considered an act of war, and dealt with accordingly."

The Coordinator sighed and flicked the comm back on. "Why Colonel, we wouldn't *dream* of defying our *King*," she said. "We are, after all, *loyal subjects* of His Royal Majesty. We'll be pleased to receive your emissaries."

The Colonel nodded curtly, and his face vanished, to be replaced once again by the Royal seal.

"Fardling urgofs! C'mon, Tisa. Let's see what they want this time." Her voice was feisty, but Tisa was not taken in.

"Should I notify anyone?"

"Why? Only rile 'em. Maybe it's not us they want. The Queen *is* still missing, after all. Bet that's who they're after. The way this heap smells, they'll not stay long. You watch." Her eyes narrowed as they pushed their way through the corridor to the docking bay. "Whatever it takes, I'll get our people out of this. And I'll get them a home!"

They clung to their hopes and the hull stanchions as the airlock recycled. The inner iris door yawned. Seven uniformed men hung in the airlock with phase scanning automatics in their hands. Leading them was Colonel Lar himself.

The Colonel's displeasure at the lack of gravity was evident, and he curled his lip in disgust at the stench. He looked unhappily down at the scruffy welcoming committee of two. "Commander Duvou," he said at last," Your vessel has been confiscated by the Crown, pending inspection. As of now, I am in command of this ship. You will do what I say."

"You can't do that!" the Coordinator protested.

"I have already done so, Madam." Lar lifted a finger, and a battery of phase weapons zeroed in on the two women. Lar pointed at

Duvou. "Now that you understand, I will speak with you in private. Alone." He then nodded briefly to his men, and flicked his fingers at Duvou. "Move along now. Surely there is some room nearby where we can speak."

The Coordinator looked briefly into Tisa's eyes, and pushed off toward the adjoining cabin. The colonel followed. His men blocked Tisa's move to join them.

The room was small, and contained conduits and spare parts, secured haphazardly. "Now then," Colonel Lar began, "let's not waste any more time. I will make this simple, and I will make this plain. I know your plans. I know about your Matrix drive, and I know about Kellierin. Furthermore, I know precisely where it is, which you do not. You have nothing to lose by following my instructions precisely. You have everything to gain. There is no room for negotiation. I have limited time. Now, this is what you must do."

Duvou looked up at Col Lar. His uncompromising visage would brook no defiance. All hope fled.

Chapter
18

Melion shifted fitfully beneath diagnostic lights, in a semiconscious fugue state. The open compartment was crammed with special instrumentation, but Melion's best life support sat by her side, focusing his energies. Dal was preparing to "guide" her through a Crisis peak. Katayan sat next to Melion. His long ears twitched and his eyes were alert.

Kimmer took her patient's hand and looked over at her two. "It's up to you now, Dal," she whispered, controlling her own emotional state carefully. She didn't want her energies to encroach on the delicate balance he needed for such work.

The biomonitor on Dal's arm alerted Kimmer to his readiness for attunement. She carefully placed Melion's hand in his. Dal's monitor lights flickered erratically as he bridged the gap to Melion's psyche. Then, one by one, they resumed their previous state.

As Dal drifted deeper into empathic linkage, he relaxed completely. Kimmer watched his face closely for any signs of disturbance. What was going on now between Dal and Melion was beyond science's ability to monitor. She did her best to match her own respiratory pattern with Dal's even breathing. Dal started to sway slightly, moving with the flow of healing energies.

Melion continued to move restlessly, but Dal kept her clammy hand in his warm grasp. His breathing became deeper and more audible. Kimmer watched intently, darting a glance at the monitors every few minutes.

Time passed. Kimmer realized that she had been caught up in the overflow of the powerful exchange, and had drifted into something of a fugue state herself. Melion was in now in a deep, healing slumber. Katayan was snoozing peacefully beside her with his nose on his paws.

She leaned over and put her hand firmly over Dal's. No response. She squeezed. He blinked suddenly, and Melion's lights flickered, and then resumed their steady glow. Dal turned his golden eyes to Kimmer.

"She'll be entranced for a week or so, and then she should come out of Crisis. She'll be fine," he said softly.

"Dal, will you recover by yourself, or do you need support?"

Dal stood on shaky legs. "I'm ok, just drained. I'll take some extra vitamins and fluid, and a little time for meditation. I've been overusing my body and neglecting my mind, but so have we all."

"True, Dal," Kimmer admitted, "but the rest of us don't have extra neurotransmitters amplifying every twinge and pain. You *have* to take it easier."

"I don't think I'm cut out for colony prep," Dal remarked. "It's harder than exploration, and minus the rewards."

Kimmer frowned and shook her head. "Maybe if you weren't so negative about it, it wouldn't seem so bad." She removed Dal's biomonitor strip. Flicking her medimonitor wristband on remote, she checked it with Melion's panel. "Move it. We're wasting time," she said brusquely. "Do I need a vest?"

"No, Kimmer. It's gotten warm." Dal said cautiously. He searched Kimmer's face for the cause of the abrupt change in her mood, but she avoided his eyes. With a last glance toward Melion, Kimmer marched out of the cabin. Dal followed, shrugging it off. She'd get over it. Kimmer's abrupt mood swings had been taxing lately. But they were all tired.

He looked across the meadow to where the crew had assembled. Renzec and Leh were in animated discussion, constructing another part of an epic saga concerning their mission. It had something to do with Cren. He sat on a downed tree trunk nearby, doing his best to disregard their chatter.

Kimmer plunked down beside Leh, pointedly turning her back on Dal. Dal gave her a long look. He tried to monitor her feelings, but bounced off a mental barrier. There was a good and a bad side to amplified feelings, he mused. This hurt.

He walked over to Cren, who welcomed the distraction."How're you holding up?" he asked.

Cren laughed. "This work is teaching me about anatomy. Especially muscles," he said, rubbing his biceps ruefully, but his twinkling eyes took away any negativity. Outdoor life agreed with him. His face had filled out, although some of that was due to bug bites.

"Have you thought any more about the last pulse test?"

"Yeah, but I need to talk to Mel. How's she doing?"

"Better, Cren. But it'll be a week yet."

"We should be grateful we got no response to the pulse. The first one was enough for me. Sit down, Dal," he said, patting the trunk area by his side. "While we're waiting for the Chief, maybe you can answer a few questions about the Tav."

Dal smiled, also relieved for a diversion. "I guess I'm the resident expert."

"Are all Tav Survey craft staffed with empaths?"

"No, Cren. Some of the people Koof lost were not empaths."

Dal sat on the dry wood, glad of the chance to stretch out in the sun. He glanced over at his two. Kimmer's hair formed a near-white aura around her head, and her warm eyes glowed with all the wonder and magic of a child. She looked radiant and desirable. Why was she so moody lately, especially the rare times when they were alone?

"What did Koof mean by his comments on the pulse?"

"He believes there is a manifestation of their holy Light developing in the sun. He suggested that it would evolve here along with life in this system."

"What's this 'Lady of Light' bit? I thought they believed in a 'Lord of Light'."

"I'm not sure, Cren. I'm sorry I can't be of more help, but the Tav mentors I had at the Academy were close-muzzled about anything other than basic empath training. I don't think there is any specific identity, either male or female. I think those are simply convenient labels for something far beyond their understanding. If so, it would certainly be beyond mine."

"Seems kind of wifty. Like in a space vid"

Dal chuckled. "No more incomprehensible than our Guardian. Some argue that they are the same. Although the Tavian light manifests itself physically at times. At least, *they* feel it does."

Rising voices disturbed their dialogue.

"That's you're opinion, Kimmer, not mine," Renzec exclaimed hotly. "Look, I'll volunteer for all the Survey work you want, and then some, but no way am I going to be stuck in a colony with a thousand screaming larval-stage humanoids. Not in winter, when I can't get out. From all the signs, it's going to be a hell of a winter here." Renzec stood and stalked to a large conifer. He leaned against its trunk and folded his arms across his chest, radiating anger.

"Hey, Rennie," Dal called out. "Calm your body! We don't know what is going to happen yet. None of us signed up for colony work. Chief Rial will be the one in the center of the storm when, and if, the colony ship arrives. He'll need all our support at that time. Once we help them set up, they may wish us to leave immediately. There's no sense arguing about tomorrow."

He spread his arm out expansively. "Look around us." Their ship rested near the center of the large meadow, with fragrant woods all around. "It's peaceful here now. Let's keep the peace while we can."

"Wish it could stay that way," Cren said. "Just us."

"That would be a rut. A comfortable one, but ruts are, for a while. Until you get stuck in them. Ren, where is Chief Rial?" Dal asked, to forestall further argument.

"He checked over what we built, and then he took a walk." Renzec said, mellowing somewhat.

"It's been cosmic working on the shelters, Dal," Cren said enthusiastically. "The local wildlife ran when we first felled one of these big guys," he said, patting the log. "Once we started using the cut wood, though, they came back. Some sat and watched. The brush piles are already being used as homes by some critters. They seem harmless. I wish we had more time to watch *them*. I'm beginning to see how important it is to leave things as we find them."

"Fat chance, once the colonists get here," Renzec growled.

"Have you had any luck with those bright little entities you sensed before we came down," Leh asked Dal.

"They're around here, very close by. They are not making contact, for some reason. Have you had any luck?"

"Me? Hardly, if you haven't," Leh snorted. "I've tried a few times. Got nothing, though." She chuckled. "Except once or twice, and that was you, searching as well."

Dal smiled ruefully. "We did bump into each other, didn't we."

"What's it feel like, with your mind all stretched out?" Cren wanted to know.

"Nothing like what you'd think," Dal explained, turning slightly to face Cren. "We send out tendrils, and then add more of ourselves as we find the path we want. It's like a grid we can sense and travel along. Only the grid is more than three dimensional."

"*More* than three dimensional? Perhaps that's why we haven't been able to measure it," Kimmer suggested.

"Could be." Dal smiled at her encouragingly, and she smiled back, adding her sunshine to the warming day. "Cren, when you have some free time, if you want to hitch a ride, why don't you find out for yourself?" Dal offered. "I've taken others along."

Cren looked dubious. "I don't think I'm ready for that."

"I wouldn't fret about it, kid," Renzec growled. "You won't have any free time soon."

It was near noon, and the last remnants of morning mist had burned away. Rial Jennery gazed out over the still surface of Lake Korenaui- a mirror reflecting the snow capped peaks and forests surrounding the far shore. A few white, fluffy clouds drifted aimlessly across the deep azure sky. He opened his arms wide to the joy of this sweet view, and breathed in a deep draft of springtime. The lake was a fitting memorial. Deep, rich and clear, and abundant with life and promise. He thought of the children who would someday play in this lake, and the lives that would be nurtured and enriched by it, and he was content with their choice. He gathered his pack and hiked back to the ship.

He met Leh there, foraging for food bars for her crewmates.

"Hah! Caught you!" he cried. "Why aren't you eating *real* food? We haven't had a decent meal since we set down."

"No time, Chief. We've been waiting for *you*," she shook a finger at him, "and you're late."

Rial's hearty laugh was interrupted by comm link activation. "Maybe I thought you needed to *make* some of that time to rest and regroup. Go on, Leh. I'll catch that," he said, indicating the comm. "Maybe it's Koof. Grab a food bar or two for me."

Leh's grin filled the cabin as she made an obvious show of counting *three* more bars to add her carrier. Chuckling softly, she went out to her crew mates. Dal had moved to a low, clean-cut stump. The others chatted around him, but he gave them no heed. He had his elbows propped on his knees, and his chin rested on his hands. His mind was lost in somewhere else. Kimmer smiled fondly at him, amused at his powers of concentration, and glad of his recent willingness to display them. As he grew comfortable with the gifts brought by his Change, he was shedding some of the unnatural reticence that he once wore like a cloak. Cren had helped with that. Laughter came easier for him now, and his overwhelming seriousness and shyness had all but fled. If only he were happier about the colony, and what it entailed. Sitting as he was, Dal resembled a creature from one of Leh's stories, more of magic and moonbeams than of theories and facts.

Kimmer went over to sit at his feet. She reached up and touched him, bringing him back to the here and now.

"Dal, have you ever seen such a place? I wish Melion were well enough to be out here. It seems so healing."

"That it does, Kimmer," Dal agreed. Then he sighed deeply. "If we only knew more about what's coming. And who is coming."

"The Chief is taking a comm call right now," Leh spoke up.

"It could be Koof," Dal speculated. "He could lend us a hand. Or a rather large paw," he amended, and a smile flickered across his face.

Kimmer smiled, and Leh let out a quick hoot. Chief Rial smiled too, as he joined the group. He made his way to a comfortable, mossy area that had been left for him, and settled the bag he'd been carrying by his side.

"Koof and his crew will bring their own problems, don't forget. Fifty kids!" Renzec griped, "Got no time for kids!"

"The logistics alone could be staggering," Dal agreed. "I know we're taught to make positives out of negatives, but I'm at a loss to know how to make me out of this." His face brightened briefly and he wacked the tree remnant, raising his eyebrow. "You might even say I'm stumped." Everybody groaned, except Kimmer. She was not amused.

"Actually, Ren, when you think about it, it might not be so bad," Dal explained. "The school ship holds fifty people, true, but some of those will be adults. Tav adults. Never underestimate the power of the Tav. Those kids will be bright, empathically adept, and Tav trained. They won't be infants."

"Infants have rights too," Kimmer bit off.

"Of course they do. No one said otherwise." Dal shot a pointed look at Renzec, and the surly engineer decided not to challenge that, and shut off his retort. "What has you on edge lately, Kimmer?" Dal said testily, wearying of the exchange.

"What has *me* on edge? You and Renzec and your negative mind set towards children! That's what!" Kimmer accused.

"Children need supervision. Constant care. We do not have the manpower to provide that. Guardian knows what state the colonists are in. We're Survey, Kimmi," Dal pleaded.

"Not nannies," Renzec added bitterly.

"Let's halt this right now," Rial said firmly, as Kimmer was about to deliver a caustic reply. "As Dal stated, the kids from the school ship are not your average kids. They're brilliant."

Renzec groaned. "So was I, when I was a brat. That makes it even more likely they'll get into trouble."

"You're still a brat, Rennie," Leh gibed, but the mood would not be lightened.

"I can't abide kids," Renzec insisted. "They pester. They want things. They get in my way. Look, I'll help to get us through this mess, but don't tell me I have to like it."

"Maybe we'll get lucky, and there won't be so much as one little Rennie among them. We'll find out soon enough if they're part of the solution or part of the problem. My guess is, they'll be a little of both," Rial commented. "Now Renzec, how goes your assignment?"

The tall engineer had been cautiously chewing on the end of a stiff blade of grass. He took it out and inspected the gnawed end critically. "This stuff isn't bad. Sweet, even. Shame we can't digest it. There are plenty of things here we can eat, though. This is a good place. Even these flowers are edible," he remarked, indicating the puffy, colorful blossoms scattered about the meadow. "They're all over. The 'corder says they're real good for us," he said with a gleam in his eye. "We may be able to process them into food."

Cren stooped down while Renzec talked, snapped off one of the blossoms and inspected it quickly. Then he popped it into his mouth and chomped. Immediately, his eyes bugged and started to water. "Ghaaaak", he sputtered, spitting out the mouthful. "Akkk! It's awful! Agh! Yuk!"

Kimmer glared at Renzec. "That was *mean*, Ren!" she protested.

Renzec placidly watched Cren's frantic efforts to rid his mouth of the foul-tasting plant.

"Maybe, Kimmer, but useful. Cren, I've been telling you all morning, don't rush things. You won't forget the lesson Nature taught you. The stuff tastes about as bad as yorbot smell. Just because the 'corder says something is *good for us* to eat, doesn't mean it's automatically *good to eat*. These blooms are loaded with nutrition. If we can find a way to change the taste, we'd have a substantial addition to the colonist's larder."

"Ugh, damn," Cren spit, wiping his mouth on his sleeve. "How," he grimaced, "do we find out what something tastes like?"

Renzec smiled wanly but said nothing.

Chief Rial chuckled. "The only way is the way you found out,

Cren. You can get an *idea* with sensors, but somebody always has to be the first to taste. "Next time you try something, after it scans safe, take a small bite and chew. Then wait until the next day before you try more. Some times there are aftertastes, or after effects.

"Beware, all of you," Rial cautioned. "If I know engineers, Renzec will try to con somebody else into tasting everything before he does. Cren, too."

"Live and learn, Chief," Renzec drawled. He reached into his belt pouch and pulled out a flat pack of yellow lozenges. He handed them to Cren.

"Try these," he said kindly. "Kimmer made them for dry throat. They're juicy and tart. I didn't think you'd eat a whole one, honest. It's persistent, that taste."

Cren viewed the offered packet with distrust, shifted the distrustful look to Renzec, and popped one of the small, yellow ovals into his mouth. Within seconds, his features softened. "Thanks, Renzec," he said, "I think."

"Well," Rennie said, continuing his interrupted report, "the water here is as perfect as can be." Cren squinted at him, wary and waiting. Renzec laughed, holding up his hand in a peace gesture. "It tastes great, too. I swear it." He glanced in the direction of the lake. "No problem with drinking from *Lake Korenaui*," he said. "We can use it just as it is. There's an abundance of life there, including decent sized fish. They're all compatible with our biochemistry. Most of them use EM energy for something.

"Cren, here, has been a great help with building shelters. He thinks like an engineer, when all is said and done. All he needs is some practical experience." Coming from Renzec, that was the height of praise. Cren beamed.

"Once our company comes, they'll have to sink some wells. They need to construct a community bathhouse attached to that septic system we put in. We made a peat bog system. Should handle things for a while, but they'll need a few more, with automatic recyclers, before the weather turns cold. There's endless projects that need doing," he said bleakly.

"We got a few shelters up fast because we used materials right to hand. Anything we build from now on will take more time, more planning, and lots more builders.

"Surely," Kimmer teased, "an *engineer* can find a way to build emergency shelters out of practically nothing!"

"Give us time," Renzec said, only half in jest. "For now, we need help to get anything more accomplished." He scratched a bug-bitten ear. "I guess that last goes for us all."

"What's your first priority?" Dal asked Renzec.

"Selectively clearing more of the surrounding area. Make some more of those." He nodded at the two massive structures on one side of the meadow. "We've been using repellor and tractor fields on the 'hoppers to position the wood from conifers. Crude, but it fills the need. Smells good, too.

"Of course, all we built were shells. Still need innards. Have to bring people down. Get them organized. Get them farming, too. The season is short. It's planting time *now*. The snow must get pretty deep here, come winter. That'll help insulate. They'll need a sizable place for the ship to land. Then they can use the ship itself for quarters, and. . . ."

"Hold it, Ren," Dal interrupted. "They won't land."

"What do you mean?"

"The colonists escaped Tagur because their leader refused to cannibalize the ship for easy shelter. She insisted on leaving it intact in orbit. Koof says we'll never convince them to land it," Dal said.

"Dal", Renzec argued, "just because Koof says. . . ."

Dal interrupted again. "Koof *knows*, Rennie. After mind-link, so do I." he said firmly. "They will *not* yield on this."

Renzec threw his arms up. "Then let them stay up there. Ablebodied adults can come down. Won't get any work done once the kids land."

Kimmer's face darkened, but she held her tongue.

"What's the most we can house immediately, Ren?" Dal asked.

"With crowding, maybe two hundred. Nothing fancy. The colony's going to need every bit of spring and summer to ready for winter, so farmers and builders have to come down first."

"I agree with Renzec," Rial said. "We've got to get farming ASAP.

We need to find edibles to gather. I have no idea of the replicator capability on the Tagur ship."

" 'Guardian's Reprieve', Chief. That's the ship's name. We better start using it. Koof said to avoid saying 'Tagur' around the colonists."

"Good thought, Dal. I hope they have seed and embryos. It would be a blow if we had to start from scratch."

Renzec stood straight. "We? What's all this 'we' stuff? I thought *we'd* get them started, and then take off."

"Maybe we will, Renzec," Chief Rial said calmly. "Maybe we will. Some of us may choose to stay and help explore Kellierin. Remember, there's a war on back home, and we are short of staff. You done, Renzec?"

"Go, Chief."

"I'll try to pick up the slack in the geology department, but, like primitive ironwork, I've gotten rusty from disuse. This is what I've found so far.

"The substantial hyperilon deposits on the desert continent may come in handy someday for building. If we can't come up with anything else, we may need to start a minimal facility for windows and domes. For now, we'll stick to the immediate area for building materials. There are caves to the north, but they show signs of occupation. Beasts may use them for hibernation during the winter.

"I, too, would like to have the ship as building material. That would save a lot of time. The wood we cut, we have to cut carefully. Save every bit of scrap as potential heat source."

"Primitive, Chief."

"So it is, Ren. But wood heats. That's what we have to go with. Unless there are any other ideas."

"Consider the possibility of a small breeder reactor, Chief. We have the materials, and it's safe as long as they're mindful of precautions. We can train techs, and leave step-by-step manuals. It would provide their energy needs for the foreseeable future, yielding minimal waste. That can be reprocessed, and what is left would decay rapidly."

"We'll have to see how technologically savvy they are, or are willing to become. It would be a shame if they polluted this place with fossil fuels. I got something else, but let's wrap up the reports first," Rial said cryptically. "Kimmer, what do you have on the local biome?"

"It's a well-mixed forest, Chief. Conifers predominate. The ecology looks stable, and we want to keep it that way."

"The Unifieds are ecosensitive, Kimmer," Dal said.

"They were," Kimmer agreed. "Who knows what the experience on Tagur has done. Their world betrayed them. They must not take out their anger and frustrations here.

"The reddish conifers that Renzec and Cren have been using for construction are similar to the ones on the outer planet. They serve to cut down on the wind. I think that's going to be important. I know we need cleared space for agriculture, but there already are sporadic clearings in the forest. I suggest that we utilize them as much as possible, and delay unnecessary tree cutting until we see what the colonists actually need.

"By the way, these trees are resinous, so watch it. Don't sit on freshly cut wood."

Dal looked startled, and stood up quickly, brushing the seat of his stretchsuit.

"Once it's had a chance to dry, it's fine," Kim explained with an impish smile. Renzec promised they'd dry everything they cut. The resin forms a waterproof surface. I've even found it petrified."

"We've been allowing a layer of fresh resin to form on cut wood," Renzec explained, "then passing an arc heater over it to smooth it out. The colonists may be crowded, but they'll be dry. "The trees have thick bark, grown for insulation. I have yet to discover how the wildlife survives, above and under the snow pack."

"Kimmer," Cren asked, "what about those trees with the shaggy bark. Could they infect the other trees?"

Kim smiled. "I thought it was a disease process too, Cren. It isn't. The bark is thin, and peeling off in layers. Those trees shed their outer layer of bark every spring. Don't know why.

"I saw a few volcanos on my overflight of the mountain range on the other side of the lake. They appear dormant, but we should monitor them.

"I've checked the immediate area for bogs and quicksand soils. Haven't found anything dangerous. There is the peat area Renzec and Cren tapped for septic filler. We're close to one crevasse, to the southwest. When you clear, guys," she directed, "don't clear in that direction."

"Gotcha," Renzec agreed.

"That's it for me," Kimmer said.

Chief Rial looked in Dal's direction, but Dal was lost in thought. He looked worn out.

"How about you, Leh?" Rial asked, continuing to direct the meeting.

"This grass would be fine for a dairy herd. If those blossoms don't destroy the taste of the milk." Her eyes were animated. "There's lots of life here, but not much variety. Few species, but lots of sub-species. That's unusual, and I want to know why. Right now I have more questions than answers. There's lifetimes worth of work here," she said, looking like she'd be more than willing to do it all.

"I found several kinds of herd beasts, but not in the immediate area. The ones to the north resemble korets, and I've been calling them that. Their smaller. They're still shedding winter coats. Motley looking, but healthy. They've started to drop young. The foals are all female. One stag per herd.

"The ungulates to the southeast have thick, padded, broad hooves. They're mostly in summer coat now, but there are patches of winter fur left on shrubs where they rubbed it off. It's white, hollow, and air-filled. Perfect for insulation. Extremely thick, with an undercoat that is water-repellant. Maybe the winter sheddings could be used woven into clothing or used as building insulation. The undercoat might be a felting material. Those long-eared jembits have thick, insulated coats too. That says cold winters to me. I haven't had time to make a detailed assessment."

"Anything else?" Rial asked.

"The birds are spectacular, and their songs individualized. I'm sure you've noticed the chimers," she smiled widely. "If I never did anything but listen to them for the rest of my life, I'd be content. They can sing more than one note at a time!

"There are reptiles around. Some have come within eyesight, but they're very cautious. I could live without some of the insects. They bite. The bites swell up and itch for days."

"Tell us something we don't know, Leh," Renzec grumbled.

"Even those wretched creatures have their place in the ecological system, Renzec," Leh admonished. "Although I haven't figured out how they live through the winter.

"Almost all of the animals and plants I've scanned have their own electromagnetic signatures. Some are bioluminescent. Some communicate using EM waves. We have flutterbys here, similar to those on the outer planet. Nothing dangerous so far.

"Oh, and speaking of dangers . . . not that it's dangerous, but I thought it was for a moment. It took me by surprise, is all. There's this bird," Leh explained, more excited than ever. "I want everybody please to be mindful of them. I heard this big flubby buzz next to my ear. Sounded like a monster insect. I'm ashamed to say I batted at this jewel of a bird. It's only about the size of one of my fingers. Didn't hurt it, but I scared the little thing, and I haven't seen one since. It was a metallic blue, with golden wings. It darted away, and then hovered a bit a few yards off. I was around those big, yellow-brown trumpet flowers at the edge of the clearing. If you see one, get a scan of it, if possible. It was fast. I've been calling it Mr. Flubbyfeathers in my mind, but that seems a clownish name for such an elegant thing."

"If we transplanted some of those flowers close to the ship," Cren suggested, "we might attract the bird."

"When, kid?" Renzec groaned. "We're going to have to find a way to work and sleep at the same time! Not to mention eat. Priorities, fella."

Cren looked at Renzec thoughtfully and shrugged. "All morning, while we've been constructing the shelters, I've been thinking a lot about Father, and how one-dimensional he is. Maybe we have more options than we know. I'm trying to evolve, ok Ren?"

"Thanks for trying," Leh said softly to Cren, favoring him with her magnificent smile. He beamed. Then she turned to Renzec.

"It's difficult, isn't it? We don't have any time to cover anything in depth. It's bound to be frustrating."

"There's never enough time," Rial agreed. "But it doesn't have to be frustrating. Think of it as a million wonderful things to do, while a whole world slowly unfolds her mysteries. This is a chance we don't often get. Let's make the most of it. As Renzec said, priorities. Just note any questions in the log. Requests also. We'll take the tasks one at a time.

"I do think, Dal, that you should focus on finding that sentience you mentioned. Try to set up a dialogue before the crowd arrives. Otherwise, they might doubt our intentions."

"The little guys are around, Chief. When I feel their voices, on the edge of my mind, I try to focus on them. But they vanish. Their presence seems strongest near sunset."

"Have you tried doing a 'sending', Dal? Calling to them?"

"No, Chief. It's always too fuzzy."

"If you remember to take your meds, you'd have a clearer mind and maybe get a better reading," Kimmer advised. "You'd be less distracted."

Dal grimaced. "We have so little time, it's a shame to spend any sleeping."

"That kind of thing can't go on much longer." Kimmer warned.

"I know. I'll get some sleep tonight. The EM forces here are fascinating, but they get me wired. With all the work, it's been a constant adrenalin rush. It's hard for me to settle down. I'm glad that there are light trees here. They're magnificent. I just wish we didn't have the biting insects as well!"

"Have any of the repellents I've given you done any good?" Kimmer asked.

"You kidding?" Renzec said with disgust. "They swim in the stuff."

"The bites are basically harmless. I checked them carefully."

"Right, Kimmer!" Renzec complained. "Have you tried working up a sweat lately?"

"Yeah," Cren said with vehemence. "When we sweat, they eat!"

"You've tried every bug deterrent I have in stock," Kimmer said. "Maybe I'll find something in the local flora. That's often the case."

"Kimmer, you have no time for that. I want you to help Dal track that sentience," Rial ordered. And you two get yourselves in sync again, he thought. "See he takes his meds and rests this afternoon. Take stunners along. Kimmer, stay close to Dal and observe him carefully. You know how preoccupied he gets when he's doing his thing.

"Now that we've covered the necessities," Rial continued, "we received a signal from the relay buoy. An unidentified vessel broke out of Matrix. I don't think we have a Kellierin day ahead of us before we get company."

"The colonists?" Dal asked.

"The Matrix signature indicates a craft too ancient to be anything but. When she broke out, it looked for a moment like there was an accompanying craft. When I zeroed in, it was gone."

"Koof's ship?" Dal asked, with hope in his voice.

"Or a military escort from Metrowyl," Rial said in a worried tone. "Could be they'll dump the passengers and take the ship. And maybe us and our ship as well."

Cren stood up in alarm, and Renzec swore.

"Let's fight our battles when they come, and not before," Rial insisted. "Another reason to track down that sentience now. We can use all the help we can get. Shame we can't move those caves." Cren narrowed his eyes at that.

"Anything else?" Dal asked. There were no comments, but Cren looked antsy. "Cren, something struck you when the Chief mentioned caves. You said something earlier about more options. If you have them, we need to know now."

Cren looked hesitant. "Think about our landing on the other planet."

Everyone looked blank. Dal's brow furrowed as he thought of possible connections. Then it clicked. "Oh no. You can't mean what I think you mean."

"Hush, Dal," Rial said impatiently, waving him quiet. "Go on, lad," he encouraged Cren. "Tell us what you've got."

"We can't move *those* caves. But maybe we can *make* caves! Tunnels, anyway. Then we *would* be making shelters out of nothing. Remember how the sides of the tunnel fused? They'd be waterproof. We could do it! Make them shallow. Even put in skylight windows someday, when we get something to put into them. Like transparent hyperilon."

Renzec looked smug. "See. I told you the kid had ideas."

"I still haven't gotten over that first tunnel," Dal said apprehensively, rubbing his neck.

"You don't have to do it," Renzec promised. "Me and the kid, here. Leave it to us. We'll work it out."

"We can't afford to crash the ship," Dal objected.

"Don't need to. We'll use 'hoppers, like this morning. We can modify the tractors to work as repellors. Give us width. Not as big as the ship, but if it works, it'll do us fine." Renzec oozed confidence.

"I feel better about the shelter situation already," the Chief beamed. "Good thinking, Cren."

Cren glowed.

"See what you two can create this afternoon. If you can make something a scanner can't penetrate, so much the better," the Chief added, glancing up at the sky. "Before we split up, I have something here." Rial stood and dug out a thermal flask and cups from pack he'd brought out. "We haven't had a true landing ceremony. I have here water from Lake Korenaui. It seems fitting." He poured, and handed the cups around. Then he turned to Dal. "This is for you to do, Dal," he said.

Dal looked surprised, but he raised his cup. The others stood and followed suit. "To adventures which await, and to questions to be answered. To this world, and the next, and to the long voyage after." The crew echoed his words. Only he was aware that one voice was missing on the last sentence.

Dal only drank half his water. Then he fumbled in his pocket. He brought out a small circular case, and retrieved his meds from it. "It seems fitting that I prepare for the search for sentient life with water that's a memorial to the lives we lost," he explained. Kimmer deliberately put her cup down as he spoke, and left the gathering. Dal looked after her and sighed as he picked up her brimming cup. He finished it, and his own, with his meds.

By the time they split up, Kimmer was halfway to the ship. "Kimmer," he called, "wait up!" He lengthened his stride and caught up to his two. He was dismayed at the storm clouds on her face. Her eyes were filling up. "What's wrong, love?" he asked tenderly. "You're having more mood swings than a Changer, lately."

Kimmer avoided his eyes. "Nothing's wrong," she said brusquely, brushing him off. "I'm tired, that's all."

Dal sent out a gentle mind touch, but was repelled by strong mental blocks. "It's more than that, Kimmer. We have to talk."

"Not now. I *said* I'm tired. Now leave me alone. I need some space, ok?"

Dal stood as if rooted, watching Kimmer cross the meadow and enter the ship. By the time he followed her in, Kimmer had already retired to her compartment and sealed it tightly. He paused outside it and touched the hard wall gently. He could make out muffled sounds of sobbing inside, but he dared not attempt a mind touch. He stood there a long time, at loss as to what to do. Then he checked on Melion. The monitor outside her compartment indicated she was still soundly entranced.

He took a sonic shower, but it did nothing to relax him. It took all his self-discipline to crawl into his lonely compartment. His body ached interminably, but the ache in heart was harder to endure. He left his compartment open, and took a stronger dose of relaxant. After a period of hard-won meditation, he drifted into a troubled sleep.

Chapter

19

"Don't stray from me," Kimmer warned nervously, as Dal moved into the sea of tall grasses. Evening was approaching. The rest of the crew had gone into the ship, and all was quiet save for the wildlife. They were in a cul-de-sac at the edge of the clearing, outside the ship's protective fields. "Don't go into the woods!" she called.

Dal smiled resignedly and returned to where she stood. "Don't fret so, Kimmi," he entreated softly. "Trust me, ok?" He brushed his hand over her silky hair. "I'm going to that jumble of rocks ahead, by the edge of the clearing. The life forms are close. I brushed the edges of their thoughts. Inquisitive and cautious, but friendly. Please don't broadcast apprehension. Be silent, Kimmer," he added, "no matter what you see, unless you're *sure* I'm in danger. On the other scout ship, Cren misunderstood Koof's sign of friendship and trust. He thought Koof was going to bite my head off. Different beings have different ways."

Kimmer gave Dal a disgruntled look. "I'm *not* a novice."

Dal grinned and gently tugged a loose tress of her hair. "Then quit acting like one. I'll let you know when to approach, and I'll try to make it soon. Now hush. That's an order."

"Yes *sir*. Understood *sir*," Kimmer replied stiffly, but in hushed tones. Then she smiled to take the edge off her words, and reached up to brush the forever-flopping lock off Dal's brow.

The sun hung heavy on the horizon, diffusing lingering light in the already darkening sky. The ship looked small and far away, burnished with sundown's pink highlights.

Dal fingered his headlamp and night goggles, but didn't flick them in place as he glided away quietly. Kimmer stayed, but kept her hand on the stunner. The grasses swished and swayed in the evening breeze. Trumpet flowers bobbed their heads gently. Kimmer let her mind relax, mindfully centering her thoughts to avoid interfering with Dal's, but she kept her eyes open and watchful. It was pleasantly warm, and her mind began to float on the intoxicating air. She could feel the edges of Dal's mind, reaching out, reassuring, anticipating, calling. And something else.

The first nibble began tentatively, almost like a question. Soft, rounded sensations came from the direction of the rocks. A feeling of peace and contentment filled Kimmer and bubbled over, body and soul. She couldn't remember when life seemed so utterly blissful.

In the dim light at the edge of the clearing, thin, glowing bands of liquid light flowed across the rocks. Different streamers of color followed. Kimmer activated her scanner, using minimal movement. Reptilian, with bioluminescent lines on their skins. Each being had a slightly different EM signature. She reached up carefully and pulled down her nighteyes. The "lines" metamorphosed into trails of bright dots. They'd flow forward, and then hesitate a moment before advancing again, always moving closer to Dal. He continued his empathic call, and they were answering. She could pick out tones of relief coming through their ocean of joyful peace. Without words, Dal widened the scope of his gentle summons to include his two. She felt him paint an interpretation of their contact. This was followed by an answering and growing confusion from the tiny creatures.

Kimmer started moving slowly and quietly toward Dal and the moving trails of light. She felt the first specific alien thought patterns brush her mind, more like a melody than a verbalization. Trusting Dal's acceptance, she opened to the tendrils of thought. Her earlier feelings of joy intensified, and the confusion vanished, to be replaced by a sense of wonder.

Dal stretched his arm out to the rock. A slender lizard, less than a foot long, slithered onto his forearm. Dal brought his arm, and the lizard, up to his face. The lizard cocked its radiant triangular head, humming and chirping. Its long snout opened wide, then snapped shut with little force. Dal laughed. "Yes, I see you have but two tiny teeth, and they are not going to be used to devour us. We have many teeth, but do not plan on eating lizards with them." He opened his mouth wide and showed them, and laughed again. That launched the remainder of the lizards into a responding chorus of chirps and twitters that resembled birds in the morning.

As Kimmer reached the rocks, the lizards hushed both mind and audio voices. The two reptiles closest to her turned and inspected her, bobbing their heads comically. Then they emitted a strange sound, like a chime. She holstered her stunner, and stretched her hand flat on the rock in invitation. Immediately, she felt the touch of tiny, rubbery feet as one of the creatures climbed up her hand and onto her forearm. When she moved her arm, a tail gently encircled part of her wrist.

The lizard was about twice as long as her hand and fingers combined. Phosphorescent spots glowed above each nostril, matching bright lines running along each side of the central ridge. She could see now that the ridge ran from the top of the head to the tail tip.

Soon she had a lizard with neon green lines on her left wrist, and a blue one wrapped around her right. Their skin was soft and leathery smooth, dry and cool against her arms. Their tiny eyes were hooded, and appeared black in the night.

Dal was rubbing his lizard's ridge. It responded with a warm, cooing noise, and the ridge unfolded into a multicolored, ribbed fan.

"They're oogeecheela, Kimmer," Dal explained in a low voice. "How much of what they say are you getting?"

"Say? Nothing at all, Dal. Just feelings. Good feelings. And something else, but I don't know what."

"Probably curiosity. They don't know what to make of you. They've been lonely, wanting other sentience for company. When we were in orbit, they felt my presence. Kimmer, all life on this planet connects on a basic level, using the EM spectrum. They picked up Leh and Katayan, but the rest of us were "silent", and they were afraid. They thought we were hiding something. They have been communicating by floating concepts at me, like mental songs with emotional overtones."

"I got a sort of dreamy happiness overlying everything," Kimmer said. "It was almost overpowering at first."

"That's their defense mechanism. But it's honest. They *are* benevolent. They seem to have a sense of humor, as well."

"They're also truly beautiful," Kimmer added.

"Yes," Dal agreed, as he put his hand down on the rock. The bright little beings scampered down his arm. One of them turned and sat on his haunches, using the long tail to balance. The lizard faced Dal, upper legs extended. Tall and skinny, he swayed with the breeze as he chimed and gestured to help get messages across the bridge between the species.

"Yes, little friend," Dal said, and he laughed softly. "You have been lonely. More of us *are* coming soon. Not too many. Only to this area. Yes, I promise," he nodded, and the lizards echoed the motion. All around them, lines of color bobbed in the night, and they were washed in an assurance that the little beings knew nodding meant agreement. "Thank you for your welcome," Dal continued. "We promise to be careful of your forest. We will cherish this planet we call Kellierin, for which you have no name. We will treat her with respect. Some of us to come will be younglings, with time to play. Some will not be silent of mind to you, like most of us are. There will even be beings not like us, and they will have the clearest voices of mind, and will honor your friendship."

Dal held out his hands to Kimmer, and the lizards flowed swiftly from her arms to his. He put them all down gently on the rocks. "They aren't nocturnal, Kimmer," he explained aside. "They've been observing us since we landed, but have stayed out of sight in the trees, until they were sure we were safe."

He turned to the lizards. "Good night, oogeecheela. Pleasant dreams, if you dream," he wished them softly. Then he took Kimmer's hand and started to lead the way back to the ship.

Kimmer chuckled. She had kept her night glasses on and her wits about her. Dal's night glasses still perched on top of his head, and his light was out. At other times after alien contact, she'd witnessed a preoccupied Dal walk into a tree or fall over a branch. Mindful of the fresh tunnels Cren and Renzec had dug, Kimmer held Dal back and fitted his night glasses snugly over his eyes. Then *she* took the lead to the ship.

They found Red Team anxiously waiting in the cabin. Cren sat mugs of unfamiliar but aromatic hot tea in front of them. They sipped it gratefully as they recounted the first contact.

"These beings aren't pets, Cren, just because they seem to enjoy life and place a high value on play." Dal warned sternly. "They are first-order sentients with thought patterns unlike ours. They have the ability to broadcast positive thought patterns, which may help with the colonists. Whether they can safely approach people so troubled is another thing."

"Dal, what effect would an oogeecheel have on someone who was ill?" Kimmer asked.

"You mean Melion?" Dal asked.

"Exactly. You seemed to feel better when we were with them."

"I still had my aches, Kimmer," Dal said thoughtfully, "but it was easier for me to detach from the pain. But I had taken meds, which have the same effect. The oogeecheela might simply have intensified that sensation.

"Perhaps contact with Mel would be painful to them. Tavs say empathy is a knife sharpened on both sides. Healing empathic contact can be exceedingly draining for the empath, even dangerous. I don't want to expose the oogeecheela to that, not without their consent."

"There are times when we'd be in trouble if our senses were altered," Renzec cautioned.

"It's in their best interest for new contacts to love them on sight. I got the sense that the oogeecheela can modify their sensorial blanket, but I don't think it's in their nature to broadcast negativity. They'd feel it too. But it could be a powerful weapon.

"Say, Cren, speaking of feelings of well-being, this tea is great," Dal smiled. "I feel energized. What is it?"

Cren smiled smugly. "Even you would never guess. Leh worked magic on that yukky flower. Its nutrition was too good to pass up. She found a safe but volatile sulfur compound that can be driven off by heat."

"It's revitalizing and flavorful too," Kimmer commented, finishing her cup. "I can use this in my medical stores. I wonder what else this planet will hold? I better go check Mel," she said as she stood and stretched, checking the status board. "I had no idea it had gotten so late."

"You go, Kimmer," Rial said as he entered the cabin with Leh, "as long as you come right back. You," he said, pointing at Dal, "stay and fill me in on first contact."

"Isn't White Team supposed to be resting?" Dal said accusingly, as he made a show of checking his comm band.

"Tried it, Dal. Didn't work," Leh explained. "We wanted to hear your report."

Dal filled the others in while Cren prepared more tea. They had boiled a quantity of blossoms that afternoon, and Leh regaled them with her adventure trying to mitigate the smell. But the oogeecheela kept creeping back into their minds and conversation.

"So you're not actually talking with them, then," Leh said.

"No, but we're communicating, Leh. Maybe they aren't as highly evolved as we are," Dal mused. "I can't be sure."

"I wonder if they feel that way about us," Leh laughed. She turned to Cren. "You be on your best behavior with them."

Cren grinned. "Don't worry, Leh," he assured her. I've been taking lessons from him," he said, jerking his thumb at Renzec."

A look of exaggerated alarm flashed across Leh's features. "Great Guardian of the Universe, preserve us all!" she cried.

Renzec threw a console cushion at Leh, who ducked, caught it, and deftly threw it back. Soon the cabin filled with storm of flying cushions and the thunder of hearty laughter.

Finally, Dal put his arms up and commanded, "Truce!"

Renzec couldn't resist throwing one last cushion at Cren's unprotected back. Cren swore, held up a cushion, and promised, "I owe you one." Then he plunked on a pile of cushions with a sigh of contentment.

Kimmer returned to the cabin and nodded her approval at the disheveled state of affairs. The crew had been overdue for a healthy letting off of steam. "What's in this tea, anyway?" she joked.

"I checked it for psychoactive substances, Kimmer," Leh replied seriously. "It's safe. Honest. How's Mel?"

"The same," Kimmer replied. "Everything's quiet."

The comm alert 'pinged' to give lie to her words. Chief Rial dropped his jovial expression along with the cushion he'd been using as a shield. With a quick glance around to his crew, he opened the comm link.

"This is Chief Rial Jennery, speaking from the planet Kellierin. Identify yourself, please."

"Norian Killain Duvou, in the ship, 'Guardian's Reprieve', in orbit around the planet Kellierin," the message crackled.

"Commander, we are experiencing heavy interference on the comm," Rial said. He loosened the high collar of his black uniform, and leaned closer to the comm, aware that he was setting the scene for future relations between the two parties.

"Don't doubt it. You got a lot of junk in the atmosphere. Where're you out of, Jennery?" Through the static, Rial detected the guarded note in the voice.

"HomePort, Survey Service, Metrowyl," Rial said, and quickly added, "We don't dock often, Duvou, and don't dawdle when we do." He gave a little, going along with her choice of folksy tone, but wouldn't use her title if she didn't reciprocate.

"Wise choice," the voice said tersely.

"Guardian knows," Rial replied. "What's up back home?"

"Lots." The Coordinator cleared her throat, but no more words were forthcoming.

Rial raised his eyebrows and shut off the transmit. "Dal, are you sensing any emotions in her voïce?"

"Wariness," Dal said.

"Thanks for the news," Rial muttered, and reopened the channel.

"Feel free to scan the shelters we've built," Rial offered. "Everything we've discovered is positive for colonization."

"Settling."

Rial narrowed his eyes in confusion. "We're glad you find that information comforting," he continued in even tones. "We've had a major breakthrough in shelter production today, and we look forward to sharing your input on colonizing."

"*Settling!*" the voice repeated stridently. "'Guardian's Reprieve' is *not*, I repeat *not*, a colony ship. *We're settlers!*"

The Chief paused as Dal moved quickly to his side. Rial looked up to see pain on the empath's face. Dal waved him to continue, and turned away.

"Well, "settling", then," Rial countered, confused at Dal's distress. He tried to catch the attention of his empath, but Kimmer was ministering to him and blocking his view. Something was up. Meanwhile, Rial had other pressing business. "Tomorrow we'll clear space for your ship," he said, trying to put a positive spin on the degrading conversation.

"You want to clear, clear! Don't let me stop you. But clear for shelters. We'll need 'em. 'Guardian's Reprieve' stays-in-orbit. We're *not* bringing her down. Maybe not *ever*."

Rial leaned back and closed transmit. Oops. Now he was in for it. He could hear someone behind give a low whistle. Renzec, probably. He opened the comm, but hesitated when he felt a light touch on his shoulder. Rial jerked his head suggestively to the link panel, but Dal refused the comm. Dal held his forefingers wide apart, pointed to Rial and then spaceward, and then brought his fingers together.

Rial nodded, and leaned into the comm again.

"Perhaps it would be better if we met face to face. The static is worsening," Rial dissembled. "We have no awareness of your present status. We know of the disasters that hit your col . . . ah, settlement."

"*That was* a colony," Duvou corrected.

Rial shook his head in confusion, and then stopped abruptly as it started to throb. He looked toward Dal for support. Pain swept across the empath's face, and his eyes closed, but still he said nothing. "We could send up a 'hopper for you," Rial offered. He was finding it difficult to keep up his side of the conversation, with so much of it going on above his head in many ways.

"Send it up. You be on it. We talk *here*," the voice ordered.

"We'd be able to provide more comfortable surroundings," Rial suggested. "You could take a look around the area."

"No doubt. We'll meet here."

"When would you like us to arrive?" Rial said, trying not to grit his teeth.

"As soon as possible." If there was any more of the message, interference crackled over it.

"Early tomorrow our time, then," Rial said agreeably. Dal put an unsteady hand on his Chief's wrist, and indicated he wanted the comm. The Chief couldn't remember when he had seen his empath so shaken.

Dal leaned over so that his face was close to the comm link. "Coordinator Duvou, this is Dalrion Darnel, second in command. Do you require medical assistance?"

"We require just about everything," the voice replied, "but we have no medical emergencies. None you could fix. You a medic?"

Dal noted her caveat. "No, an empath. We do have a medic here."

"We'll need both, eventually. Thanks for asking." The gruff tone didn't mellow.

"Coordinator, what is the status on Metrowyl?" Dal asked. "We heard from a Survey ship that war was declared. A Survey Ship with a *Tav* Chief," he added suggestively.

"That'd be Koof," the Coordinator said. "I know 'em."

"What's happening on HomePort?"

"Nothing now, son. Nothing at all. HomePort's blasted. So's the whole planet. Damn fools." The voice dripped with bitterness. "I don't have to spell it out. You know."

Dal drew his breath in sharply. "Yes. You told us. You're *settlers*."

"Smart boy," the Coordinator said wearily. "Metrowyl must of

sent all her brains to space. No Metrowyl, no colony. Maybe somebody survived underground, I don't know. The surface is dead."

"I needed to hear you say it," Dal said softly.

"Rial, you there?"

"Here, Coordinator," Rial replied in a strained voice.

"Bring that empath along, here?"

"Agreed."

Duvou broke contact. Rial stared blankly at the comm. Finally he
raised his eyes, to find Dal comforting a sobbing Kimmer. Renzec
stared, glassy eyed, looking at nothing in particular. Leh was sitting
still, with her eyes closed. Tears fell silently, leaving glistening paths
down her smooth cheeks. She gripped Cren's hand hard as he
kneeled on one knee next to her, and she patted his back unconsciously. Cren looked lost.

"People," Rial's voice snapped through the shock, "let's not imagine scenarios. Metrowyl could have been evacuated. We have no
way of knowing."

Dal walked over to stand next to Rial, and paused as the crew absorbed the hope in the Chief's words. He wore a new air of command that was palpable, and he drew their total attention.

"Our *immediate* challenge is to build a settlement and help these
people. *That* is our prime focus. We have *no* time and *no* energy to
waste on things we can't change. We're scrapping the duty regimen.
I want everyone up and going at full speed, first light or before. The
Chief and I will meet with the Coordinator on the 'Reprieve'. The
rest of you prepare accommodations for the refugees. Use time and
energy wisely. Be alert for the oogeecheela. We need them. Pray
that Koof gets here with his charges as soon as possible. He may
have more information, as well."

"That's right," Chief Rial agreed as he took the medication Kimmer dispensed. "I'm tempted to take the whole ship up instead of
the just the 'hopper. Bring back able bodied workers."

Dal looked grim. "We'll be less intimidating in the hopper."

Chief Rial clapped Dal on the shoulder, mostly because he felt
the need to touch another human being. He smiled ruefully. "Son,

I don't think we have to worry about intimidating *her*. But that's a good point. She specifically asked for you. *Your* job will be to persuade *her* to work with all of *us*, especially *me*. I don't know how we can do this otherwise."

Dal and Rial blocked out their plans and set all stations on automatic, with protective fields on full. It would be a long night, with a longer day to come.

Chapter

20

Rial adjusted the focus on the view screen. "Looks like a bullet," he remarked.

Dal shook his head. "Bad imagery," was his only comment as he modified their trajectory to intersect "Guardian's Reprieve".

"What's 'abullet'? Cren asked.

Dal laughed, finally breaking his melancholy mood. He had been gloomy because Kimmer declined to come along.

"It's a type of primitive projectile ammunition, Cren, used in hand-carried weaponry. It's not 'abullet'," Rial explained. " 'Bullet' is what they called each piece of ammunition. I saw a real bullet once, on Kalerian IV. Bullets could be many shapes, but the type I saw was like that ship out there. A squat, smooth cylinder. One end pointed, the other blunt. The Kalerians shot their bullets out of long tubes. They used small explosions at the near end to supply the force to do that. They killed people with them."

"Barbaric," Dal commented as he flipped on the automatic blinker to notify the "Reprieve" of their approach.

"Undoubtedly barbaric," Rial agreed, "but effective as well. Dal, once the "Reprieve" acknowledges, Let's skim the hull for an overview of their outer damage before we dock."

The "Reprieve" did not acknowledge until Dal had jockeyed the small craft into matching orbit. By then, the refugee ship had lost

all resemblance to a bullet. Projecting remnants of broken anten-
nae and assorted unidentifiables protruded from the patched hull.
Its stern was marred by an enormous dent, as though some inter-
galactic giant had connected with a mighty kick to punt it into space.

"By my grandmother's cross-eyed yorbu," Chief Rial whispered,
"I can't believe this heap made it out here."

Dal agreed. "I stand in awe of people who'd risk their lives
through Matrix transition with this . . . this . . . *this*! Words fail me.
There's got to be a world of pain on that ship. I feel anxiety, but not
a lot else, and I don't know why."

"You should have asked Kimmer about that," Cren suggested,
and a shadow crossed Dal's face.

"All things happen for the best," Dal replied evenly. Keep in
mind, this ship *has* saved their lives," he warned. "Let's avoid refer-
ences to its failings, when possible."

"Good idea, Dal. Still, the appearance of this ship makes me reassess what these people were fleeing from, as well as the state of
their resources," Rial mused.

"Chief," Cren asked tentatively, "does the captain of a space vessel have command authority once that vessel has landed?"

"The captain, no," Rial said carefully. "But the Coordinator of a
colony, or a settlement, does. A captain has no power on the ground.
Unless that captain happens to be the Chief in command of a Survey scout, and the planet has not been cleared by a SiTeam."

"In which case," Dal added, "the captain's word is law for his crew.
Once the colony has been granted clearance, which this one hasn't,
that word must still be taken under careful advisement by the colony
leaders in matters regarding exploration of the planet."

"For how long?" Cren asked, regarding Rial with new eyes.

"As long as the Survey Chief stays on planet," Rial answered. "In
cases where a Survey team stays until a SiTeam comes on site, the
Survey Chief is in charge until he or she leaves, and directs SiTeam
deployment as well as the Survey crew.

"Survey has been called in to do recon, or to open up new areas
for an established colony. It's rare, but it's happened. In such a case,
the colony leader is in charge of the colony, and the Chief runs the

Survey crew and any colonist or SiTeam member involved in the operation. In *no* case does the civilian command take precedence over
the Survey commander," Dal explained.

Cren nodded at the ship filling the view screen. "Does *she* know
that?" he asked.

"If she doesn't, she will," Rial said grimly. "Remember, this is a
diplomatic mission. Keep a *firm hold* of your temper," Rial ordered.

"I will, Chief," Cren promised solemnly.

"I know, son," Chief Rial confessed, "I was speaking to myself."

Dal shook his head, but kept his peace.

The docking bay was worn, but in good repair, and their docking
was uneventful. Rial kept a close eye on Dal as they closed the hatch
and waited. No visible signs of distress.

The airlock interior was not up to standards. Stained and discol-
ored gasketing showed no obvious cracks or bulges, but portions
were decidedly thin. With some misgivings, they watched their ship
vanish from sight as the iris of the docking bay closed.

The soft wushing of in-rushing air commenced. Immediately,
Dal cried out. So great was the intensity of his pain he couldn't
block the rebound, and the others were caught up in a wave of
empathic outwash. Stunned, they watched helplessly as Dal
clutched his helmeted head. The movement sent him tumbling.
He struggled to erect defenses against the onslaught, and at the
same time tried to block the spill-over hitting his companions. He
had succeeded at the latter when empathic jaws clamped his gut
and started them churning. At the same time, a sense of overwhelming helplessness disoriented him. He would have fallen, had
they not been in null-grav.

"Dal," Rial commed as he desperately clutched the empath's flail-
ing arm, "what's happening?"

Dal moaned and clung to Rial as best he could, trying to stabilize
body and mind. Clammy chills shivered up his spine, and waves of
nausea shook him. "It's not me," he gasped. "It's these people. Their
desperation. The pain." His compassion began to overcome the misery, and his eyes filled with tears.

"We've got to get him out of here!" Cren cried with alarm. He began to search frantically for a way beck to the ship.

"No," Dal insisted. His voice was strained, but firm. "We stay. These people live with this grief and pain constantly. *They're* the ones we have to get out of here. I can handle it for a little while."

Rial looked doubtful, but motioned to Cren. Wordlessly, they positioned themselves on either side of their comrade. The overhead light turned green, indicating breathable air. Metal surfaces complained as the heavy doors struggled open to reveal another worn hatch. Rial and Cren helped Dal with his helmet, and then cracked their own. A squalid stench assaulted them, and their eyes teared.

"Agh! Even yorbu was better than this," Cren cried.

Through a haze of pain, Dal muttered a warning at Cren, and looked in the direction of the monitors. Cren cast down his eyes. "Sorry," he whispered, and hushed.

The hatch door opened, revealing a small, barren room. Dim corridors branched out in all directions, save for that of the outer hull. A small women in a rumpled beige jumpsuit glided in. Coasting behind her was a large, shaggy Tav. Except for black legs and tail, his short fur was predominantly grey. His bearing was poised, but the relative size of his large black paws and long legs indicated that he was young. A wide black line wandered along the edge of both ears, sweeping down and over the ridges above bright emerald eyes. The lines joined at the center of his chiseled triangular face, and blended toward a rich, black muzzle. The effect was striking and handsome.

"Welcome to our ship, such as it is," the woman said with a smile. Her voice suggested less age than her lined face. "My name is Tisa," she added, "aide to Coordinator Duvou, although we don't go much for titles. This is Eyth," she said, indicating the Tav.

The Tav blinked huge eyes and yawned politely, showing a vast cavern of red, rimmed by sharp, gleaming white teeth. His mouth closed with a snap, and he cocked his head to study them, one by one. He then focused intently on Dal, eyes brimming with compassion. "I am pleased too meet youu," he said formally. "I believe youu know my fatherr, Awrr'Koof." He then turned and kicked off, gliding over to a nearby padded bulkhead. There, he dug in his large hind paws, expressing long, razor-sharp claws. He pushed off, propelling himself rapidly down the corridor. "Follow, please," he called over his shoulder.

"Our Coordinator awaits in the meeting room," Tisa said with a weary smile. Then she glanced toward the bulkhead, and shook her head ruefully at the long, scored claw marks on the surface. "He's new here," she explained.

"Excuse me," Rial said, "our empath is unwell. Your Coordinator requested his presence, but emanations from this ship are causing. . . ."

"We know, and we apologize," Tisa said somberly. "It's necessary for a brief time. Follow us, please. It's not far." She kicked up to a row of hand-holds. "We unclawed types propel ourselves along with these. As you must have guessed, we have no working grav on this ship, and haven't for some time." She demonstrated, moving with agility along the narrow corridor.

They followed, Rial first. Then came Dal, moving slower, hampered by the emotional torrent bombarding him. Cren brought up the rear.

At the end of the curving corridor, Eyth waited for them by the door of an old-fashioned lift. Tisa reached for the controls, but Eyth stayed her hand with an oval paw, graceful for its size.

"Wait. Therre is something I *will* doo firrst," he said. Eyth turned his attention on Dal, regarding him thoughtfully.

"But the Coordinator. . . ." Tisa protested. Eyth lifted his paw inches before her face and expressed his impressive claws to their full extension. The emerald eyes regarded Tisa thoughtfully. As she nodded, the Tav retracted his claws and turned to Dal.

Dal immediately felt a gentle, soothing, inquiring mind touch. He peered at the young Tav through half-closed eyes. His pounding head had lost its powers of concentration, and it was becoming increasingly hard not to lose his breakfast as well.

Eyth nodded gravely, and extended just one claw, with which he pressed the panel, and the lift doors opened. "The ship is causing yourr prroblem," he diagnosed. "Something else as well?"

"I've just emerged from the Season of Change. Are you familiar with it?" Dal asked in a strained voice as he entered the lift and grabbed a hand hold. He looked at the big furry face so close to his own. Eyth was radiating sympathy. Dal's fogged mind remembered. *Eyth must feel this emotional onslaught too!*

"Youu cannot rride the lift like this," Eyth said earnestly, placing his paw, claws in, on Dal's arm. "If youu will allow me too help?"

"Anything," Dal pleaded.

Eyth placed his other paw on the center of Dal's brow. Instantly, relief washed over Dal like cooling water pouring on his brain cells. But there was no thought transference. None.

"Eyth," he cried out, "that's marvelous! I am still aware of the refugees' emotions, but I don't *feel* them any more. Whatever you did, thank you! Thank you, my friend."

Tisa frowned.

Eyth's claw hooked out, leaving a stab wound on the lift control, and the mechanism engaged. "I took the liberty, while I was therre, too moderrate yourr pain arreas as well," the Tav admitted gravely. "It is just temporrarry. Until youu can modify yourr electrromagnetic patterrns."

"I don't know how," Dal admitted. "I'm just learning."

"Whoo is yourr teacherr?"

"I have no teacher. I have had no acceptable choice, Eyth."

"Maybe naow youu doo." The Tav retracted his black lips somewhat, revealing fang tips in one form of Tavian smile.

"I'd be happy for anything you can teach me," Dal said earnestly.

Eyth huffed a laugh. "Therre arre betterr teacherrs."

Dal shook his head. "I don't know them. I haven't felt this good since I held the oogeecheela."

"Oogeecheela?" Eyth and Tisa asked at once.

"An empathic life form we found on Kellierin," Chief Rial answered. "Dal and our medic found them, that is. No one else has met them. If *you* want to meet them, we'd better get to the Coordinator. We're keeping her waiting," he reminded them.

"She's expecting delay," Tisa said cryptically.

"Speaking of which," Dal asked Eyth as the slow lift chugged to life, "why haven't you relieved the refugee's burden, like you did mine?"

The Tav looked crestfallen. "But my frriend," he said sadly, "I have! That is one reason why Tavs arre herre. We arre few, but the ship morale is much imprroved. Youu could not have surrvived it beforre. You arre morre sensitive than even I, and youu arre without filterrs!"

While that statement registered, the lift stopped. Eyth turned to Cren. "Please forrgive me, Crrensed. I am sorrry I can doo nothing about the offensive smell," he said.

Tisa groaned. Cren tried vainly to melt into the wall.

"I should *not* have said this?" Eyth asked Tisa.

"Probably not, Eyth," she said patiently.

"But the smell *is* bad, Tisa! Even my furr tastes awful when I grroom. They arre guests. It distrresses. Shouldn't I. . . ."

"It isn't something we discuss in polite company."

"I see naow why youu humans have so many prroblems," Eyth nodded sagely.

Tisa rolled her eyes. She turned to the others as she pressed the door panel. "I'm sorry about it, too," she apologized to the Survey crew under her breath.

"I imagine you get use to it," Cren said gallantly as the lift shuddered to a halt.

"No," Tisa replied shortly as she turned her attention to the door panel, which was refusing to function. "Excuse me." She pulled a short-handled mallet from her belt. She rapped the offending button sharply with the mallet. Rial and Dal grimaced. But she was rewarded by an answering scrape of machinery. The lift door slid aside. They had not quite come to the desired floor, but in null-grav, that caused no hardship. It did, however, add another piece to the puzzle that was the "Reprieve".

"Things falling apart, huh?" Cren asked, oblivious to the reproving looks from his shipmates.

"I believe, 'have fallen', is the prroperr tense," Eyth corrected.

Tisa rolled her eyes again, and then gave up. "Ain't it the truth," she muttered under her breath.

She led them out of the lift and down a short length of badly lit corridor, where she pressed a panel adjacent to a large set of double doors. A comm link activated. "We're here," she announced.

"What you waiting for, then. Get on in here," a familiar, gruff voice ordered.

Tisa put her thumb in a depressed area of the panel, and the doors opened. She ushered them into a narrow, bleak room, nearly devoid of furniture. At the end of the room hung a small view screen, displaying the planet below. Beside this floated a frail, diminutive old women. Only the firm jut of her jaw gave some hint to the iron will behind the watery eyes. She displayed no badge of rank, but then, she had no need. The otherwise barren room was replete with her presence.

"You know who I am, and I know who you are," she snapped. "By now, you know we need this planet bad. So we'll dispense with small talk. We're dying up here. We need to go down. And we need to go *now!*"

Chapter
21

Duvou stabbed a gnarled finger at the group hovering in the door-way. "You!" she barked. "Don't hang! Get over here, and make it snappy! You're wasting time, and we don't have any to spare." The Coordinator had stabilized herself by hooking a foot on the bracket at the far end of the grey room. Beneath and to her right stood an ancient computer console. The rest of the room had been stripped.

Rial bit his tongue and worked his way along strategically placed brackets, as his mind interpreted incoming data. The center "floor" showed remnants of pedestals for a sizable table and chairs. Bases for dias and podium stood uselessly under the Coordinator's hover-ing form.

The Chief began, "I'm. . . ."

"Yes, I know! You're in black. Guardian! You think I'm blind! You're," she narrowed shrewd eyes on Dal, "the empath!"

Dal clung to a bracket and said simply, "Yes."

"Good," she approved. Then she looked accusingly at Eyth. "You relieved him."

"The point had been made, Madame Coorrdinatorr," Eyth said, blinking his slitted eyes calmly as he remained by the entry with Tisa.

Rial frowned. "You specifically asked for our empath, knowing the pain it would cause?"

" 'Course I knew!" Duvou sighed tiredly. She turned to Dal. "*You* understand?"

Dal regarded her thoughtfully. "I concede your point."

"Aha!" The Coordinator then glared at Cren. "*You*, I *don't* know."

"Crensed Jorien, Ma'am," Cren said briefly.

Duvou's head snapped up so sharply she began to drift. Once more, her practiced foot hooked on a bracket to check her glide, as her eyes blazed at Cren from a nest of wrinkles. "You're not kin to that land-seizing, money-clutching power broker Jorien, are you? Never mind," she said abruptly, cutting off Cren's reply before his mouth opened fully. "You are," she continued. "Look like him, you do. Well, that's the way the tayelo plops."

Duvou turned on Chief Rial. "Enough chit chat. Start moving us down. Now." she demanded.

Rial was taken aback, but he made a quick recovery. "We can do that only if you let us use this ship. If not, you'll have to reconsider. Although, I must admit, seeing its condition. . . ."

"Never happen," Duvou said shortly, jabbing one thin arm at him. She shook her finger like a nanny scolding a toddler. "Let me make this plain. My people were all for taking her down to that Guardian-forsaken hell-hole we got stuck with last time. The planet that *your* Survey Service said was just *great* for a colony. 'Save time', they said. 'We need the materials', they said."

"I had none of it then. I'm having none of it now. *This ship stays in orbit* until I say otherwise."

"Coordinator Duvou," Rial explained patiently, "our ship is not a passenger ferry, and. . . ."

"Jennery, you seem like a person endowed with at least a modicum of common sense," the Coordinator purred like a Tav. Then she shouted, "*Please-grant-me-that-same-allotment!*" Each word was emphasized with that jabbing finger. The Chief opened his mouth to reply, but she cut him off.

"We named this ship "Guardian's Reprieve". Took the idea from Tavs, naming things. She may look like scrap to you, but she is our salvation.

"We were damned surprised when Koof showed up. An answered

prayer, if ever there was. Nevermore complain about fur in the food, I swear. Anywhile, Koof told us to wait where we were. That he'd be back with help. Where we were was *lost,* by the way. In the nebula. If it weren't for Eyth, bless his black lined ears, we'd never have made it." Her expression mellowed. "Eyth got us through the nebula.

"Anyway, when Queen K, Guardian's angel as she is, gave us the go-ahead, we hopped. Actually, she had already promised us the next habitable planet."

"You got official . . . ?"

"She *told* us. We're *here.* That's official as you get."

"And what . . . ?" Rial began. Dal could feel the Chief's frustration build like magma in a volcano.

"Later," Duvou said briskly, dismissing Rial's question with a wave. "I need my people down. Now. How you going to do it?"

Rial bit back his desire to tell her exactly what he'd like to do. "Do you have any functioning scouts, or tenders that . . . ?"

"We got three tenders. They can hold forty adults per trip, if you supply pilots. Don't have much fuel. Don't want to bring the "Reprieve" closer with them radiation belts."

"Coordinator Duvou, could you tell us where Queen Kelli . . . ?"

"Later. Right now I want. . . ."

"*Qui-et!*" Rial bellowed in his best command voice. Silence spread out, save for the echo rebounding off the bulkheads.

"I've had *enough,* Madame! You *shall* quit interrupting me!" he ordered. "Furthermore, you *shall* listen to what I say."

"*You* listen, Jennery!" Duvou screamed back as she leaned into the fight. "While you've been hopping 'round in your sleek ship, and sitting on your rump on that fat, green world, we've been stuck on this malfunctioning bin of reeking humanity!" Her eyes narrowed even further, and she pointed her finger at him, holding her position with the other hand.

"Do you have *any idea,*" she ranted, "what it's *like* to be stuck with screaming babies in null-grav? Hundreds, with hardly any functioning adults to give even minimal care?" she cried. "I sometimes wonder how many ends each child has! Surely, you've noticed the fragrant air, flavored liberally with baby barf. Poo, too, but at least we can wrap that end so its product doesn't fly across the cabin." Her voice cracked with the strain, and suddenly she ran out of fuel. Her eyes watered as she stared at Rial. Then she added softly, "I can't endure any more. None of us can," she sighed.

Rial allowed his eyes to soften a little. "Madame Coordinator," he said gently, "I understand your frustration. The dread of being surrounded by demanding infants is one of the reasons I signed with Survey. And look what happened! They caught up with me halfway across the galaxy." His eyes twinkled, and he caught a gleam of humor in the old lady's face.

"I know you have troubles. I still haven't grasped their magnitude. But communication must go at least two ways. I intend to be part of the solution, not part of the problem. With respect, I ask that you do the same."

Duvou took her time, reevaluating the Survey Chief. As she did so, her countenance changed.

Rial acknowledged this by allowing his smile to widen. Duvou relaxed visibly, and met it with one of her own. Her smile kept on growing. She started to chuckle softly, and then to cackle, holding her sides with one arm as she struggled to keep her hold on the bracket with the other.

Tisa and Eyth witnessed the metamorphosis with amazement; Dal and Cren, with considerable relief. The generals had called a truce. When the laughter subsided, Rial asked gently, "Got it all out of your system?"

The old lady sighed weakly, wiping her eyes. "You beat all. I tell you," she gasped. "I been afraid to let go, even once." Then she sighed and grew deadly serious again. "But Rial, my babies *are sick!* The medics think extended null-grav after the evacuation is the cause. We lack care givers. Our replicators are minimal. Our nutrition is abominable. We *have* to get down."

Curiosity got the better of Dal. "How did this happen? Why so many babies?"

"You're Survey, not Colony." She favored Dal with a week smile. "Colonies, and settlements, breed. Our priority is to survive. We do that by building up the colony. Development is window dressing. People! That's what takes time to build. We need lots of kids. When the worms hit, the parents were outside working. Older kids were outside, too." Her eyes were lost for a moment, remembering. Then she straightened her shoulders and sloughed off the past, shaking her head.

"Outside! I *need* outside. Guardian's truth, I can't abide this stench. Our air purification system doesn't work well. Our mechanics know farm equipment. Not the same."

"Granted," Rial allowed. He grinned. "My grandmother's cross-eyed yorbu smelled better than this."

Cren rolled his eyes.

Duvou snapped to attention. "You have yorbot down there?" she said with incredulity.

"No," Rial admitted.

Duvou's face fell.

"But Koof has one on his craft," Cren interjected.

"Damn!" Duvou grinned. "He said nothing, the old kroypol!" Her lined face softened. "I had a yorbu once," she said wistfully.

"Figures," Cren muttered. Dal surreptitiously poked him in the ribs.

"I still miss the beastie," the Coordinator mused. "Nasty wretch, that. But it loved me." Then her face hardened. "It died on *Tagur*," she said, slowly emphasizing the hated name. "We don't allow that name spoken on this ship," she warned. "Except as a curse."

"Understandable," Rial agreed. "Can you commence farming as soon as you're down planet? It's spring at the site."

"Pretty much so. We salvaged most of our equipment. We've repaired it while we waited."

"Seeds?" Dal asked.

"Seeds we got," Duvou acknowledged. "Kept a store on board. No stock, but we have embryos. We'll keep half up here for a while, as insurance. Like we did before."

"Marvelous," Rial beamed. "Seeds and embryos don't function the same once replicated. We've found food sources on Kellierin, but best to get farming underway as soon as possible. We can squeeze ten adults in our ship. I strongly suggest you come down as well. You need to see what's available on Kellierin."

The old lady nodded and grinned. "Guardian's favor, but I'd give anything to get off this tub. We all would." She gave herself a shove towards the computer console, made contact, and punched up a roster. She frowned.

"You could take adults down on your tenders," Rial suggested.

"*Babies* go in the tenders. *Right away!*" Duvou insisted. She pointed to Dal. "Tell him."

"That's out of the. . . ." Rial began, when he was interrupted, and not by the Coordinator this time.

"Chief, she's right. The babies have to come down," Dal insisted.

Duvou smiled smugly.

"Why?"

"The youngest are desperately sick, and rapidly getting worse. They're not absorbing nutrition. Gravity may help. There are a *lot* of infants, Chief."

Rial looked at Duvou suspiciously. "How many? I was told you had a thousand people on this ship, total."

"Tisa, get a breakdown of ship's complement, by age."

Tisa launched herself over to the computer console, grabbed its edge and swung her lithe body around to face the panels. She entered the request manually.

"We heard about the windworms and whip snakes," Dal said, "but what caused your hull damage? It looks like it's been through a war."

Tisa looked up. "You don't know about the meteors?"

Duvou looked grim. "Fill them in, Tisa. I don't want to be complaining all the while. You complain for a bit."

Tisa set her lips in a thin line as she retrieved hard copy from the console and handed it to Duvou. "They hit as we were evacuating the last of the colony. The ground shook. I was with the last contingent on the planet when the first wave fell. The survivors took off for the 'Reprieve'. A second wave hit before we reached the ship. We had six tenders before, you see." Tisa's face aged with the telling.

"We were *lucky* when the meteors hit," Duvou said sarcastically. "They traveled with a comet. A *big* comet. It missed the planet, and us. The ship was in none too great shape to begin with, you understand," the Coordinator apologized. "That's what happened to my conference table, and lots of other things besides. They're shoring up hull plating.

"Then came Metrowyl. Wouldn't even let us dock. The kids got sick. Then the war. Don't even know who fired first. We took off. So did anybody else who could."

She looked at the report in her hand. "We have 943 people left. 476 are children between six months and three years old. Most of these are sick. All we've been doing is feed one end and clean the other. The adults have been spending their waking hours trying to fix things, if they're able. Most aren't.

"Here," she said, thrusting the readout into Chief Rial's hand. There are only twenty children between the ages of twelve and sixteen. They were going through Change when the windworms fell. They were inside. 82 of us are over 65."

"Some of these are infirm?" Dal questioned.

'All of these are infirm, in one way or another," Duvou admitted. "Don't let these statistics lead you to believe we have over 300 able-bodied. Not so. Some are kids over three, but they're doing ok. There were some folk had indoor jobs. They were spared the worms. Most of those had allergies to something on that place. Never did find out just what. And there's those with post-trauma shock. We have special quarters for them. They can't abide open spaces. Afraid something's going to drop on them and kill them. Then there are those who lost limbs. . . . You get the idea?"

Rial nodded, and his face grew somber. "How about a compromise? We'll take five tenders of the sickest children now, plus one complement of adults of your own choosing. That last must land first, to be caretakers for the kids. We'll need what medics you can spare."

Coordinator Duvou ruminated on that for a moment. "That would take the pressure off. Whoever remained would see that things are moving. I agree, with one addition."

"That being?"

"Send a tender back with an engineer to fix some of the problems we can't fix ourselves. That would be a moral booster to those who stay."

"I have just the person," Rial smiled. "I need to comm the camp. Get them thinking of the best way to accommodate your needs. Meanwhile, Dal and Cren can see something of your situation first hand."

"Agreed, Rial. I'll take you to the bridge. Eyth, lad, show young Jorien the tenders. Tisa, you take our empath to the Baby Chamber. And Calista's Room. Eyth, he going to be ok without you?"

"He will be as any would at the sight." The Tav cocked his head at Dal and regarded him seriously. "Think on me," he advised, "if youu experrience difficulties. Humanoid infants arre not at all like Tav kits. Kits smell warrm and arre soft and clean. Human kits arre. . . ."

"Eyth," Tisa warned.

The Tav huffed, and his eyebrows raised. He cocked his head at Cren, and Cren grinned. "I know *exactly* what you mean, Eyth," Cren whispered conspiratorially. "Let's take on the machines."

Tisa glanced encouragingly at Dal as she pressed the panel opening the way to the corridor. "Keep close. It's easy to get lost at the intersects."

"I'm amazed the corridors are so empty," Dal observed as they traveled quickly down the tube. "Considering the number of people on this vessel, it seems odd."

"Corridors are off limits to all but necessary personnel most hours," Tisa acknowledged. "Almost everybody who is able is working, or asleep."

"Have you been with the Coordinator long?"

"Since Metrowyl. *Before* the colony," Tisa said. "We would do anything for her. We'd. . . . I don't know how to put it."

"Follow her through hell?"

"We already did," she grimaced. She halted at a large door. "This is the 'Baby Chamber'. The kiddies up to fourteen months are in here. Let me know if it gives you problems, and we'll leave. I don't understand this empathy thing. I always thought it was an advantage." She pressed the door.

"It has it's moments," Dal agreed as he followed her through. He winced. "This, however, isn't one of them."

The stench inside was overpowering. Interior bulkheads had been removed to create a vast, cylindrical cavern. The outer bulkheads had been padded with soft, waterproof material. The inner layer was human. Babies were secured with strap restraints in pockets in the padding. Some had pacifiers and were sucking listlessly. Most just hung silent, pitifully waiting for deliverance.

There were a few enclosed areas off to the "sides". An elderly woman was exiting from one with a tiny bundle under her arm.

"Hi, Teese," she hollered, without pausing in her flight. One of the other attendants approached the visitors.

"Kreen," Tisa introduced, "this is Dal. He's from the Kellierin Survey crew."

"Good to greet you, Dal," Kreen smiled appreciatively. "Hope there are more like you below," she winked. "Had to come over. Can't believe I'm actually seeing a new face! Guess you understand."

"I'm learning," Dal said.

"Can't wait to see Kellierin! Have to go back now. Get us down *soon*, please," she pleaded as she turned and kicked off to check an infant that had started to fuss. Dal was startled. Her right arm ended slightly below the elbow.

Tisa noticed his attention shift, and explained in a whisper, "Kreen was outside toward the end of worm fall. Her hands weren't covered. Our medics could only save one."

"I'm surprised she's so cheerful. She's good maneuvering in null-grav, too. I would have thought the loss of a hand would throw off her balance.

"She learned it the hard way, the way they all did. Bouncing off walls," Tisa explained. She sighed deeply and lowered her voice even more, leaning very close to Dal. "Kreen's cheerful because she's tranked to the eyebrows. Most of the amputees are, although we use a lot less meds now that Eyth is here. Guardian knows, we could use a lot more Tavs.

"The babies wailed constantly at first. I thought they'd never stop. We couldn't sleep ourselves, with the horror of it all, and there was so much to do right after the tragedy. Patching the people. Patching the ship. We had no time for the kids. This area is soundproofed, but most of us couldn't rest for thinking of them. We knew they were still awake, screaming. Then, it was like they gave up." She looked forlorn. "The medics from the school say they may never come right. But they're better since Eyth worked with them."

"Medics? From the school?"

"Yes. Ours are dead. Koof brought us some. From 'Path of Light'. Queen K's ship. They won't find her," Tisa promised. "Not with Tavs along."

"You left-that planet-a while ago. Why are there so many infants?"

"A lot of the women survivors were pregnant. We lost a most of the moms. The babies often survived. They have gut cramps, because they have problems digesting concentrates.

"Those little rooms are where they're changed. They're fed in position. Concentrates and water. That's all we have left. When we still had formula, they started projectile vomiting that, so we switched to concentrates. You can't believe what happens with barf in null-grav!"

"I have some recent experience with that, actually."

"Oh? Anyway, the recyclers are in those rooms. We've kept up a supply of waterproofs." She sighed. "Believe me, it's a priority. Before food, even."

"I want to work with Eyth. With his guidance, maybe I can help the children."

"Do you like babies? Eyth says you have great empath potential. Even better than some Tavs. Says you can provide a 'different ingredient'."

"I don't know about that," Dal said sadly. "I'm not trained properly. I've just gotten over the Change."

"Out here?" Tisa said incredulously. "Alone?"

"Yes, out here. And no, not alone. Our crew is family. We've got another going through a Change Crisis right now."

"You must have had it rough, with your talents."

"It was bad for a while."

Tisa keyed open the door with her palm, and waited for Dal to exit. After they cleared the door, Tisa held it open for three children. They entered the room with a rush, acknowledging Tisa and Dal with barely a glance.

"It's important to remember, to be aware all the time, that our people are impaired." Tisa warned Dal once the door closed behind the youths. "Physically and, well, otherwise."

"Otherwise?" Dal asked, listening closely.

"You see the outer wounds, like the amputees. In some cases, though, the people most traumatized were the ones who were spared. There's a room for them. They're like the infants. They don't move. They don't talk."

"You seem to have survived intact, Tisa," Dal remarked as they paused before another large door.

Tisa rolled up one of her sleeves to the elbow. Long, runneling scars snaked their way up her slender arms. Deep, puckered holes remained where worms had been gauged out of her flesh. She met Dal's apologetic eyes without flinching. "I was wearing gloves, Dal. And a hat. Outside. My hands look fine. Remember! The pain runs deep. But you're an empath, right?" Then she rolled down her sleeve, and wordlessly opened the door.

Chapter

22

"How come you're at the comm, Renzec?"

"Happened to be in the ship getting food, Chief. Kimmer asked me to spell her while she checked Mel."

"How's Mel?"

"Coming out already. Kimmer can't figure it."

"We mustn't refuse a friendly murdle. Give thanks for our blessings and continue on. Her expertise in geology will come in handy."

"True, Chief," Renzec said, puzzled. Chief Rial was not one for small talk comming from a ship.

"Better get building, son. Get me Leh or Kimmer, please."

"Right, Chief."

While Rial waited, Cren and Eyth came onto the bridge. Cren looked excited as he maneuvered over to Rial. "Chief, are you ready for this? The tenders are fitted with floor padding. If they bundle the babies and strap 'em in, they can fit eighty tots per trip."

"Eighty! She said forty!"

"That was adults." Eyth clarified. "These arre babies. Babies arre smallerr."

Rial brought his hand up to support his pounding head. "Continue," he moaned to Cren.

"It's amazing" Cren exclaimed. "By the time Eyth and I left the tender area, they were starting to load infants. These people know how to move!"

Rial's lips thinned, and he bit back an expletive.

"Don't worry, sir," Cren finished. "They've pre-packed the kids' needs. Already on the tender." Cren hesitated. "There *is* a problem."

Rial sighed deeply. "Yes, Cren. I know. I'm in null-grav without a table."

"Table, sir?" Cren looked dumbfounded.

"Yes, Cren. So I could rest my head on it and weep. Never mind," Rial amended stoically as he saw Cren's confusion. "Tell me the problem."

"They need pilots for the tenders."

"I would be glad to rrun as many trrips on a tenderr as needful," Eyth volunteered.

"Good man, er, ah, thank you, Eyth," Rial said. "We may need your empathic skills more than your piloting ones, though, once the first load lands. The children will be stressed, first with the trip down, and then the shock of gravity after so long."

The Tav looked pleased. "Underrstood, Chief Rrial. Feel frree too utilize my talents as youu see fit."

The comm sputtered, then came to life. "Chief Rial, are you there?"

"Here, Leh. Kimmer with you?"

"Standing by, Chief," the medic's voice answered.

"Renzec there?"

"No sir," Kimmer answered, puzzled. "He told me to get the comm. He went back to tun. . . ."

"Good," Rial interrupted. He filled his people in. ". . . and we'll need lots of bedding. I'll leave that to you. There will only be two attendants for each tender."

"Two handlers for eighty kids?"

"They've been coping. Start thinking what we can use for diapers. We can't tie up recyclers with mundane things."

"Diapers aren't mundane if you don't have them," Leh said. "Especially if the wearers have diarrhea."

"Well put. But try to think of a resource available locally. Ideas, please. Simplify, modify, and improvise."

"We'll think of something, Chief," Leh said agreeably, warming to the challenge. "We'll put all the babies in one shelter for now."

"We'll house adults in a separate shelter," Kimmer said. "Someplace quiet where they can sleep. Have to darken it. One of the tunnels!"

"We can set up one shelter for food prep, " Leh added.

"These folks are used to doing without. Be careful what you tell Renzec. Tell him we need a hot-shot pilot who's willing to transport difficult cargo. Don't specify. Carry it through," Rial ordered, and disconnected. Rial knew his people were already flying to their tasks. He also knew everything else was rapidly flying out of control.

Chapter

23

Once in the door, Dal and Tisa were immediately confronted by an opaline, translucent barrier unlike anything Dal had ever seen. It looked like a gel membrane, blocking further entry.

"What in the Guardian's Name is *that*?"

"Don't know. Tavs made it," Tisa said. "Come on. We need to go through." She kicked off the wall, diving through the membrane.

Dal hesitated. He touched the barrier gingerly. It yielded, stretching as he pushed. Without warning, Tisa reached into the membrane and grabbed his hand, hauling him through. The gelatinous substance resisted his passage slightly, making a definite sucking sound as it released him on the other side. Dal felt an immediate lightening of spirit. He and Tisa were in a small antechamber, facing another grey membrane.

"That was bizarre," Dal marveled, a bit shaken. The membrane had stripped residual electromagnetics from his skin. He wondered what else it had done.

Tisa grinned. "Some people never get the hang of going through by themselves."

Dal moved back to the initial barrier and sniffed it. It smelled like hyperilon adhesive. His brow creased as he pondered its makeup. "Are both membranes the same?"

"Who knows?" Tisa said. "Eyth calls it a 'psychic blotter'. It clings, but then slides right off and forms a wall again. The Tavs are using it to isolate the toddlers. Otherwise, the ship-wide depression magnifies itself. We adults have tasks to occupy our minds, but the kids just absorb the negativity. That's why they got hit so hard."

"Makes sense. I've always thought empathic talent was merely a matter of degree. And belief. Some things have to be believed to be seen and utilized." Dal paused. He could see objects hurtling through the air on the other side. "This membrane? It's a slow liquid, isn't it? In a constant state of flux?"

Tisa thought for a moment. "I guess. Ask Eyth. We coated the whole room with the stuff. Eyth says it messes up his fur, and doesn't like going through it."

"What's going on in there?"

"Go on in and find out," Tisa said with a grin.

Dal glided up to the sticky polymer, braced himself on the wall, closed his eyes, and plunged through. He was instantly hit with a blast of happy bedlam. He looked around, amazed. Small children were flying unchecked through the air. They spun, tumbled, and whirled in all directions. Shrieks of glee pierced the room. The bulkheads shouted with loud colors in a mismatched patchwork of designs and materials. Dal could tell that the bright fabric was a recent addition, placed on top of the psychic buffer and utilitarian padding.

"Something, isn't it," Tisa shouted over the din. "Shows what proper child care can do."

In the center of the orchestrated melee, an adult Tav serenely monitored traffic. Elegant tawny fur contrasted with slender black legs and tail. Her finely chiseled features were highlighted by the same black pattern Eyth wore.

"Yes, childrren," the Tav encouraged. "Rride the airr as if it werre a wild drrog-beast! See what youu can doo with it. Use all thrree dimensions. The airr in null-grrav is yourr playgrround, and yourr frriend. Enjoy it!"

One energetic bundle of child was catapulting out of control, on a collision course with the Tav. She twisted in mid-air, nonchalantly plucking him out of danger by catching his waist with her agile tail. She spun him off on a slower, safer trajectory. The youngster squealed with delight. Dal noticed several older children cavorting with their juniors. They could have been helpers, or maybe they were just having fun. He looked at Tisa and grinned. "This is marvelous!"

"It's new," Tisa shouted over the din. "Actually, we owe this to you."

Dal looked puzzled. "Why?"

"This room was as bad as the Baby Chamber. The children were dreary and irritable. They couldn't understand what happened, only that their parents were gone, and their world as well. They were confined, with nothing to amuse them. Then a scout ship appeared. It was Awr'Koof. Because of what you told him, he came looking for us. Then he took off. He went to the school for help."

"Tisa, I can't hear most of what you're saying over this pandemonium," Dal shouted.

Tisa laughed and came closer. "We were powering up when the scout ship returned with Eyth. Plus a few medics. Human ones. Awr'Koof brought us his two for these kids. Only Tavs don't call them twos. His mate, I think. Tavs have an odd system. Name Children, and all that." Tisa looked at Dal with a predatory gleam. "Do you have a two?"

"Yes," he said emphatically. "Kimmer would love this room." He recognized that gleam, and wanted to deflect it immediately.

"Ah, well." Tisa turned and caught the eye of the feline educator. "Calista," she boomed out over the uproar, waving, "can you come here please?" Then she turned back to Dal.

"Calista is Master Teacher of the Queen's School Ship. Queen K renamed it 'Path of Light' . Calista came in here and took matters in hand. Um, in paw," she corrected, grinning.

The elegant feline glanced around for a brief check of her younglings before responding. "Childrren," she called out," *activate 'Plan Secrret'.*" The racket ceased instantly, although the activity level hardly dropped. Calista launched herself gracefully toward Tisa and Dal, artfully avoiding living projectiles in her path.

She caught a pawhold on a nearby bracket to stop her movement. She twined her slender black tail around the bracket, and stretched her body out long. A delicate, oval paw snicked off the broadcast comm she wore as a pendant. Then she composed herself, crossing one front paw over the other, and awaited introduction.

"Calista, this is Dal. He's one of our rescuers from Kellierin. The planet, not the Queen. From the Survey Ship."

"Ah," the felinoid said in a quiet voice that carried, even without the comm. She regarded Dal thoughtfully. Her ears pricked forward, and her white whiskers twitched against her black muzzle as she sniffed him politely.

"Theirr empath! So." Her green slit-eyes grew large, and she nodded sagely. "*The* Dalrrion Darrnel then. At last!"

This confused Dal. "I am the only one I know about. Thank you for your 'volume control'. That's a handy trick."

"Silence is a useful safety skill for little ones of all species." The Tav tilted her head to one side and studied Dal thoughtfully. "Yourr potential forr empathic development had much too doo with prrompting Queen Kellierrin too found the school. She had herr eye on youu. Wheneverr yourr ship docked at HomePorrt, she trried too meet with youu. Youu neverr stayed long enough, and she was busy with herr dual role."

"It wasn't healthy for us to stay, Master Teacher," Dal said. "I'm sorry we couldn't connect. We had reason for worry."

"So it would seem. Therre is someone waiting forr youu on the school ship. Youu will evolve togetherr. Youu arre awarre of the networrk of possible paths?"

"I can sense it, sometimes. Even see it, like a grid stretching out in all directions, when I'm focused and my mind is clear. Especially when I do a sending for other life forms, or try to connect with a planetary harmonic."

"So. Youu have done much on yourr own. We have a grreat deal too talk about, when therre is time. Youu belong with us."

"Master Teacher. I am still unsure of my talents. I would be honored."

Calista made the huffy sound of Tavian laughter. "Please, call me Calista. It seems a waste too stand on cerremony, when we stand on nothing at all," she purred, sweeping one exquisite dark paw to indicate the empty space beneath them. She began to purr softly. Dal had never before heard that rumbling sound, but it held a quiet joy that gave him peace.

"You have made a great difference here in a short time, Lady Calista," he said respectfully. "Is there nothing more you can do for the infants?"

Calista's eyes saddened. "Dalrrion, we arre limited. Ourr medics have paws full keeping them alive until we get on the grround." She sighed deeply.

"It must take a totally different teaching strategy, coping with traumatized children. What a challenge, after educating the gifted! I thought all you could do would be to feed and clean, like with the babies."

Calista huffed. "That *would* be a chorre! That, also, is beyond me. How tedious! But youu arre rright. Dealing with them is verry differrent. But not the way youu arre thinking.

"These catlets get into *much* less trrouble than ourr students! They obey me, as well. Childrren, especially empathic ones, arre the most challenging too teach, and totally impossible too contrrol. One can only hope too *channel* theirr enerrgy.

"I have a grreat advantage here. I rremind them of a big, furrry toy. They listen too me. It has given me an opporrtunity forr me too see things thrrough new eyes. And it is a chance too strretch my claws a bit. Childrren need theirr claws strretched, as well. That's one of the things wrrong with the Baby Chamber." A shudder rippled down her fur. "Childrren this age arre full of questions. Theirr minds arre rripe forr learrning. We simply cause that prrocess too be fun. It pains me that we have nothing too offerr the babies naow."

"Lady Calista, it's so quiet over there, in the Baby Chamber. Music, or even soothing noises, might help. At the minimum, it would help the caretakers."

"We trried, Dalrrion! The planetarry noises we played, such as waterrfalls and brrooks, caused the infants too become frretful and fearrful. Perrhaps memorries of . . . that place. Music we trried was even morre disrruptive."

"Tavian music?"

"Yes, of courrse! We brrought the verry best with us. They had nothing herre on boarrd."

The thought of Tavian atonals made Dal's ears ache. Some notes were above the range of human ears. Unfortunately, most were not. "I'll send some blocks of human music over. They may be more soothing to round ears. Have you thought of sending some of these children over to play with the babies? Or even to talk to them."

"We will be glad too trry it. The tiny ones are so sensorry deprrived. Some of these olderr childrren could surrvive brrief times outside the barrrier naow."

"I am so pleased too meet youu at last. I am sorry youu must still wait for she who waits forr youu," she said cryptically. She gave a fond look over her shoulder at the room full of bouncing children. "I must rreturrn too class now." She looked deeply into Dal's eyes. "Youu *will* have a place in my school, Dalrrion Darrrnel," she promised.

"I know," Dal smiled. "I look forward to it."

She slowly closed her eyes at him, and leaned forward to sniff his hand, to remember. Surprising himself as much as Calista, Dal leaned forward to sniff the side of her face, and lightly brush her soft fur with his cheek. Then she swiveled her slender body and called, "*Secrret's out!* Storry time, childrren! Everry one in place!"

Noisy once again, the children scrambled in a boisterous rush to the other end of the room. The older ones started strapping the youngest down. Calista leaped gracefully into space, flicking on her broadcast comm as she soared in an arc to a suspended pad slightly above the gathering.

Dal met Tisa's eyes as they left reluctantly. She shared his disappointment at missing the story. The cares of the rest of their existence had vanished here, and they were reluctant to take up their burdens once again. Leh and Calista would have future joy in swapping tales.

The 'Path of Light'! Dal got a feeling of "rightness", whenever the school was mentioned. Perhaps adjusting to life outside the Survey, and to children, especially children like these, could be a pleasant possibility after all.

Chapter
24

"I'm at a total loss," Kimmer said dejectedly. She looked drained, and she had lost weight. Another day of running futile tests on unresponsive infants had taken its toll.

"Why am I here?" Cren questioned.

"We have no time for philosophical inquiries, Crensed," Rial said. "Stick to the business at hand." He too was exhausted, and getting punchy.

"Chief, I mean here at this meeting," Cren said earnestly. "I don't know anything about babies."

"We need a breakthrough, Cren," Kimmer explained wearily. "You have a good track record with your tunnels."

"We're damn grateful for those shelters, too," Coordinator Duvou rasped. She leaned over and patted Cren on the arm. "They offer a real sense of security to the settlers. Give us an update on the tots, Kimmer."

"The change to gravity helped. Their eyes followed us around, and they started eating. Two hours after we tried them on formula, though, they developed cramps and couldn't hold anything down. Now they're all on intravenous feedings." Kimmer pushed back a stray wisp of damp, pale hair. New lines showed on her face, with dark half moons supporting her troubled eyes. She stifled a yawn.

Dal went over and placed a hand on her shoulder. "Kimmer, you need to take better care of yourself," he reproved gently.

"It should be obvious even to you, Dalrion, that I've had more important things on my mind."

Hurt registered briefly on Dal's face. The others showed concern at the exchange. Cren, especially, looked at Kimmer with disbelief, and, to his surprise, felt Dal's pain.

"Dal made a good point," Chief Rial said carefully, measuring the fragile state of his medic's nerves. "It won't do to have our healers fall ill."

Kimmer gave an enormous sigh. "I know, Chief." She looked up at the weary face of her two. "I'm sorry, Dal. It's just so frustrating. The more I try to help, the worse things get. We've gotten nowhere!"

"That's not true, Kimmer. We've been able to rule out a lot," Dal said encouragingly. "There isn't an infectious agent involved. I get an impression that their condition has multiple causes."

"You're probably right." Kimmer admitted. "But we've taken such care to eliminate variables. What else is there?"

"We could isolate the critical care facility. That would take care of the air, not just water and food," Dal suggested.

"It wouldn't be difficult," Cren added.

"They were sick before they had Kellierin air, but they didn't have gravity then. It's another combination," Kimmer agreed dubiously.

"Are you sure the formula was sterile?" Coordinator Duvou asked. Now it was Kimmer's turn to look hurt.

"I can verify that, Coordinator," Malindrin, one of the medics from the "Reprieve", answered. She smiled in an attempt to buffer the Coordinator's words. Kimmer gave Duvou a peeved look, but said nothing.

"How about trying yukky tea?" Cren suggested. "It's not baby food, but it's nutritious. It's easy on the tum, too."

"I don't know, Cren," Kimmer said doubtfully. "It has complex constituents." She sighed again. "We have to try something though. I'm scared."

"We all are, child," the Coordinator said. "Have faith, Kimmer."

"I'm doing my best," Kimmer said, an edge of resentment creeping into her voice.

Dal massaged her tight neck and shoulder muscles, wishing he could comfort his two with his empathic talents, but respecting her recent insistence for privacy. "We know, Kimmer. We've all had far too much work lately. Come on. I'll help you set up the tender."

"I'll be glad to prepare an infusion of yukky blossoms for the infants," Malindrin offered.

"Mind, Malindrin, that you use ultrapure water," Duvou directed as she left. "We don't need any more variables."

Malindrin nodded assent, casting a telling eye at Kimmer and smiling tolerantly. She touched Kimmer's shoulder gently. "Don't take what the Coordinator says personally. It's her way. It's been eating her up inside, too. She knows you've been living for those kids. Don't give up hope."

Kimmer smiled wanly. "Thanks, Malindrin. Sorry I've been touchy lately."

"It's to be expected. Don't fret on it."

"How's Melion doing?" Dal asked as the group broke up.

"Exceedingly well, Dal," Kimmer said, glad to discuss her one recovering patient. "I have no idea why she came out of Crisis so early, but she's itchy to get back to work. I don't know that she's ready for a duty rotation though. Maybe I'll put her to work in the isolation tender. She'll be under my eye there, though I'm sure she'd be much more comfortable handling geological data."

Dal laughed.

"What's so funny?"

"Of all the people in the universe, we're the strangest bunch of people to be given the care of sick infants!"

Kimmer smiled ruefully. "I'm not so sure," she said. "The Guardian provides us with what we need most. Maybe we've been too focused on data and exploration. When I hold those tiny hands, I feel the future in them. And lately, I've felt it slipping away." She looked up at her two, and her eyes were full of pain.

Dal embraced her gently, and she responded, hugging him with a fierceness that surprised him.

"Oh, Dal, I ache for them. I feel so helpless. Just like they must feel. They've lost hope."

"That's why you mustn't, love. We must carry them on *our* hopes. It's vital that you keep positive thoughts, Kimmer, and I could help with balancing. . . ."

"No, Dal!" Kimmer abruptly pushed him away. "I can't. Not now. Trust me on this. How is Rennie doing? I know you and the Chief have been doing a fast dance to keep him away from the kids."

Dal sighed with the abrupt change of subject. "With the workload, we're not having any difficulty keeping him occupied. He did a stint on the 'Reprieve', and fixed most of the major mechanical problems that were fixable. There are no end of projects for him here, and he's been attacking them with a frenzy. Of course, he's been rather vocal about his feelings concerning settlement work."

Kimmer grimaced. "Moaning and groaning?"

"That about sums it up. Says he wants to get this over with so he can resume Survey tasks," Dal sighed.

"Before the settlers came, you expressed much the same sentiments, Dal. How do you feel about it now that you've had some experience working with the settlers, and see their dreams taking shape?" Kimmer asked cautiously. She breathed deeply, closing her eyes and shoring up her psychic barriers against the answer she feared would come.

"I've been giving that a lot of thought, Kimmer. I've considered myself career Survey. Like Chief Rial. I love my work, and I'm certainly prepared to take out a ship of my own. I find the job rewarding, and thoroughly enjoy visiting new worlds. But with the devastation of Metrowyl, things changed.

"The Kellierin system is intriguing. There is much to be done here. There is much to *discover* here. But as to what to do with the rest of my life, I have worthy dreams of my own.

"My path lies with the Queen's school ship, Kimmer. I need empath training. My talents continue to develop, and I must learn what they are and how best to deal with them. Both Calista and Koof have told me that I need the school to complete me, and that the school is where I belong. For far too long I have felt incomplete. Now I know why.

"Calista told me about a person who is waiting there for me. She's the empath who will complete me, and enable me to develop my full potential. Sometimes I imagine I can hear her mind calling out to me, from somewhere up in the heavens, wherever the school ship may be."

Kimmer looked at him through a veil of longing. She yearned to reach out and hold him tight, and never let him go. But he was staring up at the sky, as though he could see right through space to wherever the "Path of Light" was located. She felt his utter absorption and desire, and weighed it against her own needs and dreams. Behind her psychic barriers, her heart began to ache anew.

The trial of yukky tea caused a bout of colic for the few infants who received it. They were immediately switched to concentrates, but one by one, the babies all lost ground. In the space of three days, the settlement added eleven tiny mounds to their rapidly growing cemetery. Kimmer took each death as personal failure. She hardly spoke at all. Melion found work in the isotender increasingly depressing, and the negative environment began to slow her recovery. When Kimmer suggested that she might be better off in the lab, Melion immediately agreed.

The geologist wrapped an insulating blanket tightly about her thin shoulders as she leaned into the gusty wind that smacked into her, feeling a twinge of guilt. Kimmer hadn't been happy about her eagerness to escape. Then again, Kimmer didn't seem too happy with anything lately. Or anyone.

Although the lab was immediately adjacent to the tenders, Melion headed off in another direction. She made her way carefully amid the maze of new tunnels and mounds in the clearing. Swaying slightly, she stumbled over tree roots and stones. She was more unsteady than she'd dared admit to Kimmer, but she felt driven by need to talk with Dal.

As she entered the ship, Melion immediately felt enveloped by an unexplained gladness of heart. Dal was hard at work at his station. He was engrossed in his task, and as was so typical, his focus was so intent that he failed to sense her presence. She rested a moment in the doorway, basking in the strange and wonderful peace that enveloped her. Then she noticed the neon lizard snoozing on Dal's shoulder.

"Good Guardian, what's that!" she exclaimed. The tiny lizard's head shot up at her words, and it began an excited whistling.

Dal looked up in surprise. "Melion! It's great to see you," he said, setting aside his sketch. "How long have you been out and about?"

"Just now," Melion admitted. "I'm getting my land legs back. What's that?" she asked again, scrutinizing the lizard. It clung tightly to Dal's uniform, craning its head up and around to get a better look at Melion.

"This is an oogeecheel. Remember the bright sentience I felt in the ship? This is it," he said with obvious affection.

Melion's puzzled expression prompted Dal's memory to clear. "That's right! You wouldn't know. You were heading into Crisis." He looked introspective for a moment. "Kimmer didn't fill you in on these little empaths? They broadcast positive emotions. Like all life forms we've found on Kellierin so far, they utilize electromagnetics in some way. Kimmer and I even discussed bringing one over to you. Then the tenders arrived, with the sick infants and the endless work projects. Negativity floats like a low lying cloud around some of the refugees. Oogeecheela are shy, and the idea of non-empathic sentients is new to them. This little lady came by only this morning. They transmit concepts and not words, but I think they have the capacity to verbalize thoughts. It's like learning a new language for both of us."

Melion sat very still and held her hand out to the little reptile. The tiny eyes regarded her thoughtfully, and the triangular head cocked first to one side and then to the other. Melion smiled encouragingly and tried to send positive vibes, although she had minimal empathic talents. Then the lizard moved toward her, tentative at first. Melion felt little feet climbing up her wrist. She slowly brought the being close to her face, and warmed to the soft, cooing sound. She echoed the coo, and suddenly a burst of joy washed over her.

"Delightful!" she exclaimed. "What do they eat?"

"They absorb some types of EM for energy. They can eat plants.

They also eat those wretched biting insects, which is even more of a reason to have lots of them around. But I haven't heard that type of sound from them before." Dal sent out empathic feelers, and found that the little lizard was at work, soothing and balancing Melion. He sent a wash of gratitude to the oogeecheel, but got no response. The lizard seemed totally absorbed with Melion.

He looked at his crewmate, and assessed the state of her health. Her reddish-brown skin lacked it's normal glow. Her hair was dull, and her eyes seemed dimmer than normal. And something heavy was on her mind.

"How about a cup of tea?" Dal suggested, and he walked over to the center console and picked up two cups and a large thermos.

"Yes, please." Melion put the oogeecheel back on Dal's shoulder, where it circled once and settled down. "Are all oo-gee-cheels so vi-brantly colored?"

"So far as I know. The bioluminescence has something to do with their EM receptors," Dal replied as he poured the steaming tea into the cups. "By the way, the plural is 'oogeecheela'."

"They *are* specific in their communication. I can't hear a thing. But I certainly am aware of the comfort she broadcasts. I felt it as I came in." She sipped the fragrant liquid. "Speaking of comfort, I've had yukky tea before, in the isotender. It wasn't like this at all."

"How so?"

"It tasted pleasant, Dal, but that was it. This is revitalizing. Al-most as good as choc. I feel energized."

"It is restorative. I haven't had time for regular meals lately," he admitted, "or for anything much else than work. This tea keeps me going."

Melion looked thoughtful. "You've lost weight," she observed. "Kimmer says you need a keeper."

Dal nodded thoughtfully. "She has always said that. She's always been right, too."

"That's what I want to talk about, Dal," Melion began.

Dal looked perplexed. "A keeper?" Then he smiled.

"Be serious. I mean Kimmer, Dal. I'm concerned. Have you no-ticed anything unusual?"

"Melion," Dal said regretfully, "I haven't seen Kimmer at all lately. We've been going full speed on different projects. The sick babies take all her time, energy and devotion. The settlement and the crew take mine. She's always asleep when I get to bed. Usually in her own compartment. She's let me know that she doesn't want my company lately. Something has happened between us since you went into Crisis, and I don't understand it at all." Dal sighed, momentarily allowing his pain to show. "When I try to contact her empathically, I meet mental blocks. Yet our love is still there, and stronger than ever. It's been awkward. I know she's in pain, and yet she won't let me help."

"Oh, Dal! That's so sad. You need each other more than ever. I *have* been around Kimmer a lot lately, and I am seriously concerned for her health. Her mind wanders. She's preoccupied. I know that her digestive system is acting up, although she tries to hide it, and she's lost her appetite. I'm no medic, and certainly no empath, but I believe it's more than depression due to the infant dilemma. I've observed her carefully, Dal. Somehow, she isn't...Kimmer. She's acting strange, and it seems to be getting worse."

Dal looked worried. "Melion, I have never known you to be wrong in your observations. I could easily have misjudged the situation. I haven't scanned Kimmer for some time. She asked me not to." He sipped his tea thoughtfully. "I think we've been too close to the problems we're trying to solve. Fresh eyes might spot solutions we're missing. Fresh eyes like yours. Thank you for your information. I will act on it.

"Melion, you've been in the isotender. Do you have any suggestions on the baby situation? Their health is rapidly deteriorating, and that is affecting us all."

"Has anybody tried the yukky tea?" Melion offered.

Dal groaned. "Everybody says that. We did try it. It was a disaster."

"What about the oogeecheela? Wouldn't their positive emotions help the infants?"

"The Coordinator vetoed that. She refuses to allow any unnecessary life form in the isotender. Or anything else that isn't sterilized eleventy million ways. I haven't pushed her on this issue, because we didn't have any oogeecheela, and there was nothing to be gained. She's one tough lady. She seems to specialize in stubborn. Eyth and I tried to help the tots with empathic balancing, but it didn't seem to have any effect that we could tell."

"Eyth?"

"Eyth is a young Tav. He piloted the ship that guided the 'Reprieve' to Kellierin."

"A Tav? Here?" Melion's eyes sparkled with new life. "I want to meet him."

"You will," Dal promised. "When last I checked, he was out on the meadow by the lab, on the sunny side, rolling in the grass."

Melion was taken aback. "Rolling in the grass! That doesn't sound like the Academy Tavs."

"They were somewhat more formal, I grant you," Dal agreed with a chuckle. "You have a treat in store. If you think the oogeecheel is a wonderment, wait until you meet Eyth!"

"Dal, why haven't you taken an oogeecheel to the babies in the second tender?"

Dal leaned back, surprised. "Well, probably because I didn't have one to take until today. Coordinator Duvou certainly wouldn't approve, if she knew." His eyes gleamed. "But she hasn't specifically vetoed it! I can do stubborn too. I'll take this one over and see what happens, if she's willing to make an attempt to ease the infants."

"And I will look into the mystery of the changing tea," Melion promised. "My first assignment." She drained her cup and stood.

Dal rose also. "This sketch is ready. Windmills, Mel. We have enough wind, so why not use it? Let me walk you to the lab." Dal paused and concentrated a moment, and the oogeecheel began to chirp excitedly, swaying her head back and forth and dancing little steps on Dal's shoulder. He smiled. "She wants to help. It's worth a try. Then I'll visit Kimmer, if she allows." Then his face grew grim. "Even if she doesn't. She's my two, but I'm also her team leader, and acting commander. I tend to forget that. And so does she."

The wind had diminished, and the afternoon sun was pleasant. As they walked, Dal told Melion of some of the settlers. "There's this fellow, Dvorat. He's a great mountain of a man. He has a knack for growing things. He's taken charge of farming. He's keeping trees as wind breakers. He has legumes up already. Tubers and other stuff are in the ground. When I asked him if the plants could withstand the wind, he said, 'We'll know by the end of the year. May have to put up wind fences. Got the seeds. Got to try.'" Dal laughed. "Some of these folks were only waiting for a reason to feel positive about life. They're turning the others around. They have people fishing and foraging. Mel, they've got a plant that tastes like choc! Nearly so, anyway. And they've found a small mammal they're trying to do-mesticate. Called a 'gorda varnee'."

"Why that?"

"Because it goes, 'Gor-da var-nee'," Dal brayed at her, and she laughed.

"They're at work drying and preserving and building. And Mel, Cren has grown up overnight! He's often the one people turn to when it comes to making decisions about structures and functions. He's developing into a natural leader. I'm very proud of him." Then Dal sobered. "If only it weren't for the sick babies. They seem to waste away. The settlers are afraid to bring any more infants down."

"Maybe I can help," Melion offered.

Dal smiled at her and winked. "You already have," he assured her.

He handed his sketch to a young lad passing by. "Please take this to Renzec." The boy grinned, nodded, and took off as fast as his legs could go. The older youths seemed to run everywhere, rather than walk, once they got their gravity legs back.

Dal entered the open tender. He explained his plan to the atten-dant, and introduced the oogeecheel. The young medic was thor-oughly charmed, and encouraged by the comfort that came with the tiny lizard. Dal placed the reptile in a crib, next to one of the sick tots. The thin, triangular head swung toward the baby, then up to Dal, and then back to the baby. The infant moved fitfully. Her little hands clenched as soon as the lizard was set down. The oogeecheel began to make the soft, cooing, healing sound. It circled twice in the bedding, and then coiled next to the child. It closed its eyes and appeared to sleep, head on tail. The baby visibly relaxed, and then immediately drifted into deep slumber. Dal watched for a moment. He looked at the pale, emaciated child and sent her a mental message, inviting response, but felt nothing.

"I'll be back shortly," he promised the attendant.

"Take your time. I believe that child is sleeping well for the first time. Now I have some hope."

Dal walked over to the isotender and pressed the comm signal. He waited a moment, but received no response. Impatiently, he tapped the comm code twice, releasing the seal. As the door shut behind him, a wave of fear swept over him. He started to panic as he waited for the air to purge and cycle through.

"Kimmer!" he called through the comm. No answer. Why didn't she respond?

He closed his eyes and tried to sense her presence, but all he could feel were feeble negative sensations typical of the weakened, cachectic infants. And beyond that . . .

Dal charged through the entrance, barely noticing rows of nearly comatose infants along the outer perimeter of the isotender. What held his focus was Kimmer, collapsed on the floor, one arm out as if in supplication. He kneeled next to her and scanned her lightly. He felt the heavy pulse of exhaustion compounded by long frustration. He scanned deeper. The rhythm and flow of her body was severely disrupted.

As he reached out to lift her, his hand brushed a bright blue-streaked oogeecheel wrapped around her neck, covered by her high collar. How had it gotten in through the doorlock? What was it doing on Kimmer? He reached for it, and his mind brushed the borders of its fugue state. It was in deep sync with Kimmer, and Dal rode inward on its link. Then he probed even deeper into Kimmer's psyche. There was something there. Something strange. Something not Kimmer, not oogeecheela, and not Dal. Very deep, inside the essence of the one he loved, lurked the presence of an alien mind.

Chapter
25

Melion scrolled through the medlog. The formula for problem solving was simple. When dysfunction occurs, find the triggering imbalance. Correct the imbalance. If the correction doesn't maintain, find the perpetuating factor or factors. Find the missing link.

The lab was nearly empty. In one corner of the wooden shelter, the ultra pure water apparatus droned a monotone hum. Melion stared at it blankly, allowing her subconscious to ruminate, as she sipped the yukky tea. It's aroma tasted flat. Her eyes narrowed as she focused on the mug in her hand. She straightened up and scanned her recording pad with movements both deliberate and brisk. Slowly, she began to smile.

"She was lying there when I came in, Malindrin," Dal explained.

A frail, elderly woman behind them fluttered her hands about her face as she wept. "I swear to you, by the 'Reprieve'," she wailed, "I was only gone a few moments. She was running exams. She gave me permission. . . ."

"Don't worry, Meika," Dal automatically reassured her. "It's not you fault." It's mine, he thought, for not anticipating this, and preventing it.

Meika looked nervously from Dal to Malindrin, and then to the fallen form of Kimmer. Then she wiped her eyes and picked up the closest child to cuddle.

Malindrin slipped a medicorder off her shoulder and scanned over Kimmer's immobile form. Then she sighed with relief. "Exhaustion. Nothing else."

"There *must be* something else!" Dal insisted.

Malindrin looked at Dal quizzically. "I tell you she's fine. It's to be expected, the way she's been pushing herself."

"I could sense something strange *inside her,*" Dal insisted. "People don't faint without reason."

"True, but. You can't push yourself this hard." She touched Kimmer's forehead lightly. "Not when you're pregnant."

Shocked swept over Dal's face. "Kimmer can't be pregnant! She takes preventative. What I felt inside was alien!"

Malindrin pushed back her wavy hair and absently scratched a bug bite behind her ear. "Be that as it may, your two is *definitely* pregnant. You must have caught the emerging life force. They tend to be chaotic at this stage. Don't try to probe it for the next month or so. Trust me. There is no sign of any abnormality."

Kimmer blinked and raised her arm to ward off the light. "What happened?" she asked fuzzily.

Dal helped her to sit. He supported her carefully in his arms. "Lean on me, until you regain some strength. You fainted."

She nestled her head on his chest and sighed. "Oh, this feels good. I need to be held more. I'm sorry I got you worried for nothing. Just need more sleep."

Dal obligingly held her, trying to sort through the confusion that muddled around in his brain.

Malindrin smiled at them. "You both need some time to talk. Alone. If you need me, you know where to reach me."

"Uh, where?" Dal asked blankly.

"The lab. Where you found me," Malindrin said patiently.

"Uh, thanks," Dal said awkwardly. "Kimmer, love, can you get up?"

Kimmer looked abashed. "I'm not an invalid, Dal" she said, dismissing the incident.

Dal steadied her as she stood up. "Come out for a walk. You need a break."

"That sounds like a good idea, Dal. I can't stay long though." She touched Meika on the arm as she left. The attendant looked up from changing a baby and nodded. Kimmer held out her hand to the oogeecheel on Meika's shoulder. "I'd better take this little one out. The Coordinator will throw a tantrum." Dal, Kimmer and the tiny lizard cycled through the airlock. The oogeecheel was dropped off at the open tender, to join in helping the infants there.

Dal took Kimmer's hand and they walked silently over to the edge of the nearby woods.

"Dal, let's avoid the forest. I love it, but I lose too much blood to those insects. They've gotten bad since the warmer weather set in."

"Right here is fine, Kimmer." Dal settled on a grassy hillock over-looking the main clearing. Kimmer nestled beside him, and they watched the settlement activity silently.

Finally, Dal took a deep breath and said, "Malindrin told me you're pregnant."

Kimmer turned and searched his eyes closely, seeing only concern. She resumed the pretense of watching the bustle below. "I thought I might be."

"You didn't know?"

"I didn't want proof, Dal."

"I don't understand. What could you gain by not knowing?"

"Time. Dal, it's like this." Kimmer took Dal's hand again, and held it in both of hers. "When we landed on the outer planet, I was due for the yearly preventative. Then one thing after the other happened. Usually, I'd have a few months leeway. This time, I didn't."

"Why didn't you tell anyone?" Dal said, with more than a hint of anguish. "Why didn't you at least tell me?"

"Honestly?"

"Of course, honestly!"

"I felt I was losing you. I still do. I can't deal with that," Kimmer gulped, losing control. "We're heading in different directions, Dal. I don't want to hold you back. If we break two, I want part of you to be with me. For always. With your child, I'll have that. We've both been so busy. . . ."

Dal's usual composure was gone. "Kimmer," he said, taking her into his arms, "I love you. If you love me, how can you talk about breaking two? Just because we haven't had time together lately. . . ."

"No, Dal. It's more than that." Kimmer leaned her head on his shoulder, as she blinked away tears. "You belong with the 'Path of Light'. You told me that yourself. Even in your sleep, you murmur about the 'empathic bond' you lack. You say you want the settlement established, so you can get out from under it. I love this place, Dal. I really do. This world is . . . special. I belong here. Besides, I know how you feel about kids."

Dal hugged her close. She could hear his heart pounding rapidly. "How *can* you know, love? I don't even know. Kimmi," he said, looking deeply into her eyes, "I love working with the older kids here. I *have* been thinking a lot about the Queen's school. I *do* want to be part of it. There *is* a special person waiting. Do you know what a 'Name Child' is?"

"Sort of a fosterling, only more?"

"Much more. Their concept of 'braided lives' is alien to us. I think I'll be asked to have her as a Name Child. It's quite an honor, and a commitment. We will develop empathically together. Kimmer, I can adapt to sharing you with our baby. Can you accept sharing me with a Name Child?"

Kimmer laughed. Tears of relief streamed from her eyes. "A Tav! Dal, my love, I want in on that, too. I'm fascinated by Tavs! And I'm not going to raise our child alone, either. *Especially* if he or she is an empath!"

She hugged him tightly-a treasure reclaimed-and he returned the embrace, but much more gently. "I'm not spun gleifness, Dal. I won't crumble."

Dal met her eyes. "I thought you were going to, there for a while. Me too. We need each other."

"We do work better as a team," Kimmer agreed. "I've been miserable. And you will see how truly nasty I can become, if some of those Tagur types don't stop sniffing 'round your heels. They're the worst predators on the planet!"

"True. I try to discourage them. Perhaps we can find some sort of symbol to warn them off. Some two-sign. Guardian knows, I need protection! There is a severe shortage of men among the colonists."

Kimmer's eyes lit up. "I know the perfect thing!"

"What?"

"You'll see." She smiled mysteriously.

Dal laughed again. "Make it soon, please." Then his face sombered as he looked into the clear sky. "Speaking of the 'Path of Light', it should have arrived by now. It's been heavy on my mind. The plan is to base the school on Kellierin." He gently brushed Kimmer's hair with his hand. "You'd have known that, if I had shared more with you. We haven't had enough time alone to. . . ."

"Speaking of which," Kimmer peered over Dal's arm at a streak of grey fur bounding swiftly toward them. "What's got into him? Why isn't he using the foot path?" she asked.

Dal smiled and murmured, "I have a feeling we'll find out *real* soon. Let's make a promise, before we get distracted, that we'll coordinate our schedules. And I'd better start thinking about this baby. Neither of us knows the first thing about raising kids." His eyes sparkled. "Imagine a planet of healthy kids, raised Calista-style! Malindrin says I can make mental contact with the child within the next two months. The Tavs will show me how to help it along."

"*Raeorw!* Dal! Kimmerr!" he yelled excitedly.

"What's up, Eyth?" Dal called.

"They'rre herre!" He skidded to a halt on the hummock and started prancing excitedly in the short grass. "Fatherr! The Queen! They brroke Matrrix! They'rre herre!"

Dal, Kimmer and Eyth raced down the path to the main clearing in time to see Chief Rial and Coordinator Duvou come out of the Survey ship. Rial raised his eyebrows, acknowledging the newcomers, and addressed the small crowd gathered around the entrance.

"You probably have heard the news. The Queen's Ship School, the 'Path of Light', is a day out from orbit. We received one message through the relay, but transmission was garbled."

"So now you know," the Coordinator exclaimed, raising her hands in exasperation, "So get to work. Time's wastin'. Summer won't last forever!"

"That's right, people," Rial ordered. "Survey crew, settlement staff, meet inside. We need to gather."

"We've been able to work pretty well together, your people and mine," Coordinator Duvou acknowledged to Rial, as everyone settled in for a planning session.

"Too busy to argue," Rial Jennery quipped as he leaned against the master comm console.

"You're right about that," Duvou cackled. "Haven't worked so hard since my yorbu gave birth to six!"

"Six! They all make it?"

"That they did. I almost didn't, though," the Coordinator chuckled, remembering.

The crackle of the comm broke through the cabin chatter and stilled it instantly. All eyes focused on the comm panel, and the two leaders moved to either side of it.

A strong male voice boomed over the comm. A voice of authority. A voice expecting to be obeyed.

"'Path of Light' to Kellierin base. Are you receiving?"

Rial Jennery shot a worried look at the Coordinator, but she wouldn't meet his eyes.

"Kellierin base here," Rial replied crisply, in like tones. Something about the transmission set him on guard, and he didn't like the Coordinator's body language. "Receiving clearly. What is your status, 'Path of Light'?"

"Kellierin base. Expect recon party mid-morning tomorrow, your time."

"What sized craft, 'Path of Light'?"

"Adequate for needs, Kellierin base. We require briefing with your senior staff. We will deploy from the large clearing north-northwest of your present location. We require 'Guardian's Reprieve' to keep adequate distance from us, and refrain from further attempts to scan. Request any contingent greeting our craft maintain distance."

Rial's frown grew deeper with each word. He looked meaning-fully at Dal. Dal closed his eyes for a brief moment, sending his em-pathic reach up and out to the 'Path of Light'. Then he opened his eyes and shook his head. Nothing.

"Kellierin base, standing by." Rial flipped the comm on hold. He turned and leaned his hips against the console, crossing his arms de-fensively. "What do you make of that!"

"Nothing I like," Coordinator Duvou said in worried tones. She moved away from the comm unit, and stood with her head down.

"Could it be another ship? Not the real 'Path'?" Renzec asked.

"It's the real 'Path'. The 'Reprieve' has been tracking her since they broke Matrix," the Coordinator asserted. "We know the signa-ture." The Coordinator wasn't telling all she knew. She glanced war-ily at Dal. Tisa chewed her lip, but remained silent. Her eyes begged Duvou to speak.

"Chief," Dal interjected, "I'm aware of the 'Reprieve', in orbit. I do believe" he reproved sternly, "that Coordinator Duvou has some-thing vital to tell us. I sense nothing at all from the 'Path', and they can't be that far away."

Eyth fidgeted, but decided to keep his own counsel.

"I think we'd better prepare for more than an envoy," Renzec glowered.

"How do we do that, Rennie?" Rial sighed.

"We could send people to the caves."

"For how long, Ren?" Dal disagreed. "We need the entire sum-mer for food production and foraging. We have to get the 'Reprieve' people down and try to mend their hurts. Even if the Royalists con-trol the school, that doesn't mean they have the Queen and the em-paths. I don't know why, but I don't feel bad about this."

"That's ok, son," Rial said pointedly. "I feel bad enough for both of us."

"We're going to have to meet what's coming," Duvou said quietly. "I don't think we should say anything to the others. One more set-back would do my people in," she said tiredly. "Dal's also right. I know who's on that ship. But I *think* he's ok. I hope you can trust me on this. I hope I can trust *him*. Good Guardian, what could anyone possibly want that we have?"

"Maybe nothing," Dal said reassuringly. But phrases like, 'your special empathic potential' and 'empaths as weapons' crowded his mind. The Coordinator had impressive mental blocks about that ship, and he knew that she hadn't created them. At the same time, a strange calm settled over him. Could he remove the danger to the others? At what price? He cast a long look at Kimmer, and her face mirrored his feelings. Their hands clasped tightly. "Let's trust the Guardian on this one," Dal insisted.

Duvou rolled her eyes. "That's what I did on Tagur," she muttered. She seemed to be struggling with something in her mind. Finally she said, "Dal may be right. Things may be fine." Then she sighed. "And I may be a yorbu."

Chapter
26

Overnight rain segued into a damp, misty morning. Trees lurked like ghostly sentinels, robed in ground-hugging clouds. Then the clouds scattered, and the mist burned off. The small 'contingent' of 'personnel' waited apprehensively at the end of the sunlit clearing, dwarfed by resinous conifers.

Abruptly, a ship broke through the clouds. It was of military configuration, about three times the size of a Survey scout. Just as it began to spiral down, a young runner darted up to the welcoming committee.

"Folks in the lab want Kimmer right away," he gasped, catching his breath.

Kimmer groaned. "Thank you, Kielof. Tell them I'm coming," she said, and the boy raced away. "Not the best timing." Kimmer looked longingly at Dal. "I have to go," she said as she glanced nervously at the approaching ship. "We covered this ground last night. I can't do any good here. Maybe I can in the lab."

"I understand," Dal said, but he clung to her hand and pulled her to him. "I love you, remember that," he whispered in her ear.

"Dal, I'm going to the lab, not the next galaxy. I won't be gone long," she promised, but she turned away quickly as tears started to flow.

Dal's eyes followed her as she ran down the path. Then he turned to face Rial and Duvou. "I'm going out alone to meet the ship," he said simply.

The Coordinator looked questioningly at Rial.

"When you travel with an empath, you'd best listen to his hunches," Rial said softly. But his eyes looked old.

"I try to trust my hunches, too," Duvou rasped. "I'm riding on one now. We'll find out soon enough if I did the right thing. Go on, son. Guardian's blessing."

The war-battered craft settled gently on the far side of the clearing.

As it landed, Eyth came racing down the path. He skidded to a stop in front of the group. "What's wrrong, Dal?" He cocked his head sideways and sniffed at his friend. His tail drooped abruptly.

"Stay here, Eyth," Dal insisted. "Something may not be right. Do you recognize that craft?"

"It is strrange too me." He sat on his sleek haunches and touched one of the empath's hands with his large paw. "I wish too accompany youu," he said solemnly.

Dal leaned and whispered into his friend's large ear. "If something goes wrong out there, they'll need your talents here. Besides, I'll need you to take care of Kimmer for me."

Eyth swallowed hard, and his slit pupils narrowed. He reached up and rubbed his chin on Dal's, marking him with Tav scent. Then he backed up three steps to stand with Chief Rial and Coordinator Duvou. Rial put a calming hand on the soft grey fur of Eyth's quivering back, as Dal took off alone for the strange ship.

Dal felt terribly alone in the vast clearing. He could still sense nothing from the craft before him, nor from the 'Path' above. He took a full breath of the Kellierin air, fragrant with evergreen, as he centered his resolve.

Chief Rial glanced at Coordinator Duvou. Suddenly her shoulders sagged and she bit her lip. "Rial," she blurted, "I know that ship. It's been through hell since they boarded us, but I know it. Military Intelligence."

Rial took off after Dal, with Duvou stirring her old bones behind him. Eyth followed, about a step behind Rial. The ship door opened, and a long ramp projected out and secured itself to the turf. Eyth let out one squeak as he sensed who was aboard the craft.

A tall, stately, grey-haired man strode down the ramp alone, surveying the area. He wore Royalist fatigues, and emblems of rank gleamed in the light of the Kellierin sun. He balanced a long, metallic tube of some kind in his hand. He met Dal at the bottom of the ramp, and escorted him into the ship. The door closed behind them firmly.

Rial and Duvou swapped glances. Duvou hissed, "That's Colonel Lar! He's got Dal!"

Both humans took off for the ramp at their respective top speeds, with Eyth bounding past them, heedless of promises. They all came to an abrupt halt when the ship door reopened. Colonel Lar appeared, still carrying the slender, metallic tube.

Rial put his hand on Duvou's arm, and they halted and held their breaths. Eyth, quivering, waited beside them. Then the humans released the air from their lungs with a whoosh, as Awr'Koof followed Colonel Lar out of the doorway. Another Tav, slender and tawny with dark markings, followed Koof. At the sight of his mother, Eyth threw any remaining pretense of dignity aside and mewed high kit-cries of welcome.

The slim Tav leaped sideways off the ramp, greeting Eyth with a strange dance that consisted of a great deal of prancing and head and chin rubs. Lar threw back his head and laughed a loud, hearty laugh that carried to the edge of the clearing and beyond, dispelling any fears the small group harbored.

By the time Rial and the Coordinator reached the ship, three youths, about half Cren's age, had disembarked, followed by an attractive, lithe young woman carrying a yorbu. She was dressed simply, and her hair was bound up in a kerchief. One lock of rich, chestnut hair had escaped across her forehead. Her cheek was smudged.

Koof bowed his head in salute to Rial and Duvou, and greeted them by name.

"We have come toogetherr in safety at last," he said. "I am pleased too prresent Colonel Larr, late of the Rroyalist forrces. Without him, we would not be herre."

The Colonel stuck out his hand and shook theirs vigorously. "I have heard of your exploits, Chief Rial. And I have met you, Madame Coordinator, although I was flying under false colors at the time," he said in his deep, rumbling voice. "I am glad for you to know at last that your trust in me was well founded." His eyes twinkled with a merriment too long concealed. "I hope the uniform did not distress you unduly," he apologized. "I had no chance to bring civilian clothing with me. It was a rather precipitous departure."

"Colonel Larr was secrretly Unified," Koof explained. "So secrret, the Unifieds didn't know. He evacuated hundrreds of sympathizerrs too a safe worrld farr away. Queen Kellierrin knew of his trrue feelings. He has aided the 'Path' grreatly."

"The uniform misled us, Colonel Lar," Chief Rial admitted. "We worried about your military demeanor over the comm as well."

"I warned you not to be so officious, Lar," the women with the woman with the yorbu scolded. "I knew I should have commed them myself! You'll scare someone to his death, I just know it! Young Dal came to us as a sacrificial offering!"

"The habits of a lifetime don't fade overnight, dear lady," Lar apologized. "And you never know. This uniform may come in handy yet again, Guardian forbid its need." He reached up a strong hand and grasped the woman's arm. "Let me help you down the ramp, my dear, and also that most odorous creature to which you cling, for some unfathomable reason." The yorbu moved its head towards Lar, but seemed content to reek in silence.

"I wanted it off my ship, Lar," the woman explained. "The stench of it will abate somewhat in the open air. It will be useful here. And perhaps, in its absence, the 'Path' will become reasonably habitable once again.

Coordinator Duvou met her at the base of the ramp. "May I?" she asked, eagerness in her eyes, as she held out her arms for the smelly beast.

"Be my guest," the woman said with obvious relief, "although I must caution you, it doesn't take to strangers. But then, it doesn't care much for friends, either, so I guess it really doesn't matter." She cheerfully relinquished her redolent companion. "I think you're just annoyed that it outranks you, Lar," she said impishly as she wiped her hands on her rumpled green tunic, vainly trying to find an area not covered with long yorbu hairs. The yorbu snarled up at the Co-ordinator, and she beamed.

The Colonel grimaced at the pun, and composed himself. Then, with a deep bow, he said grandly, "Gentlefolk, it is my honor to present Her Royal Majesty, Queen Kellierin, late of the Court of Metrowyl."

The Queen favored Colonel Lar with a long-suffering look, and stuck out her hand to the Coordinator. "Don't mind him," she whispered an aside. Duvou sputtered as she shook the offered hand mechanically, balancing the yorbu in the other. The Chief just smiled.

"Chief Rial," the Queen said as she answered his smile with one of her own, "since you were so nice as to name this planet for me, I thought we'd drop in and perhaps stay for a while. Please call me Kae. Kellierin would be so confusing, don't you think. *And,*" she said, looking pointedly at the Colonel, "my former title no longer applies. Though Lar insists on its use." She lowered her voice conspiratorially. "He doesn't realize that as a school administrator, I have ever so much more power than I did at court. I can't abide fuss." Her cheeks dimpled pleasantly, and she winked at the Chief as they shook hands.

"Ah. A lady after my own heart." Rial said with satisfaction. "Now where has Dal gotten himself to?"

"He'll be along. He commed his two from the ship, to let her know all was well. Now he's comming someone on the 'Path'."

"Why couldn't he sense the empaths on the 'Path of Light'? Or on this ship, for that matter?" Rial was perplexed.

"Both ships are coated inside with psychic blotter. Dal told you about that, right?" Rial nodded. "Klev has low-order empaths working with him, you see. They aren't very sensitive, but they would have noticed our adepts in the school ship. That precaution kept us undiscovered. Our yorbu is sensitive to military transmission frequencies, as well."

"Ah. I see." The Chief began to walk the Queen to the settlement proper. "Actually, Queen Kae," he said, turning to her with a wink, "my grandmother use to have a yorbu. . . ."

"You see, I had to get the children out, so subterfuge was necessary," Queen Kae explained. They sat in the glade on logs, drinking tea. "You know," she remarked with genuine pleasure, "this is absolutely marvelous! Whatever do you call it?"

An embarrassed silence ensued. "Uh, yukky tea, Ma'am," Renzec finally responded with uncharacteristic shyness.

"What a *curious* name! How did it come by such an appellation, dare I ask?"

"The blossoms it's made from, Ma'am, before they're heated. Well, they taste yukky," he finished lamely.

The Queen laughed-a sound like a thousand tinkly bells. "How utterly appropriate!" she said. "As I was saying," she continued, "here I was in space with all these students. The hunt for us was underway, and well. . . . You know, I don't think I'll finish this story. Calista tells it better, and I believe she's with *your* story teller, Chief Rial. A lovely woman, that Leh. They are composing a glorious epic. I tend to ramble on so, and get sidetracked easily. Just let it be said that we were hiding in space, with no place to go except away. Of course, there is this lovely planet the Tavs told Lar about, which is fine for studying, but it does have its own humanoids, even though they don't take very good care of their world, and it has ever so much species variety. We have *so* many interesting embryos from there that may well be appropriate here, and they're killing them off at such a dreadful rate, so we wanted to save what we could of them, you see, while we were in the area anyway. The children learned a great deal, mostly by negative example, unfortunately. Then we heard of this lovely planet. The name you gave it seemed a sign from the Guardian."

Chief Rial grew worried. "Is there any chance the Royalists suspect where you are?"

"Klev? That impossible man! Unless he wanted something, he

never paid any attention to me. Nor to the school, until he wanted
the ship, and the trained empaths. Of course, he had no idea we
had Matrix capabilities, thanks to Colonel Lar, who pieced the system together. Lar simply loved this whole operation! Lurking
about in shadows, wearing disguises!" She smiled fondly. "Klev had
reasons to believe I'd never leave the Metrowyl system." A darkness settled on her face for an instant, and then was banished. "If
it weren't for the dear Tavs, and sweet Colonel Lar, we really
would have been finished. By personally investigating every possible sighting of the 'Path', he totally destroyed any chance the
Royalists had of finding us."

"That 'dear man' " Duvou glowered at Lar, "scared the hell out
of us before we left Metrowyl."

"I had to, kind lady. Forgive me. Iit was imperative that I give the
impression of checking all suspicious craft." His laughter boomed.
"You must admit, the 'Reprieve' is a rather questionable vessel. Besides," he said matter-of-factly, "I needed to change the Matrix pro-
gramming. I had to make sure you'd come through in one piece, and
in the right area."

"I was afraid you had bugged the ship, Lar," the Coordinator
scolded.

"*Of course*, I bugged the ship, Madame Coordinator. I didn't
know if you could make it through Matrix space with that cobbled
drive, and I didn't want to lose you!"

The Coordinator laughed so hard the tears rolled down her
cheeks. "Good Guardian, but we could have used you on the
colony."

"My heart grieved that I was unable to come to your aid, but I
needed to stay under cover. Until the very end."

"But it is not the very end just yet," reminded the Queen. "At any
whiles, the Colonel was able to divert any mention of Kellierin what-
soever from reaching Metrowyl. Only one bit of data got through,
and that only to the 'Guardian's Reprieve', sent by Tavs. We may indeed have guests, but the guests should be Survey. We'll have need
of them, and they will need a safe place.

"And now, without more ado, I must ask for *your* help. We have plants in the ship, you know, the little ship we just landed in. Some should be planted without delay. The Tavs will have need of them.

Cren leaped up. "I'll take care of it," he offered.

"There are rather more plants than one person, however strong, can handle. You'll need help." Queen Kae graced him with a warm smile, and he blushed, smitten.

Colonel Lar pulled himself up with the help of the long metallic tube, which he used as a cane. "Come son," he nodded to Cren. "You too," he said in his commanding voice, pointing to Eyth. "You can dig faster than we can, with those claws of yours, and you *enjoy* it!"

Eyth jumped up and joined them.

"Before we go, I must add another word of apology to the Coordinator. I have taken the liberty of requesting that the 'Reprieve' relieve us of the majority of our fuel. The 'Path' is off-loading while we speak. I want minimal load before we come down. I intend to bring her down myself. Right now, however, we must attend to the tayelo plants. Come on, troops! Hop to it."

"Frresh tayelo!" Eyth cried for joy. The three of them went off to the ship.

"Tayelo?" Rial asked.

"Tayelo is a vegetable, but it tastes like fresh meat," Queen Kae explained. Then she wrinkled her nose in distaste. "To a Tav, that is. They can put up empathic barriers if they must hunt, of course. That's the only way empathic omnivores can eat meat. But Tavs are known for genetic engineering. What they can do with plants, for us two-legs as well as furfolk! We have a whole ship's worth of treasures. Hardly room enough to move, there is. We have a Master Gardener as well.

"Some of our hiding was done around the home world of the Tavs. Then we fled to this Earth place. We were all aware of the tragedy your people suffered, Coordinator, so at each place we stuffed every cranny with goodies. But we must introduce things carefully. The empaths will help us to understand what niches need to be filled. We will do whatever we can to alleviate your losses."

"Queen Kae, I'm profoundly grateful. To think the Guardian was listening to my prattle all along! We're looking at a tough winter, for all its only now spring. Your ship could be the difference between rationing and feasting." She slapped her knee. "If we could just figure our what to do about the babies!"

Queen Kae's head came up with a jolt, and the blood drained from her face. "Babies? What babies?"

"The 'Reprieve' infants, Queen Kae," Dal explained. "They're ill."

"Take me to them now," the Queen ordered desperately as she stood. Then she sighed and added, "Please." She looked around her. "Will you all please forgive my rudeness? You see, the reason Klev thought I'd never leave," her eyes filled with tears and she drew a jagged breath, "is that he held my twin baby girls hostage," she forced out of nearly clenched teeth. "I don't even know if they're still alive. " She turned and grasped Dal's hand and held tight. "Take me to the children, please. Come, Shondi," she said, holding out her other hand to a very serious looking boy who had been sitting at her feet. He looked to be about twelve, although his eyes looked older. The three walked silently for a space. Then the Queen looked at Dal closely. "You aren't well yourself," she observed.

"You are not empathic?" Dal could sense no common bridge.

"No," the Queen said. "But you can't hang around empaths without picking up some sensitivity to body language. And you are important to me." She halted.

"Shondi, will you walk with Dal, please? Do you mind, Dal?"

"No. Of course not," Dal said, somewhat mystified.

The boy looked up at Dal thoughtfully. He closed his eyes a moment. Then he opened them wide and said, "Your channels are unclear." He took Dal's hand and again closed his eyes. Dal felt a powerful force surge through him. Suddenly, his muscles no longer spasmed and ached. "That will do for now," Shondi said gravely, opening his dark eyes. "We must take it in easy stages. Give your body time to adjust. You must see the Lady Ceil. She is trainer of Tavs. She will teach you what you must know."

"There is nothing I wish for more, Shondi," Dal said sincerely.

Shondi nodded. Then they commenced walking.

Shondi is our best poet," Queen Kae said fondly, "as well as a healer. The traits seem to go together, somehow."

"Really!" Dal smiled. "I'd love to read your work," he said to the boy.

"Some day you shall. When I have something that's worthy."

Queen Kae shook her head in dismay. "It's really all so wonderful. But he keeps insisting it's not ready."

"I know the feeling," Dal admitted. "I used to write poetry."

Queen Kae looked at him sharply. "Why did you stop?"

Dal thought, and then laughed. "Actually, I don't know that I have," he answered. Shondi looked up at him and they shared a brief, secret smile.

As they approached the "baby complex", Dal explained the situation. "I believe that their digestive systems have atrophied. We need to build them up, and slowly introduce them to real food. But first, we have to find a nutrient they can assimilate."

"Take me to see the most critical ones first."

"Very well, Queen Kae. We've set up an isolation tender. We wanted to keep the variables low."

The Queen nodded, and Dal pressed the comm unit outside the isotender. Kimmer's voice called out, "Who's there?"

"It's Dal, Kimmer, with some special people who wish to see the children."

"Come right on in," Kimmer said with a laugh. Her voice was light and merry. "We can use the help."

Puzzled, Dal led the way through the airlock. When the door opened, he saw Kimmer, Melion, two 'Reprieve' medics, and two nursery attendants. They were feeding babies, and the infants were sucking noisily at the feeding bulbs.

"Oh, Dal! Melion found the answer," Kimmer said, beaming.

"What's that you're feeding them?" Dal asked.

"Yukky tea!" Melion replied with satisfaction. "Made with *lake* water. It has a synergic effect, boosting the nutrition, and it also has a natural buffer. Ultra pure tea not only is less nutritious, it's also caustic, and irritated their gastrointestinal systems.

"When we ran a scan on tea made with ultra pure water, and compared it to tea with lake water, we saw what was happening. This is good old unsterile yukky tea. We can bring down the rest of the infants soon."

"We could send some tea up," Dal suggested.

"They already have plain yukky tea. We sent a supply up for the adults on return flights."

"I'll call them," promised Dal. "Right now, I want you to meet Queen Kae."

"The, the Queen? Where?" Kimmer stammered, and almost dropped the baby. Queen Kae rushed over.

"Here. Now let me have this tiny one," she insisted, and took the infant from Kimmer's arms. She started making cooing noises. "What an *adorable* child!"

"Some of these babies are seriously ill," Shondi whispered to Dal. "Which ones?"

"Not the ones that are being fed. Some of the others."

"Point them out. They can be fed next," Dal suggested. He could feel improvement in the feeding children. It was intense.

Shondi went over to one of the somnolent infants. "This one here. And that other," he nodded.

"Thank you, dear," the Queen said. "Dal, you feed that one, and Shondi, you get the other." She looked at Kimmer. "You do have extra feeding bulbs?"

"Yes. Right over here."

"Kimmi, I can't do this," Dal protested. "This child is too small."

"Take the bulb, Dal," Kimmer said firmly. "Feed the baby. Then it won't be so small." She handed Dal and Shondi full bulbs.

She looked at her royal visitor uncertainly.

The Queen looked up and smiled. "Call me Kae. Queen Kae, if you must. And please let me stay here with the children for a while."

Kimmer beamed. "That would be an honor. I'll go brew more tea. And I think I can safely disengage the airlock system."

"I could do that," Dal suggested. He looked extremely uncomfortable holding the feeding bulb of tea in one hand and the emaciated infant in the other. Shondi was already dutifully feeding the other child.

"Feed, Dal!" Kimmer ordered. "It's practice. I'll be right back, with more tea. I'll open the tender, and I'll call the 'Reprieve'."

"Take your time," Queen Kae recommended. "If need be, I can teach Dal and Shondi how to change the babies." She shared a smile with Kimmer. Kimmer caught a brief glimpse of alarm crossing Dal's face as the airlock started cycling. She just managed to wait until the first door closed before she dissolved into giggles.

It was a medium sized ship, but top of the line in every way. On the basis of hull design alone, Dal could understand Klev's reluctance to fit it with Matrix drive, and thus chance its loss. He stood expectantly with Shondi, as they watched Colonel Lar nestle the 'Path of Light' into it's own clearing, gently as a kleebfettle brushtail settling over her clutch of eggs. Dal couldn't wait to board her. He itched to see her labs. He longed for her library. And he was anxious to meet the beings whom she carried. Especially one.

Shondi stood impassively at his side, no sign of the impatience that was implied by Dal's every action. Dal, abashed, centered himself with difficulty. He would meet his future very shortly, and start down a new path. The rest of his crewmates were diligently at their tasks, and Queen Kae had refused to be parted from the infants. Coordinator Duvou had relinquished her charge over them with unconcealed relief.

As Dal calmed himself, he regarded Shondi thoughtfully. He had been a great resource, moderating ship withdrawal problems of the infants. Yet he carried a set of problems all his own.

"He was once a carefree child, so full of mirth that it made one glad just to be in his presence," Queen Kae had confided to Dal. "He had one of the highest empathic ratings at the school. That was his undoing.

"Dal, he absolutely idolized his older brother. Gorshen had accepted a post at the Academy a few years ago. They were mind linked, at the end, although Gorshen tried to sever that link. But

Shondi was the stronger empath, and he held. Strangely, what hurt the child most was that his brother struggled to break away. He needs healing, Dal. Perhaps you can help each other?"

Dal's thoughts were interrupted by a crashing noise coming from the conifers behind them. He turned as Eyth and Calista emerged from a run through the forest. The Tavs trotted slightly past them, halted and inspected the grasses. Choosing their spots carefully, they flopped down on the meadow and rolled.

"Tavs love to play," Dal observed.

"That may well be," Shondi replied somberly, "but I believe they have also found a pleasurable way to provide themselves with protection against these atrocious insects."

"What do you mean?"

"The raw yukky blossoms. I assumed that anything that tasted so bad might also be a deterrent to the insects. I have no scientific basis for that, you understand," he said earnestly. "Only observation. Calista believes it warrants testing. I have observed native animals rolling in the blossoms."

Dal grinned and stooped to pick some of the unpalatable blossoms and rub them on his skin.

"Ah, I see youu have been enlisted forr testing the prreventative powerrs of yukky blossoms," Calista remarked with a purr as she and Eyth approached them. Then she sat next to Dal and arched her finely chiseled head to regard her flanks. "What a shame we can't grroom afterr. They make furr tastc horrrid!"

"The blossoms have no discerrnable scent too humans orr felines," Eyth explained, "but the insects must be able to detect its prresence, forr we have no morre bites."

Dal laughed. He looked at the flowers in his hand. "I never noticed how resilient these are. They're barely crushed."

"Indeed," Eyth agreed. "I think that theirr pollination is accomplished by animals which rroll on them forr insect prrotection. I'm not surre. The light flutterrbys, which feed durring the day, although they mate at night, seem too like them. It will be good too have access too ourr laborratorries once again."

Dal glanced at the 'Path', which remained quiet and still on the meadow. "What's taking them so long?"

"We have a strrange prropulsion system," Calista explained. "Koof and the Colonel had too rretrrofit a modified Matrrix thrrough the coil drrive. I assume disengaging the Matrrix will be a prriorrity. Then we can use the "Path" too ferrry people and equipment down frrom the 'Rreprrieve'. Ah, therre is action at the lock."

The dual hatch slid back, and a wide ramp unfolded. The tall figure of Colonel Lar was the first to exit. He stood and raised his arm in a wave to them. "Halloo, folks," he called, his commanding voice carrying easily over the wide meadow. A line of students followed him down the ramp. Then came a delicate, very small dark brown young Tav wearing a harness. A bag hung from each side. Dal smiled in recognition. The dark Tav yawned wide, and snapped sharp teeth. Then she opened her mouth slightly and curled her top lip, showing gleaming fangs. She focused her eyes on Dal and let out a yearning cry. Then she daintily stepped down the ramp, moving as quickly as she could with her burdens. The students around her also carried bundles of belongings, as they would temporarily relocate into several large mounds until the ship's transfer tasks were accomplished.

Dal, Shondi, Calista and Eyth hurried over to greet the new arrivals.

"Youu will enjoy the company of Tikeh," Calista promised Dal. "She's come to be with youu, Dalrrion, and with yourr family."

An elderly Tav, assisted by two students, came down the ramp slowly. "That is the Lady Ceil, trrainerr of trrainerrs, and Masterr Mystic of the school." Calista looked at Dal with mock wistfulness. "I will miss youu, Dalrrion. "Yourr time will be totally absorrbed by the Lady Ceil and Tikeh, and the rrest of us will neverr see youu again."

Dal grinned. "I doubt much if Kimmer would allow that."

Calista smiled knowingly. "Ah, they will have herr too. And the childrren she carrries." Then she called out, "Teek! Herrre, let us help youu with those. Dal, will youu help please too lighten these burrdens? Shondi, please go and see too the Lady Ceil."

As Dal stooped at Tikeh's sleek side to help her adjust her harness, the slender brown neck curved gracefully around, and he found himself regarded by a pair of deep-golden brown eyes. His eyes met hers, and a spark of connection flashed between them, as each identified a kindred spirit and a longing met at last. He laid his hand gently on the short, soft fur. "I've been waiting for you, Tikeh," he said softly. "Waiting for a long time. Welcome home."

Sometime later, Dal sat with one of Teek's dark oval paws against his forehead.

"You see, Teek. No matter how hard I reach out, I haven't made the connection. I know Kellierin sings around me, but I can't find the melody."

"Ah, Dal. I see the prroblem." She took her other front paw and laid it on his cheek. "Follow thrrough my mind. Yoou look outside forr attunement. Seek forr Kellierrin within youu. And naow, within mee. Mindfulness, naow. Focus. Look inside. Ah. Therre. It was waiting forr youu all the time. Youu had too learrn too listen too youurrself, beforr youu could hearr Kellierrin."

"Teek! It's lovely. I have it now, the connection. We have it. Thank you, Teek."

Tikeh rubbed Dal's cheek with her own, and the two of them sat in harmony, listening to the music of Kellierin.

Epilogue

The keed leaves were racked and drying in the herb mound. The last iloh root had been dug, and the ships' preservers were stuffed with a variety of meats, fish, vegetables and fruits, including mounds of yukky blossoms which had been heat dried. Two whole mounds had been devoted to grains, and a supply of wensi nuts had been hoarded as treats to enjoy in the long winter ahead. The small herd of Gorda varnee were nested in barn mounds, supplying the settlement with milk, cheese and butter. Grasses had been dried and stockpiled to feed the animals.

The tayelo bushes had grown large in the hot, moist summer. The expected ships from Resniki and other Tavian worlds had never arrived. But the meaty fruit had hung ripe from the shrubs, and the Tavs on Kellierin had snatched it eagerly with lightning swift swipes of their claws. Sufficient fruit had been preserved for the winter. Talk was that one of the next projects would be greenhouse design and construction. There was much speculation as to what this first winter would bring. A series of tunnels ran between the mounds and wood shelters, so that interaction could take place in spite of any weather. The Tavian genetic engineers were developing strains of faster growing, cold tolerant food species. And the children grew strong.

Ships that arrived during the summer were all Survey craft that had been on missions when war struck Metrowyl. They brought with them rumors of further conflicts, and a tale of devastating epidemics on the Tavian worlds. All of the crews chose to stay.

To celebrate first harvest, the settlement held a feast. In actuality, it was many feasts, for the community had already grown too large to gather in any one shelter or group of shelters.

Dal sat against the wall of the first Gathering Mound, tired from the day's exertions. He had finished helping Colonel Lar secure the last of the sensor monitors. He was content with the summer's passing. He could control his empathic talent, as well as other developing abilities, and the warm steady pulse of the planet Kellierin was a comfort to him.

Kimmer napped peacefully in his arms. She wore a petrified "tree tear", captured in a silver spiral pendant-mate to the one he had around his neck. She slept a lot more lately, storing her energy for the birth of the twins. They would arrive soon. The girls had been in mental rapport with their father and Tikeh for the past three months.

Colonel Lar snoozed in the corner, a half-read report in his lap. In a shadowed corner, Renzec and Tisa spoke softly. Rial Jennery and Queen Kae sat together at a side table, sipping tea and talking in low tones. By the time other men had overcome their awe of royalty and approached the lovely lady, she had been totally smitten with the Survey Chief. It took a while for Rial to concede that he might make a fit match for the younger woman. Queen Kae had suffered much at the hand of the arrogant and conceited Klev. She delighted in the charm and wit of Jennery, and blossomed in his presence. She would not be denied.

The fire crackled and sizzled, throwing warmth and light into the dark shadows. Coordinator Duvou reclined against a pile of cured furs, absentmindedly stroking the aromatic Twik Twik and its bondmate, curled by her side.

Cren and some of the Survey additions sat watching the fire.

Koof and Calista had their chins resting on their forepaws, but Eyth had his head upside down in the Master Gardener's lap. Lynneese had a way with Tavs, just as she had with plants. Tikeh was curled at her feet, a treetear, match of the two worn by Dal and Kimmer, in a silver spiral hanging from her neck.

In the center of the Gathering mound, by the fire, Leh sat on a log stool. She wove her story with practiced skill, as her graceful arms moved in picturesque gestures to enhance her words. Her animated face was the black velvet of the midnight sky of Metrowyl, and her golden eyes held secrets. Secrets she would share with those she loved. More than one man around the fire was concentrating more on the story teller than the story.

Leh's face lit up like dawn in time-lapse photography. "And they came safely to the planet of Kellierin. And here, the school and the children flourished in happiness and peace. And the Guardian's favor rested on the settlement. The Survey crews came and added to the wisdom. And, someday, the Tav will also come to Kellierin."

With that promise, Leh brought her hands down in her lap, and bowed her head, receiving the applause of her appreciative listeners.

Dal closed his eyes and centered, finding the slow and steady throb of the heart of Kellierin, and felt at peace. Then he sent his thoughts up, beyond the mound's roof on which the first flakes of snow were falling. He whispered dreamily to himself, a promise. "Someday. Someday, the Tav will also come to Kellierin."

AUTHOR'S NOTE:
PASSING FOR HUMAN

This book is a science fiction, but remember the prologue. Do some of the symptoms of the Season of Change sound familiar to you? There is an invisible chronic neuroendocrine dysfunction known as fibromyalgia syndrome (FMS). With FMS, whenever the body enters deep (delta-level) sleep, alpha (waking) waves intrude and wake the sleeper, or jolt him/her into shallow sleep. Since neurotransmitter regulation, muscle repair, and many other vital functions take place in delta sleep, the person with FMS is soon suffering unless they get adequate medical support. To make the diagnosis more interesting, every person may find different neurotransmitters and hormones and other neural biochemical modulators affected, to different degrees. Many of the problems are cognitive — what we call "fibrofog", with short-term memory problems and other invisible handicaps. The pain and other symptoms can profoundly disrupt your life.

If that weren't enough of a challenge, another condition that often occurs with FMS is myofascial pain syndrome (MPS). MPS is an invisible neuromuscular condition thoroughly documented in many papers and two wonderful medical texts written by JFK's White House physician, Janet G. Travell MD, and her co-author, David G. Simons MD. Unfortunately, these papers and texts are for the most part ignored by your medical schools.

If these patients lack proper diagnosis and adequate support, they often become needlessly disabled. FMS and MPS patients don't look sick, so they are often victimized by clinicians, pharmacists, family, co-workers and companions. They are often treated as malingerers and drug-seekers. Overwhelming symptoms, compounded by anger, frustration and mind-numbing pain further complicate the diagnostic picture. Many valuable, creative people are being lost to suicide and misunderstanding. Families are being destroyed, homes are lost, and your health care system is severely stressed, due to lack of understanding and training on the part of the medical care providers.

If you want to learn more about these conditions, see my website at http://www.sover.net/~devstar

Devin Starlanyl
W. Chesterfield 1998